THIS TIME FOREVER

Kerry's right hand primly held the bathrobe closed at the neck. "Dale, what are you doing here?" She looked nervously at the darkened homes nearby, as if she expected the neighbors to be spying on them right now from their windows.

Dale had a bottle of chilled wine in one hand and a long-stemmed red rose in the other. "Don't be coy, Chief, you know why I'm here. I spelled it out for you over the phone not thirty minutes ago." He grinned at her, showing straight, white teeth in his tanned face.

Damn, Dale smelled good. He was wearing a pair of loose-fitting Levi's and a gray pullover shirt that displayed his pectorals to perfection. He put the bottle of wine on the coffee table, handed her the rose, and pulled her into his arms.

"How was I to know you were going to come tearing in here in the middle of the night?" She held the rose behind her as Dale pressed her closer to him.

"I *told* you I was coming."

"And I distinctly recall telling you, 'not tonight'!" She wriggled in his embrace.

"Kerry, Kerry," Dale cajoled, his tone husky, "quite contrary. Afraid of what her neighbors will think when they find out she's a normal woman with normal needs, and a man has actually invaded her territory past midnight." He released her, walked over to the big picture window, and opened the draperies. Standing in front of the window, he exclaimed, "Look at me, Dale Preston, Esquire, here to seduce your chief of police!"

Other Books by Janice Sims

AFFAIR OF THE HEART
"To Love Again" in LOVE LETTERS
ALL THE RIGHT REASONS
OUT OF THE BLUE
FOR KEEPS
A BITTERSWEET LOVE
"The Keys to My Heart" in
A VERY SPECIAL LOVE
A SECOND CHANCE AT LOVE

Published by BET/Arabesque Books

THIS TIME FOREVER

JANICE SIMS

BET Publications, LLC
www.bet.com

ARABESQUE BOOKS are published by

BET Publications, LLC
c/o BET BOOKS
One BET Plaza
1900 W Place NE
Washington, DC 20018-1211

First Printing: October 2001
10 9 8 7 6 5 4 3 2 1

Printed in the United States of America

This book is dedicated to all the sisters out there who have taken a leap of faith and decided to give love another chance. That's a heroic thing to do in this day and age.

You're a force of nature, elemental,
unpredictable and wild, at critical mass.
That's why all the times you
came in and out of my life . . .
I stood aside, and let you pass.
What a fool I was!
It wasn't the fact that you were too hot to
handle,
I'm more than man enough for that.
It was your strength I wondered at.
This time, you'll have to go through me.
I'm looking forward to it.

—The Book of Counted Joys

ONE

Dawn in Damascus.

Kerry Everett's Adidas-shod feet pounded the asphalt as she jogged down Main Street. It wasn't even 6 A.M. yet, and the temperature was already in the high sixties. Such was August in northwest Florida. Above her, the night-shrouded sky gave way to day as an orange-and-purple streak heralded imminent sunrise.

She was nearing Deeks's place. She steeled herself for the usual assault on her nerves from Atta Girl, Lewis Deeks's vicious pit bull. Deeks, a well-known racist, had a seven-foot electrified fence around his property. He dutifully raised the Confederate flag every morning, going out to put it on its thirty-foot pole for all of Damascus to see.

Kerry told herself that if Atta Girl should ever get over or under that fence and actually got the chance to follow through with all that the growling and barking promised, she wasn't going to shoot the dog, she was going to shoot the owner, because Atta Girl wouldn't do anything she wasn't trained to do.

Deeks was, after all, the one who made her that mean and ornery. Just like him.

"Aruhhhhhhhhh." Atta Girl had approached the fence so suddenly Kerry was *still* startled even though she'd known what was coming. The dog frothed at the mouth, bared yellowed teeth, her powerful body fairly trembling with menace. "Aruhhhhhh."

Kerry kept jogging. *One of these days, Deeks,* she thought.

Now heading west, jogging on the soft shoulder of Highway 441, Kerry passed the kudzu jungle on the right. It was called "the jungle" by area folks because the lush green climbing plants that covered everything made it look like Tarzan's jungle in Africa. For as long as Kerry could remember, kids had played in the kudzu jungle, blissfully unaware of snakes and other critters living in the dense vegetation. Kudzu was introduced to the United States at the USA Centennial Exposition in 1876, where it was used in the Japanese pavilion as a fragrant ornamental vine to cover arbors.

When she passed her two-mile mark, Kerry's breathing was only moderately labored. She was accustomed to jogging three miles six days a week. She took Sundays off to allow her muscles and tendons time to recuperate.

Several cars passed her, some blew their horns and she waved: Damascus residents heading to Gainesville, the county seat. Gainesville was only about twenty miles away, and many Damascans commuted. Damascus was, after all, only a small town. Though well managed, it didn't have enough businesses to employ all of its able-bodied citizens. It was, however, a wonderful place to live and raise a family. Therefore many considered the twenty-mile commute a minor liability compared to the myriad benefits of living in Damascus.

The sun was up now. A few clouds marred an otherwise clear, blue sky. Kerry figured by noon, they'd have a few showers. The weather service had recently issued a hurricane warning, saying north Florida would get several soakings before Hurricane Sonia turned its full attention to the Florida peninsula. Kerry didn't pay much heed to the warnings. She couldn't recall Damascus ever incurring damage from a hurricane in her lifetime.

Though southern Florida got hit hard by Hurricane Andrew in 1992, *they* had gotten nothing but rain. The weather service had been right about the soakings off of Hurricane Sonia, though. Every afternoon, Damascus got a good gullywasher.

She turned her mind to the day's agenda. There was the monthly duty roster to post. Then there was the meeting with the town council to discuss security at the upcoming street fair. Every year Damascus threw a fund-raising event to bring together the townspeople. This year they were rallying around the well-loved waitress from Percy's Diner, Doreen Wilkins. Doreen had polycystic kidney disease and needed a transplant.

As far as providing security for the fair went, Damascus was relatively free of crime. There *was* an ongoing problem with drugs. Kerry's department was extremely vigilant and had, for the most part, cleared out many of the dealers, who were now either serving time or had left town. There was one thorn in her side, however, Johnny Haywood.

Kerry ground her teeth at the thought of Johnny Haywood, the wily drug dealer who'd always managed to slip through their fingers! The problem was that Johnny was a hometown boy, and, for various reasons, no one would inform on him.

He'd been indoctrinated in the business by his father, Ike Haywood. Ike had been killed in prison. The two older brothers, Ike Jr. and Billy, were both at Raiford State Prison. Johnny was on the outside dealing drugs. There was only one boy left, the baby, Harold. Bess Haywood, God bless her, was trying her best to keep him on the straight and narrow. Kerry's mother, Evelyn, had often bemoaned Bess's fate at falling for a man like Ike. Bess was as good as the day was long. She was a church mother, never missing a Sunday at St. John A.M.E. Church. She volunteered with Meals-on-Wheels, deliv-

ering food to the elderly and shut-ins. There wasn't anything she wouldn't do for a friend or a neighbor.

Kerry shook her head as she continued her jog. Sometimes no matter how hard a parent tried, she couldn't
save her children. It was a crying shame what those boys
had put their mother through over the years.

"Gotcha!"

With lightning-quick reflexes Kerry leapt into a
fighter's stance and raised her fists, preparing to defend
herself, when she saw it was only Dale Preston, and
punched him hard on the upper arm instead. "Damn it,
Dale. Where did you come from?"

"Ow! I was waiting in the woods there for you to
come by," Dale said, cocking his head in the direction
of a clump of bushes. He grinned. "You know I can set
my watch by your habits. The chief should be less pre-
dictable. What if some crazy redneck took it into his
head to do you harm? All he'd have to do is lie in wait
for you like I just did, and you'd be a goner," he said.
His deep voice had just a hint of a Southern accent.

Kerry continued jogging, knowing Dale would keep
pace with her. "When did *you* get back in town?" she
asked, understandably irritated.

"Last night. And I wish I'd postponed my return."

"Why? Your phone's already ringing off the hook,"
she joked.

Dale, tall, good-looking, built, a top defense attorney,
was the most eligible bachelor in town. That is, when he
was *in* town. For the past three months, he'd been in
Washington, D.C., working on a high-profile murder case
during which he'd defended, and won an acquittal for, a
US senator.

"There's one particular female I wish I could avoid,"
he said, sounding weary.

"Jenna?" Kerry guessed. Jenna was Dale's sister.
While both their father, Dale Sr., and Dale were reputable
attorneys, Jenna, at twenty-eight, had not yet found her

calling. She drifted from one dead-end job to another. From one deadbeat man to another. Never seeming to catch on that she was the only one who could break the cycle and do something worthwhile with her life.

"She's not in any trouble, is she?" Kerry asked, concerned. In spite of Jenna's penchant for screwups, she was a good-hearted person, and Kerry didn't want anything bad to happen to her.

"Man trouble again," Dale said. "Listen, I'm sorry I even brought it up. What I really want to know is, do you have a date yet for the Sadie Hawkins dance the last night of the street fair?"

Kerry laughed. "A date?" She eyed him, taking in those fine muscular thighs, that washboard stomach, those wonderful pectorals and biceps. She'd known Dale all her days. He'd been two grades ahead of her in high school. They'd both been athletes. She played basketball, women's softball, volleyball, and ran track. He was captain of the football team his twelfth year. Ran cross-country. They'd been jogging together since she'd moved back to Damascus in 1998 after a stint as a Miami police officer.

In high school they'd flirted via eye contact mostly. Back then, it was taboo for a white boy to date a black girl. So, they were cordial. They didn't run in the same circles. When she returned home in 1998, Dale got up the nerve to tell her how he felt about her. And Kerry still didn't know how to take his attentions. Hence she chose not to encourage them. It wasn't that Dale left her cold. On the contrary, Kerry was a healthy female with healthy female proclivities. It was just that Kerry didn't dillydally when it came to sex, and she figured Dale might be another CWB: curious white boy. If she had an affair with him, he'd soon tire of her, and her heart would be broken. Then where would their friendship be? Down the drain. She valued him more as a friend than as a lover.

Dale stopped running. Kerry stopped, too, and he went to stand in front of her.

"You know," he said, peering down into her large whiskey-colored eyes. "When I was away I missed you more than I missed anything else about this town." He glanced around. Pines trees surrounded them. Narrowing his eyes, he said, "Why do I still live here when my office is in Gainesville and I accept work all over the country? It's because of you, Kerry Everett. Now, I know you feel something for me."

Kerry bit her bottom lip. "Dale—"

"No, let me finish and then I'm going home to shower," he interrupted her. Reaching out he tilted her chin up, his thumb momentarily caressing the dimple in her chin. He liked everything about her heart-shaped face, but he especially liked her chin. It was alluring and a little bit defiant, just like she was. "It's been nearly three years since I told you I loved you, Kerry. I've only grown to love you more over the intervening months, weeks, days. Why don't you marry me and move away with me? We can live anywhere. You can do anything. Go to law school. You've been talking about doing that. Do it! I'll support you in everything you do. We'd be so good together. A team. As lovers, friends, partners. I'm thirty-five. You're thirty-two. I want to have children with you. Let's not wait any longer. Take the plunge, Kerry." His dark blue eyes lovingly swept over her face. "No matter how we try to ignore them, there will always be forces wanting to tear us apart. But we don't have to let them. The future is ours, Kerry. Let's grab it with both hands."

With that, he lowered his head and kissed her on the mouth. His right hand was at the base of her skull, gently but firmly holding her against him. Kerry didn't try to resist. She'd been wondering what it would be like to be kissed by him. Would it change how she felt about him?

Would it make her stop straddling the fence where her emotions for him were concerned?

All she knew, as their tongues danced, was that Dale tasted just fine. He moaned and pulled her fully into his arms. Kerry's right hand had worked its way up into his curly hair and, Lord, she was kissing him back with as much fervor as he was kissing her. Their bodies were pressed together, and the athletic gear they wore did little to conceal the state of arousal they found themselves in. Her nipples had hardened and were visible under the tank top and sports bra she wore. She felt his manhood pressing against her inner thigh. How had her leg gotten between his, anyway?

This last thought frightened her so that she abruptly broke off the kiss. Dale's eyes were smoky with desire when he regarded her. "You can't tell me that wasn't good to you, Chief," he teased, a rakish smile on his full lips.

Kerry languidly pushed out of his embrace, her chest heaving. "I think it proves I'm a red-blooded American girl." *And it's been a long time since I've been with a man,* she mentally tacked on.

"That you are," Dale happily agreed, and hastily kissed her forehead. "I've got a meeting in about an hour. I hate working on Saturday, but it couldn't be avoided. I should be free by two, though." He kissed her again for good measure. "While you're going about your daily routine, serving and protecting our fair city, think about what I said, okay?"

"Okay," Kerry said softly. Dale smiled his pleasure, then turned and walked away.

She indulged in a few voyeuristic moments before it dawned on her: She'd just been proposed to. *I have to tell Kiki right away!* she thought as she continued her jog.

* * *

Jared Carr woke up coughing. Sitting up on the cool, damp ground, the previous night came rushing back to him. He and his buds had been partying at Dougie's place because Dougie's parents had gone out of town for a funeral. The last thing he remembered was telling Krystal Cox she had a bodacious bod, and then everything else was a blur. He must have passed out. Probably from that cheap beer they'd been swilling all night long.

Still disoriented, he tried to rise, and suddenly his stomach roiled. He made it to his knees before he started vomiting. When he was finished, he felt so empty he imagined his stomach lining was touching his backbone. Stumbling to his feet, he looked around him. Those buttheads had dumped him at Mason's Auto Parts. It was a junked-car graveyard where people went to find parts at cut-rate prices.

He wasn't angry with his friends. He'd pulled the same joke on an unsuspecting bud more than once. But he felt like crap and didn't relish the two-mile walk back to town. He supposed he could stop by Miss Viola's and ask to use the phone to call his mom. Miss Viola's place was only a few blocks away, but then Miss Viola would overhear and his business would be all over town before sundown. Plus, his mom wouldn't take kindly to having her Saturday-morning sleep-in interrupted. She worked hard at Kmart all week, and Saturday was the only day she got the chance to get a little extra rest. He didn't have to worry about his dad, because his dad had walked out on them when Jared was a kid. They hadn't heard from him since.

So, in his weakened condition, he began walking toward the chained back gate that the boys had undoubtedly squeezed through last night to leave him here. It's how they'd done it when they'd left Mark Johnson in here the last time they'd pulled this trick.

Before he made it to the end of the lot, he had to stop and rest against a battered Dodge Dart. Feeling sorry for himself, he vowed never to drink again. But, realistically, he knew that vow would be broken the very next time one of his friends phoned and said the magical word: party! He was only a seventeen-year-old kid, after all. He deserved to get totaled every now and then. Next year he'd be a senior and then he'd have to tighten his belt a lot. He didn't want his mom to have to pay for his college education. He was smart enough to maintain a good grade point average, and he played football. Plus he did community service. All things he knew looked good on his academic record. He would prove to his mom that he wasn't a loser like his dad. He'd make her proud.

Moving around the Dodge Dart, he thought he saw a man's foot, a bare foot, on the ground on the opposite side of the car. Blinking, he walked toward the foot, which was attached to a leg—and then a whole body came into view. It was a black guy lying flat on his back, wearing nothing but a pair of jeans. His arms were splayed out at his sides. His eyes were wide open but unseeing. His mouth formed an O as if he'd been surprised in death. There was a bullet hole between his eyes. His chest was a bloody mess. It looked as if someone had tried to carve something in it with a knife.

"Oh, God!" Jared cried, backpedaling so fast he nearly tripped over his own feet.

Adrenaline flooded him and the burst of energy gave him the strength to flee the scene. He ran to the chained gate and nearly tore his shirt off trying to get through it. Then he ran the quarter mile to Viola Kelly's house and pounded on her door like a madman.

He didn't know how Miss Viola, an elderly black woman who lived alone and had a problem with her eyes, would react to seeing a crazy-looking white boy at her door demanding to be let in, but he didn't care. He had the wild notion that the man he'd left dead in Mason's

Auto Parts had suddenly been reanimated and was pursuing him.

"Miss Viola! Miss Viola, it's Jared Carr. You know me, my mother's Melanie Carr, she works down at the Kmart," he called loudly, continuing to pound on Viola Kelly's solid pine door.

He was prancing as if he had to pee, glancing nervously behind him in case the dead man really was coming for him.

Viola Kelly was in her garden in her backyard when she heard the racket. She came through the back door, hurried through the house until finally she stood at the front door peering through the curtains into the frightened, sweaty face of Jared Carr.

She had on her thickest spectacles. She had several pairs in various strengths. His face was familiar. But a woman living alone practiced caution. "What you want, boy?"

"Miss Viola, you've gotta let me in," Jared pleaded. He had his back pressed against the front door. "There's a dead man on Mason's Auto Parts property. Somebody shot him, and then they cut him up. Please, Miss Viola! I'm scared!"

Viola knew fear when she heard it. After sixty-nine years of living on this earth, she was familiar with it. She quickly unlocked the door and let the boy in. Just as rapidly, she locked the door behind him.

Jared was trembling. The combination of a hangover and having come face-to-face with death a few minutes ago had taken a toll on his body. His blond hair was plastered to his head and his gray eyes had a haunted aspect to them. "Miss Viola, you've got to call the police. Whoever did it might still be out there," he warned hoarsely.

Viola pointed to a small table at the back of the room. "Phone's right there. You call 'em. But don't tell 'em you're calling from my house. I don't want to get involved. I didn't see nothing. There's no reason for 'em to come snooping around here."

"Yes ma'am," Jared said, and went to make the call.

By the time dispatcher Dera Stephenson answered he'd managed to calm down a bit. "There's a dead man on the Mason's Auto Parts lot," he told her.

"I don't *know* why he decided to ask now," Kerry told her older sister, Kiana, over the phone. "He seemed a bit more intense than he usually is."

She was sitting on the side of the bed, smoothing lotion on her just-showered limbs while she held the receiver at her ear with a little neck action. "Do I love him? Kiki, you know the answer to that. No, I don't love him. But I like him a hell of a lot!"

Beep, beep, beep . . .

"Kiki, that's my beeper, I've got to go. You and Gabriel still going out tonight?"

"Yes," Kiana Everett-Merrick answered. "Coco's looking forward to seeing you."

Kerry smiled at the thought of her five-and-a-half-year-old niece. "I'm looking forward to it, too. I'll see you at seven then."

"All right, have a good day!" Kiana replied.

Kerry pressed the OFF button on the phone, then pressed the number one which took her directly to Dera Stephenson at the police station.

"Dera, it's Kerry. What's up?"

"Kerry, a young boy reported finding a dead man over at Mason's Auto Parts. He'd been shot in the head. Since you weren't on duty yet, I relayed the message to Paul who was in that quadrant. I'm letting you know, too, in case you want to provide backup."

Kerry's heartbeat quickened at the news. "Okay, Dera, tell Paul I'm on my way."

"Do you want me to notify Clemons as well?" Dera asked.

"No, Paul and I can handle it," Kerry decided. "Thanks, Dera."

"Be careful," Dera admonished, and hung up.

Kerry replaced the cordless phone on its base, then quickly finished putting on her khaki uniform. Standing in front of the mirror in her bedroom, she tucked her shirt into her pants, fastened the black leather utility belt around her small waist, then sat down on the bed to put on socks and her black oxfords with the extra support. She did a lot of walking in her job, and good shoes were a necessity.

Her hair, which fell to the middle of her back, was in its customary bun at the nape of her neck. Not a strand was out of place.

She was five-ten, and one hundred fifty-five pounds. Jogging kept her healthy and toned. Weight lifting gave her musculature definition. She'd always been a strong woman, and she was comfortable in her own skin.

Striding over to the chest of drawers next to the door, she pulled open the top drawer and withdrew a locked steel box. The key was on a chain around her neck. Whenever she was off duty, her service revolver remained in this locked box. She had two nieces and a nephew who visited often. She was not about to be careless with their lives. No matter how frequently you warned a child about not touching guns, sometimes curiosity got the best of them.

Her shotgun and backup 9mm were both locked in her patrol car, which was a white supercharged Ford Explorer.

Fully dressed and armed, she hurried out of the house, closing the door which automatically locked behind her.

Mr. Thomas was in his yard next door whacking weeds, his favorite pastime. He paused in his task long enough to lift his baseball cap from his bald head in a salute and bestow a warm smile on her. He reminded her of a brown elf.

"Good morning, Mr. Thomas," Kerry called. She was tempted to name the weed whacker, too, it was such an integral part of the dear, sweet man. He was eighty-four years old and still able to putter around in his yard. God, bless him!

Kerry felt as if she were in a cockpit every time she got behind the wheel of the Explorer. Besides the normal accoutrements a vehicle might have like a radio, a cassette player, or a CD player, her honey of a car also had onboard navigation, a laptop computer, radar, and a fax machine. The front seat was separated from the backseat by steel mesh. In case she had to transport a prisoner.

As she backed out of the driveway, she threw her cognitive mind into action. A murder in Damascus? There hadn't been a murder in their town since 1981 when Hattie Bascom caught her husband, Alfred, in bed with her best friend and shot them both. Hattie had lost her mind after that and spent the rest of her days in the mental hospital up in Chattahoochee, Florida.

By the time Kerry had driven to the outskirts of town and arrived at Mason's Auto Parts, there were two other police cruisers, plus three civilian cars, parked at the still-locked gate. Mason's Auto Parts covered ten acres. Collie Mason had fenced in the entire area, which was packed with wrecked autos in various stages of disrepair, some more skeletal in appearance than others, depending on how many parts had been removed.

Collie was a big, shaggy-haired man in his early fifties who always looked as if he could use a shave and a bath. He was standing just inside the gate, conversing with Deputies Paul Robertson and Royce Clemons as Kerry approached them on foot.

When Paul saw Kerry coming, he pushed the gate open as far as it would go to facilitate Kerry's entrance. "Morning, Chief. I told Collie to keep the gate locked

until we completed our investigation," he told Kerry. He
looked over at the civilian cars.

"Good," Kerry said, briefly smiling at him. She could
always count on Paul to show logic and to follow procedure. They already had gawkers. When the word got
around there would be carloads of people rubbernecking,
hoping to get a look at the dead man or, at least, find
out what was going on in their town.

Paul Robertson was a couple inches taller than Kerry
with a swarthy complexion, dark hair, and dark eyes. He
was trim and wore his uniform well.

Deputy Royce Clemons was blond, blue-eyed, six-feet-
two, and rangy. He wore his hair in a buzz cut, and his
nose was invariably red, which made Kerry think he had
a drinking problem he was hiding from the department.
Anyone with a drinking problem was required to go into
a rehab program or seek employment elsewhere. Of
course, Royce could have broken capillaries, which also
caused reddening of the nose. Kerry tried to give him
the benefit of the doubt. But the fact was Royce Clemons
made it clear he didn't like her. The feeling was mutual.

"Chief," he said now, acknowledging her.

"Royce," she returned, turning her eyes on Collie Mason. "Mr. Mason."

"Morning, Chief," Collie said, a frown creasing his
brow.

They shook hands.

"Can we get this over with?" he asked sincerely. He
looked up as two more cars arrived and parked outside
the gate. The occupants got out of their cars and sat on
the hoods much like spectators who didn't want to buy
a ticket to the Damascus Springs High School football
games did. They were just waiting for the game to begin.

Kerry reassuringly touched his shoulder, directing him
toward the back of the junkyard. "Sure, sure, let's do
this."

"It was Melanie Carr's kid who phoned it in," Paul

told Kerry as the four of them walked toward the scene of the crime. "Apparently some friends of his left him here last night as a practical joke. When he woke up this morning, he saw the body as he was leaving. Scared him to death."

"I imagine so," Kerry said. She and Paul walked behind Collie and Royce. "What's your first impression of the scene?"

"Well, Chief," Paul said, as they arrived at the spot where the body lay. "My first thought was, it must have been a vigilante killing." He reluctantly looked down at the body. "Look who the guest of honor is."

Kerry followed his line of sight, and did a double take when she recognized the corpse. It was the thorn in her side himself, Johnny Haywood.

Since this aspect of her job was her least favorite, Kerry dreaded the next few minutes.

Having arrived on the scene first, Paul had marked off the immediate area surrounding the body with yellow crime scene tape. They were all standing outside the marked-off area at the moment. Kerry carefully observed the ground around them. With all the recent rain, the ground was moist and therefore more porous, which lent itself to deeper impressions.

Kerry looked up at Paul. "You're the only one who's been in the area besides the Carr kid?"

Paul nodded in the affirmative.

"Then I want you to pour casts of all the footprints leading out of here." She slowly walked the area. This done, she lifted the tape and crossed the crime scene.

Standing over the body, she bent down to peer into Johnny's eyes. They were occluded somewhat, the breakdown not as complete as on some bodies she'd seen over the years. Which meant he hadn't been dead very long. Plus there was the fact that there were no signs of further putrefaction. The body was in the early stages of rigor mortis, the seepage of fluids and malodorous smells not yet evident.

Which was good as far as forensic science was concerned. The earlier the body was found before breakdown, the better chances of discovering clues that would help in the apprehension of the killer.

TWO

"Somebody did the world a favor," Kerry overheard Royce say to Collie Mason.

Kerry had slipped on a pair of surgical gloves and was examining the victim's hands.

There was a split knuckle on his right hand plus dried blood on the palms of both hands. The bottoms of his feet were surprisingly clean. No visible muck and the nails didn't have sand beneath them. To Kerry that meant the body had been carried to the scene. Therefore chances were he hadn't been killed here.

". . . big-time drug dealer," Royce was saying. "His supplier probably offed him."

Kerry placed the victim's foot back down and rose. Looking at Royce, she said evenly, "Paul could use your help."

Royce's nostrils flared and his eyes narrowed, a sure sign of irritation. "Sure, Chief."

"Mr. Mason, I apologize for keeping you from your work. Thank you for your assistance. We will try to wrap this up as soon as possible."

Collie Mason's brows shot up at this obvious dismissal, but he held his tongue.

"Well, all right. Y'all want me to keep the gate locked a while longer? I've got customers lining up out there." Kerry doubted that any of those cars belonged to customers.

"I'm sorry, but you're going to have to remain closed until we're finished gathering evidence," Kerry told him. "The coroner's van will be here shortly. And then forensics will need more time to do their thing once the body's removed. Please be patient."

Collie walked off, grumbling about the department compensating him for lost earnings.

Kerry smiled to herself and squatted next to the body again. She felt mixed emotions about Johnny Haywood's death. He was her age, thirty-two. They'd gone to school together. Johnny and his older brother, Ike Jr., had been thick as thieves. Both of them got a kick out of tormenting her. They would pull her hair, push her down and try to kiss her, which repulsed her a lot more than a shove ever did. Her older brother, Eddie, had whipped their butts more than once. Nothing stopped them, though, until she started fighting back. The first time she punched Ike Haywood Jr. in the nose and drew blood was the beginning of the end. After that, the Haywood boys were more circumspect in their dealings with her. It helped that Kiana, two years ahead of her, usually walked her to school before going on to the high school down the street. Kiana was known as Krazy Kiki. When she got into fights with boys she knew exactly what spot to aim for. She was not averse to biting, scratching, or gouging, and had sent many a foolhardy boy limping home to his momma. Kerry had quite a reputation to live up to. By the time she got to high school, she was also known as a girl not to be messed with—which wasn't too cool if you wanted a date on a Saturday night.

"Even you didn't deserve this," Kerry said in a low voice as she looked at the bloody mess that was Johnny Haywood's chest. She could clearly make out the words carved into it: BETTER OFF DEAD, in block letters. She imagined it was difficult to write in cursive on flesh.

She stood up and turned away from the scene, drawing in a deep breath and sighing. She supposed she should be the one to tell Nicole, Johnny's wife, and Miss Bess, his mother, that he was dead.

She walked over to her deputies who were carefully removing the casts from the damp ground. It only took a few minutes for the mixture to harden. "Talk to me," she said to Paul.

"You're not going to believe this," Paul said, his dark eyes meeting hers, "but there are two sets of prints aside from mine and the Carr boy's, and they're both size-ten athletic shoes."

Kerry had asked Paul to take casts of all the footprints for a reason. She wanted to compare the thickness of each cast. Thickness was indicative of the weight of the subject. She asked Paul to point out his own cast. He did. It was thicker than each of the casts belonging to the suspects.

Paul weighed around one hundred and eighty pounds.

"They must be lightweights," Kerry said of the suspects.

"Stone-cold crackheads are usually as skinny as rails," Royce suggested. "Maybe a couple of them iced him and stole his stash."

"Maybe," Kerry said. But she didn't think so.

"Hey, Dera. How's it going?" Kerry called to the lone occupant of the room as she came through the door of the police station. It was located downtown in the new city hall, and was far more comfortable than the old courthouse had been. The old digs had been a two-hundred-year-old antebellum monstrosity. Older citizens were nostalgic about it, saying it was a reminder of a more genteel time. Kerry, and many of the other black citizens, were glad to see it go, right along with the Confederate flag that they used to fly alongside the American flag out front near the rotunda. Now the only flags flying

out front were the State of Florida flag and the American
flag.

Dera Stephenson, an African-American woman in her
late forties, had worked for two chiefs prior to Kerry. As
the department's head dispatcher, her voice was instantly
recognizable by city personnel as well as the citizenry.

Dera was fond of Kerry. She liked all of the Everetts.
She worshipped with them every Sunday morning, and
her children had all been taught by Mrs. Everett, as they
referred to Kerry's mom, Evelyn, who was a retired
schoolteacher.

Dera ran a hand through her long braid extensions.
"It's been quiet. I heard your fax machine goin' crazy a
few minutes ago, though, and went to investigate, in case
it was something you needed to know right away. Ike
Haywood's getting ready to be paroled in a couple days.
The warden thought you ought to know."

Kerry looked heavenward and issued an exasperated
sigh. "That's all I need: Ike out of jail, and his brother's
just been killed."

"Johnny?" Dera gasped. She got up from behind her
desk. Five-three on a good day, her head came to Kerry's
shoulder. Dressed in black leggings and a long denim
shirt, she affected a young attitude that defied aging.
Leaning on the corner of the desk, she regarded Kerry.
"Poor Miss Bess," she said with a sad shake of her head.
"Hasn't that woman been through enough?"

"Indeed, indeed," Kerry commiserated, heading for the
inner office. "I've got to do the paperwork on it, then
head over to Nicole Haywood's to break the news to her;
then it's on to Miss Bess's. I don't look forward to it."

"Mmm-mmm-mmm," Dera intoned just as the 911
line lit up on the complicated computer-operated system.
She reclaimed her chair behind the computer and said,
"Nine-one-one. What is the nature of your emergency?"

In her office, Kerry put her gun in her desk drawer
then sat down and logged onto the computer. Seconds

later, she'd accessed the FBI's database and entered the pertinent preliminary info about the murder of Johnny Haywood. Then she waited for the program to compare her information with previous input. It didn't take long for her to find out that the modus operandi of her suspect matched several methods of three serial killers the FBI was presently in pursuit of.

One of them plied his trade exclusively in the South, including Florida.

She pressed the PRINT key and made a hard copy of the findings. She didn't know what, if anything, the FBI would do with the information she'd supplied. This was the first time she'd ever had to log on and fill out their form.

Finished with that, she filled out the reports that would go into the City of Damascus Police Department's files.

Dera stuck her head in the door just as Kerry was typing the last sentence. "Chief, the mayor is here to see you." She rolled her eyes. *Self-important blowhard,* was how Dera usually referred to His Honor out of earshot.

"Tell him to come right in," Kerry said, quickly typing the remaining words. She made a hard copy while she waited for Reginald Washington to make his entrance.

Reverend Reginald Washington. He was also pastor of a local African Methodist Episcopal Church.

"Kerry, what is this I hear about a murder in my town!" he demanded, jowls flapping.

Taken aback, Kerry scowled at him. "Who told *you?*"

His jowls settled back down, making him look like a hound dog. "Collie Mason phoned me, saying the city was accountable for any damage done to his property and any earnings he might lose due to the extended period of time you all are spending out there. Who is it, Kerry? Who got killed on your watch?"

Kerry got up and walked around to stand in front of the mayor, who was two inches shorter than she was and a hundred pounds heavier. Kerry didn't know why the man wore a tie; with his double chin it looked as if he were hanging himself!

Though he was African-American, he was very light skinned, so much so that whenever he became enraged he turned a nice shade of pink. Like a Christmas ham. His natural hair was red and tightly curled. The tips of his ears were nearly crimson now.

"Johnny Haywood."

"The drug dealer?"

"Do you know another Johnny Haywood?"

"How did he . . . ?"

"Bullet between the eyes."

"Execution-style?"

"Execution-style, or just a lucky shot, who knows? The man's still dead," Kerry said, impatient. She turned to go to her desk drawer and retrieve her gun. After checking the ammunition, she looked up. "I was just on my way out to deliver the news to his wife and mother. Would you like to ride shotgun, or can I assume this meeting is over?"

"Just do your job!" Reginald blustered, moving out of her path. "And do it quickly," he added, his beady brown eyes resting on the play of her hips in those khaki pants as she walked through the door.

A woman chief of police. He would never have hired her if it had been up to him alone. A woman was good for two things, as his wife, Marisol, knew well. She'd given him six children, and she was one hell of a cook. Marisol was perfect in every way.

The Haywood home was a new split-level sitting on two acres on the outskirts of town. There were two cars in the driveway: a late-model black Lexus and an older-model white Jeep Cherokee. Kerry parked on the edge of the yard and got out. In a fairly new subdivision, the Haywood home was one of only four on Magnolia Street.

The lawn had recently been laid, and they hadn't done much landscaping. The house next door didn't have grass in its yard at all, just rocky soil.

Kerry rang the bell and removed her sunglasses. She hoped this would go well. If Nicole Haywood didn't become too emotional upon hearing of her husband's death, Kerry wanted to get a statement from her.

"Who is it?" came a sharp female voice.

"Chief Everett, Damascus Police Department," Kerry said with authority. "I'm here to see Nicole Haywood."

The door was yanked open, and Nicole Haywood stood there in a nightgown with a matching bathrobe over it. Her short, brown hair was in disarray and there were bags under her eyes. She looked unbearably tired.

Kerry guessed she couldn't be more than twenty-five, but today she looked ten years older. She noticed something else too: the left side of Nicole's face was bruised and swollen, as if she'd recently taken a lick there. They'd never met until now. Kerry had heard Nicole's family was from Gainesville.

Kerry was just about to launch into the reason why she was there when a small boy, who looked barely old enough to walk, came toddling into the room. He had a bottle with apple juice in it in one hand and was dragging a rather battered stuffed rabbit with the other. He wore only a soiled white T-shirt and a diaper that, even from this distance, Kerry could tell was pretty ripe.

"Mama," he whined, going to his mother and grabbing her around the legs, which wasn't easy since he wasn't letting go of either the bottle or the stuffed rabbit to do so. Nicole bent down and angrily snatched him up into her arms. Looking at Kerry she said, "I guess you can see I have my hands full, Chief. What's so important you had to come here this early in the morning?" Kerry's watch read 11:13 A.M. "You can save your breath if it's about that sorry-ass husband of mine. If y'all finally caught up with him, he can rot in prison for all I care."

So, she knows what he did for a living, Kerry thought. *No use postponing this any longer.* "Mrs. Haywood, I'm sorry, but it *is* about your husband."

The toddler had begun drinking his juice and his sucking seemed to further irritate his mother. She took the bottle from his mouth and bent to set him on the floor. Turning cold eyes on Kerry, she said, "I told you I don't want to hear anything about him."

"I'm sorry, Mrs. Haywood, but your husband is dead." There, it was out. There was no way to deliver news of this magnitude nicely. You just had to say it and get it over with. Nicole's eyes stretched wide, and she simply stood there a few seconds in shock, her mouth hanging open and her head cocked to the side, staring at Kerry.

The little boy started bawling. Kerry looked down and discovered Nicole had unintentionally stepped on his foot and she was still standing on it. Kerry calmly reached out and grabbed Nicole by the shoulders and moved her off her son's foot. Then, she picked up the baby. Nicole hadn't moved. Her eyes were following Kerry, though, so Kerry knew that some part of her was cognizant of what was going on.

With the baby on her left hip (her gun was on the right side), Kerry took Nicole's hand and began walking toward the back of the house. "Your son needs changing. Sometimes it helps to do normal things if you've had a shock. Show me where his bedroom is, where you keep his clean clothes."

As if she had no will of her own, Nicole allowed herself to be led along. Kerry talked while they walked. "Is there anyone here with you? Someone who can stay with you a while after I've gone?" There had been two cars in the driveway, perhaps someone else was in the house.

Kerry got her first response. Nicole shook her head in the negative.

After peering inside two bedrooms, Kerry finally came to the nursery. It was a brightly decorated room, and it was neat compared to the rest of the house. Though the furnishings, carpeting, everything in the house appeared to be new, it could use a good cleaning. Kerry had seen it before: drug money could buy every conceivable luxury, but if you didn't have the training or the discipline to maintain those pretty things, it all soon went to pot. But, of course, with money like that you just bought new things when the old stuff wore out.

Looking at Nicole Haywood, Kerry realized this kind of life had a terrible effect on a person. Nicole was standing in the middle of her son's nursery, pulling her hair. When she removed her hand, a spiky tuft remaining standing.

The blinds were shut, throwing the room into semi-darkness. Kerry went and opened them. After that she immediately saw the disposable diapers, wipes, and baby powder on the changing table next to the window.

She went and placed the baby in Nicole's arms. She felt Nicole's hold tighten around her son before letting go. "You're probably much better at this than I am. It's been a while since I changed a diaper."

Besides, she wanted Nicole to *do* something. It might snap her out of her present state of mind. Nicole gazed down at the top of her son's curly head. "Jack," she said in a low, tortured voice.

She went into action, deftly swinging her son upright and onto her shoulder; then she gently placed him on his back on the changing table and made short work of cleaning him up. Kerry stood to the side, watching, wanting to breathe a loud sigh of relief, but afraid to make any noise for fear it would interrupt Nicole's return to normalcy.

Soon little Jack was sweet-smelling and dressed in a clean T-shirt and a pair of shorts. It was summer, after all,. and his mother wanted him to be comfortable.

Nicole placed her son on her hip and regarded Kerry with clearer eyes. "Do I need to go identify him or something? I see that on TV all the time."

"That isn't necessary," Kerry told her. "We have a positive ID."

Nicole led the way back out to the living room. "I killed him," she said, her tone so bereft of hope that Kerry felt her stomach muscles tense in sympathy. She didn't believe Nicole was confessing to her husband's murder; it was guilt talking. Regret for hateful words spoken, or loving words left unspoken. Either way the grieving partner usually experienced guilt when her mate died.

"Do you think you're up to answering a few questions?" Kerry asked. Nicole had sat down on the sofa and motioned for Kerry to sit down, too. Kerry took the chair directly opposite Nicole's. Nicole put Jack on the floor. He immediately rose and went to get his bottle of apple juice, which had been left in the center of the large, airy room. As soon as he put the nipple in his mouth, he plopped down on the floor, content.

Nicole's big brown eyes were tear-filled. She wiped them with the back of her hand. "Last night he came in after being gone I-don't-know-where all day long and started in on me. 'Why can't you clean this place up?' he wanted to know. 'I buy you the best of everything and you treat it like crap.' I told him it was because I hated how he bought these things. He knew I hated what he did. I wanted him to get out, but he said he couldn't get out, not alive anyway. After that, I yelled at him that I was leaving him. I couldn't live like this anymore, and that's when he hit me. I was so angry with him I told him I wished he were dead; then, at least, Jack and I could live without fear."

A sob escaped, and she took a deep breath. "Something in him snapped. He started hitting me and hitting me. I have bruises all over my body. I passed out, and when I came to, he was gone. I mean he just *left* me here alone with a baby in the house. I could have choked on my own blood and died, but did he care?" She paused, maybe remembering that her husband *was* dead. She sighed. "I didn't mean it. I didn't really want him dead. I just wanted him to quit dealing drugs." She looked up at Kerry, a frightened expression on her face. "You don't think whoever killed Johnny would come after me and Jack, do you? Maybe think since I was married to him I might be hiding some drugs or money? Because I swear I didn't know anything about that business. He didn't tell me anything! I didn't even know where he would go, who he would be with. He never had them phone here, not here, just his cell phone. I swear, I don't know anything!"

"Calm down," Kerry said reassuringly. "That's not why I'm here. I just wanted to know the approximate time you saw him last. And if you had any idea where he might have gone after he left here."

"It was around ten last night." Nicole eagerly supplied the answer. "I knew it was ten because the early news was just starting when he came in. We only argued about fifteen minutes . . . God, it seems like much longer now . . . and then he punched me and I can't tell you anything else after that."

Meaning she couldn't tell Kerry what time he left the house or where he was going.

"All right," Kerry said, rising. "If you think of anything else, give me a call." She reached into her breast pocket and retrieved a business card. "You can call me anytime, day or night. Understand?"

Nicole accepted the card and got to her feet, preparing to walk Kerry to the door.

"One more thing, Chief," Nicole said, her hand on

the doorknob. She bit her bottom lip and frowned before continuing. "How did he . . . die?"

"He was shot," Kerry simply said. She left before Nicole could ask any further questions. Soon details about her husband's death would be coming out of the woman's ears. If she could spare her some pain right now, then good.

In the Explorer, she dialed her mother's number as she was driving away from the Haywood house. Evelyn Everett answered on the third ring.

"Everett residence, Evelyn speaking."

"Good morning, Momma."

"Hey, baby girl. What is this I hear about Johnny Haywood getting killed last night?"

Kerry felt like screaming, she was so frustrated. News traveled fast in small towns, especially bad news. And she had yet to get over to Miss Bess's house to break the news to her. What if some big mouth blurted it out before she could get there?

"Momma, I hope you haven't called Miss Bess, because I haven't had the chance to tell her yet. How did you find out?"

"Big head Reggie Washington was at the garage for a tune-up this morning. He told your daddy, and your daddy phoned me. Don't worry, I haven't told anyone else."

"Good," Kerry said, sounding relieved. "I'm heading over to Miss Bess's now. I had to break the news to Johnny's wife first. The reason I'm phoning you is to ask you to call the troops. Nicole Haywood and Miss Bess are going to need the comfort and covered casseroles of the sisters of good old St. John A.M.E. Church. Oh, and enlist a few hearty souls who don't mind getting their hands dirty. Nicole's house could use a little tender loving care. You know there'll be people in and out before and after the funeral, and I'm sure she isn't going to feel up to cleaning it herself. And, please, choose ladies who're not going to be judgmental while doing it. The woman has been through hell."

"Kerry, I assure you, none of the ladies in my group would make the child feel self-conscious at a time like this," her mother said, aghast.

"Yeah, right. I remember the time Mrs. Young told a grieving widow, right in front of everybody at the funeral, that she was showing too much cleavage."

"Okay," Evelyn had to admit, "Enid is an exception. She's much too candid for her own good. We'll leave Enid at home."

Laughing, Kerry said, "Thanks, Momma. If someone could get over to Nicole's place as soon as possible, I'd really appreciate it. And give me about an hour before you all report for duty at Miss Bess's."

"I'll get right on it," Evelyn promised.

"I knew I could count on you," Kerry said. Then, they rang off.

Kerry pointed the Explorer back toward Damascus. Miss Bess lived in town on Delancey Street, only a few houses down from her parents' bungalow.

Kerry noticed the first fat raindrops as she passed the WELCOME TO DAMASCUS sign. *Great,* she thought, *now bad news will be accompanied by thunder and lightning.* It seemed like death and rain went hand in hand. How many times had she been at an interment, and as the casket was lowered into the ground it started to rain? Too many.

When she was a little girl and that happened, her mother would tell her, "It's okay, sweetie, God is crying, too."

Elizabeth Haywood, called Bess by all who loved her, was busy canning tomatoes in her kitchen. It was hot work, but her garden had yielded more tomatoes than she'd been able to give away this summer, and she wasn't about to let them go to waste.

Times were hard when she was growing up, and she still remembered the scarcity of food. How her parents had scraped for a living. Going to bed hungry. Getting up hungry. That's one thing she swore her children would never experience: hunger.

At the stove, she turned the heat off under the glass jars filled with whole, peeled tomatoes. She would allow them to cool to room temperature; then she'd store them in her pantry.

She peered up at the clock hanging on the wall above the sink. Nearly noon and that boy was still in bed! Wiping damp hands on her colorful apron, she walked through the kitchen and into the hallway, then turned left. Twenty-two years old, and he couldn't hold a job to save his life. Did he expect to live with her, rent-free, forever?

She'd like to have her house to herself just once before she died. At sixty-two, she was still a handsome woman with warm brown skin, beautiful black hair with silver streaks in it. She was short, but had watched her weight; couldn't keep any weight on her what with worrying about her boys all the time.

But, she thought, as she put her hand on Harold's doorknob and turned, *the Lord has brought me this far, I guess he'll take me the rest of the way.*

"Harold Haywood, if you don't get out of that bed and in that yard and mow the grass I'm going to pull your mattress out to the front yard and set it on fire with you still on it! I mean it, Harold. Get your butt up right now."

Harold knew those strident tones well. He sat up in bed rubbing the sleep from his eyes. "Aw, Ma. Dude can't get no rest around here."

Bess humphed and tossed over her shoulder as she left the room, "Nobody told you to stay out until four o'clock in the morning. There are things to be done around here. And as long as you're sleeping in my bed, eating my food, using my electricity and water, without giving me one thin dime to help pay the bills, I'm going to get it out of your hide. So, get up. After mowing the lawn, you can wash my car."

THREE

Special Agent Maceo Kent rounded the corner, heading to the assistant director's office. He was coming off a difficult case, an interstate child-kidnapping in which the father abducted his own child and threatened to kill her. They'd managed to rescue the six-year-old girl, but her father had blown his brains out before they could disarm him.

Mac knew their priority had been to bring the girl home safely, but felt the father's death was senseless because anyone, in his opinion, could go a little crazy after a divorce.

If the poor guy had just taken the time to *think* before acting on emotion alone, he would have realized his wife leaving him for a younger man was not the end of the world. Just a change in the lineup. That was the problem with domestic cases: emotions ran high, and emotions could get your ass killed if you weren't careful.

Mac stopped at the assistant director's secretary's desk.

"I'm expected," he said.

Candice Price, an attractive twenty-three-year-old African-American woman, looked up and smiled slowly. Except for a darker, richer skin tone and that barely noticeable scar on his cheek, she could swear that Mac

Kent was the actor Boris Kodjoe of the Showtime series *Soul Food*. Yum, yum!

"Go right in, Agent Kent," she said, full lips parting to reveal straight, white teeth.

"Thank you," Mac said, as if he were totally unaware of his effect on her, which was far from the truth. He knew that hungry look all too well. She wasn't his type, though. Young, beautiful, ambitious women like Candice Price were never satisfied with men who were looking for a lasting relationship. They needed a high level of excitement and plenty of disposable income. Mac was past wanting to be any honey's Mack Daddy. At thirty-seven, he'd had his fill of transient relationships. He was a bachelor, but not a confirmed bachelor. There had been one woman he would've married in a heartbeat, but the time hadn't been right for them.

Mac paused at the mahogany door before turning the knob and going inside. Why had he thought of her? Now that she *had* crossed his mind, he wondered what had become of her, and if she was still as wonderful as he remembered. It was certainly worth thinking about.

"Agent Kent." Assistant Director Palmer offered his hand. After they shook, he indicated with a nod of his head that Mac should sit. Assistant Director Palmer was invariably formal when talking business, even though he could toss back a few drinks with the best of them when off duty.

"I've got something I think will interest you," he told Mac, sliding a single sheet of paper across the desk. "There's a possibility your vigilante has struck again."

He waited while Mac quickly scanned the report.

"It does sound like his handiwork, it's true," Mac said. "But this says there were two sets of footprints at the scene. Our guy works alone. Could be a copycat."

"You've got a dead drug dealer with the exact words our suspect has used every single time. What's more, three months ago when he struck in Maryland, he stashed the body at a used car lot. This person stashed it at an auto parts place. Even if it *is* a copy cat murder it's still worth your time. Go to . . ." He couldn't think of the town's name.

Mac read from the report. "Damascus, Florida. Pop. 5,643." He raised his eyes. "Could be a setting for an episode of the *Andy Griffith Show.*" Then he read the name of the officer who had provided the data: Chief Kerry Everett. It couldn't be *his* Kerry. It most certainly could be. Whom was he fooling? Of course it was his Kerry. Her hometown was Damascus, Florida. He wasn't about to forget that.

"Bears looking into," he said to the assistant director.

Assistant Director Palmer gave him an imperceptible nod. "All right. I suggest you go in undercover. Only the chief of police should know who you are. We don't want to scare off our guy if he's in hiding in Damascus. At any rate, Chief Everett can probably use your expertise."

Mac stood and shook the assistant director's hand. "I haven't met a small-town chief of police yet who welcomed our interference."

That elicited a chuckle from the taciturn assistant director.

Bess grimaced when she heard the rain on the roof. She looked across the room at Harold who was taking his time eating a bowl of cereal and drinking what was left of the coffee she had brewed that morning. If he'd risen earlier, he could have had a hot breakfast with her. But Bess made it a point of never cooking food for Harold and keeping it warm for him. To Bess, it demonstrated a lack of character for someone to linger in bed while the day passed them by. She rose at six each weekday and at seven on the weekend. Her behavior was habitual. No alarm clock was needed to get her out of bed each morning. Sometimes it took a blast of dynamite to get her youngest son out of bed.

"I guess you know it's raining," she said as she dried the extra lids and jars she hadn't needed for the canning. She waited for some response. Perhaps the sound of regret in his voice for having missed the opportunity to prove his worth.

Harold looked up at her, mouth full of cereal, and shrugged his shoulders.

"I'll have to wait until the grass dries out now," he said almost cheerfully. "Can't cut it while it's wet. Daddy taught me that."

"Yes, well," Bess returned, ready for his excuses, "the garage needs cleaning out, and you can do that rain or shine."

The crestfallen expression on her son's face was all the reward she needed. She left the kitchen merrily humming a hymn.

"Aw, man!" she overheard Harold moan as she turned the corner. Bess smiled.

The doorbell chimed.

Bess looked through the peephole before pulling the door open and smiling at Kerry Everett. She was always happy to see any of the Everetts on her front porch. "Kerry, I haven't seen you in a month of Sundays. What brings you here?"

Kerry lowered the hood on her rain coat, pulled it off and left it on the hook on the post nearest the steps. Miss Bess had put it there for that very purpose. Kerry wiped her feet on the mat before stepping inside. The smell of tomatoes assailed her nostrils.

"You've been canning, I see," she said, smiling down at Bess.

"Yes," Bess said, and pulled Kerry into her arms for a warm embrace. Their faces briefly touched, and Kerry thought Miss Bess's face felt just like her mother's, velvety soft. Miss Bess's fragrance was a combination of

Obsession by Calvin Klein and the faint scent of cooked tomatoes.

Bess released Kerry and closed the door. Gazing up at Kerry with a smile, she said, "I bet I know why you dropped by, to tell me about Ike Jr. Somebody from the prison, I can't recall the name, phoned yesterday morning and told me he would be released on Monday of next week." She directed Kerry toward the living room with a gesture of her hand. The living room was decorated in Early American, overstuffed couches and chairs covered in a pastel floral print. An inviting, neat, yet lived in room. A piano was in the corner. Bess had tried to teach all her sons to play. None of them showed any interest whatsoever. But with their father calling it a sissy pastime, how did she think they would react to her lessons? That was Ike, tearing down everything she tried to build up. Including her boys.

After both she and Kerry were seated on the couch, Bess sighed. "I suppose he'll come here when they release him. The prison official told me they were giving him a bus ticket, a small amount of cash, and the possessions he had when he went in. I know he won't try to go back to Jenette. She divorced him while he was inside, you know."

Kerry nodded in the negative. "No, I didn't know."

"Yes, she said she loved him but didn't love what he'd become." Bess's brown eyes were a bit watery. "I can't blame her. God knows I wish I'd left Ike earlier. Maybe my boys would have had a chance. Growing up watching their father con his way in and out of trouble. Me, working my fingers to the bone as a domestic to keep food on the table. Whom do you suppose they would look up to? The con artist whose tales always seemed exciting to young ears, or the mother who was constantly telling them crime doesn't pay?"

Kerry was willing to sit there and listen because she didn't want to deliver the news she'd come to deliver, anyway. And, who knows, Miss Bess having her say might soften the blow of what was to come. So when Miss Bess breathed in and out, as if she was getting her second wind, Kerry let her talk.

"After I put Ike out of the house, just before he went to prison that final time, the boys were so angry at me for 'abandoning' their father. When he came by, he'd pull up in a fine car every time. He'd flash rolls of money big enough to choke a horse with. Bought them useless gifts, toys they broke within thirty minutes of playing with them. Clothes so outrageously hip, the boys were ashamed to wear them to school for fear the other kids would pick on them. These were things Ike would bring back from his travels to the Big City. That's what he called any city bigger than Gainesville."

Kerry smiled at Miss Bess's description. She remembered Ike Haywood. He was fast talking, wore clothes that you could see from a mile away they were so garish. But there were good things she recalled about him, too. He would stop the ice cream truck in the middle of the street on summer afternoons, and treat every kid in the neighborhood.

"You think he's going to make it on the outside?" Bess asked, bringing Kerry back to the subject at hand, Ike Jr.'s parole.

"That's entirely up to Ike," Kerry answered honestly. "I hope so."

Bess shook her head sadly. "Me, too. There's always a chance he'll straighten up. He has three sons of his own to think about. I pray for that all the time, that Ike Jr., Billy and Johnny will see the light and become responsible men."

Kerry felt like a heel at the mention of Johnny's name. How could she just sit here and pretend she'd only come to tell Miss Bess her son Ike Jr. was being paroled, when she'd come for a much more serious reason? *Coward,* she called herself.

She reached over and clasped both Miss Bess's hands in hers. Blowing air between her lips, she said, "Please forgive me, Miss Bess, but I'm not here to tell you about Ike."

Bess noted the sympathetic expression in Kerry's eyes, and the pressure with which she was holding her hands, as if she had to hold on tight because what she had to say would undoubtedly cause a shock to the system.

"It's Johnny," Kerry said.

With those words, Bess knew. She simply *knew*.

There had been too many times in her life when someone had to deliver bad news. In each instance, when the person had a sliver of human kindness in his heart, she'd seen that look she was seeing in Kerry's eyes now.

Sometimes Bess wished they would just come on out with it. Spill it with the first words issuing from their mouths, instead of allowing a few words to escape at a time. It seemed so much harder when they drew it out for fear of seeing her pain. Pain would come whether they said it slowly or dropped the bomb on her so fast it left her dizzy.

"Johnny's been arrested?" Bess told herself she could hope. She could hope that that was why Kerry was holding her lips together so tightly her mouth was one thin line.

Kerry pried her lips apart. "We found—"

Bess screamed. She caught Kerry off guard, and Kerry let go of her hands. Hands she had meant to hold onto no matter what transpired in the next few minutes. Bess careened sharply, pushing herself up off the couch and standing. Holding her head in her hands, she cried, "No, Kerry, you didn't come here to tell me my son is dead!"

Kerry rose too. "I'm sorry, Miss Bess."

Bess keened like a wounded animal. "Oh, God! How? How did he die?" She looked at Kerry with a frantic expression in her dark, inexpressibly sad eyes.

Kerry was about to reply when Harold came running

into the room, looking from his mother to Kerry and wiping his mouth with the sleeve of his shirt. "Momma, what's going on?" His eyes rested accusingly on Kerry. He didn't trust the police. Nor the justice system. It had killed his father and imprisoned his brothers. "What are you doing here?"

He went to his mother and pulled her into his arms. He looked over his mother's head at Kerry. "What did you say to her?"

Harold was a big man, six-three and over two hundred pounds. He had played varsity football, but after he'd allowed his grades to drop his senior year, hadn't been picked by any of the college coaches to play ball for them. Some said that that failure made him give up on doing anything else. If he couldn't do what he had his heart set on, playing college ball, he wouldn't do anything. Kerry had to assess size and mentality when in situations like this. Domestic calls were unpredictable at best, and could become violent, worst-case scenarios. So now she chose her words wisely, and cautiously.

"Your mother's upset because I came here to tell her that Johnny is dead, Harold. We found his body at Mason's Auto Parts this morning, and, from all evidence, it was a killing." She tried to keep her voice as soft and authoritative as possible. But Miss Bess's crying was affecting her, and it was difficult to control her emotions.

Harold hugged his mother tighter. "Shh, Momma. We'll find the person who did this to Johnny. I can promise you that." He spoke with such ferocity, such conviction, that a chill ran up Kerry's spine. She instinctively knew what he meant. Ike Jr. was getting out of prison, and the Haywood boys were going on a vigilante hunt for the killer of their brother.

Kerry moved close to Harold, her eyes just as fierce as his. "Listen to me, Harold, Johnny was killed on *my* watch, in my town. I *will* find the killer and make him pay for what he did."

Harold actually laughed as he rocked his mother. "You're gonna find the killer? You people are probably celebrating down there at the police station. I know how badly you wanted to catch Johnny, but he was too smart for you. I wouldn't be surprised if he was killed by one of *you*. One of those rednecks you have working for you, or one of the Aryan Nation boys that drive around here with Confederate flags on their pickup trucks and shotguns in the back windows. Well, you can tell them for me that by the time I'm finished with them, they'll be swimming in their own blood."

"Stop it, stop it!" Bess cried, twisting out of her son's embrace. She took a step back and slapped Harold's face. Slapped him so hard, tears immediately came to his eyes.

"I don't want to hear you talking like that, Harold," she cried, her bottom lip trembling. She stepped forward and grasped him by the upper arms. For a tiny woman, her hold was biting. "Johnny is dead because of what he did for a living. He lived by the sword, and he died by it, God rest his soul." Her eyes were pleading when they ran over his much-loved face. "I don't want you losing sight of that fact, Harold. Your brother is dead! He'll never get the chance to see his own son grow up. He'll never get the chance to change his way of living, if that was in his heart. I know you only remember the boy you grew up with. You turned a blind eye to his drug dealing. Maybe you even thought it was cool. I knew you accepted gifts of money and other things from him, so maybe that was your way of condoning what he did. But that was wrong, Harold. Those who do what Johnny did, dealing drugs to people who are hooked, people who don't know or care where their next meal is coming from as long as they can get another hit, people whose lives are ruined, and whose children's lives are ruined because of drugs! They're pitiful, Harold. They deserve your pity. But the man who sells it to them, he doesn't deserve your pity, he deserves your contempt.

Because a man who will do something like that to his own people, just for money, has no heart, and has sold his soul to the devil."

Harold stood there, tears rolling down his cheeks. All the fight had drained from him. He just wanted to mourn the brother he'd loved before he'd become the man his mother was describing. He just wanted to remember that man for a while.

He regarded Kerry. "You really gonna try to catch whoever did this?"

"With every ounce of my being," Kerry assured him. And meant it.

It was still raining when Kerry left Bess Haywood's home. She stood on the porch a moment, getting her bearings as she slipped on the hooded raincoat. Sympathetic tears rolled down her cheeks. As long as she was in their presence, she'd been able to hold the tears in check. How would it look for the chief of police to cry while on duty? Not very encouraging to someone you're supposed to be serving and protecting.

She knew what it was like to lose a loved one, though. And that was why their pain had affected her. Less than two years ago Kerry's older sister, Dionne, and her husband, Kevin, had been killed in an auto accident. A drunk driver ran head-on into them. Their then four-year-old daughter, Courtney, had miraculously survived the crash. Courtney was now being raised by Kerry's sister, Kiana, and her husband, Gabriel, who was, coincidentally, Kevin's older brother.

Kerry glanced down at her watch as she carefully walked down the steps and hurried toward the Explorer. It was a little past one in the afternoon. The emotional intensity of the last few hours left her drained. She longed to call it a day and head over to Kiana and Gabriel's house where she'd spend the evening babysitting her niece. Nothing soothed her more than listening to Courtney chatter about anything and everything while she ate her dinner, took a bath, then settled down to watch a Disney video, which she invariably fell asleep to. Kerry would have to carry her to bed, whereupon Courtney would stage a comeback and stay awake long enough to be read her favorite African fairy tale: *The Girl Who Loved Butterflies*. Any other tale would do after it was read, but she had to have that one read to her first.

No rest for the weary, Kerry thought as she pulled into her parking space at city hall. There, near the police station's entrance, was the WJXK News van. A Gainesville station, WJXK's motto was *We're There When You Need Us.*

Just as Kerry was climbing from the Explorer, news anchor Denise Capshaw came running out of the police station, a cameraman following close behind. Kerry narrowed her eyes. Denise, a tall brunette in her early twenties and eager to make a name for herself so she could move on to a big-city affiliate, shoved the mike under Kerry's nose.

"Chief, what can you tell us about alleged drug dealer Johnny Haywood's death?"

Kerry squinted under the glare of the camera's lights. "It's much too early to report anything about Mr. Haywood's death, Miss Capshaw. We're conducting a thorough investigation. I have no comment other than that."

"Is it true that a message was carved into his chest?" Denise asked. Kerry was appalled by the look of morbid curiosity in the woman's green eyes. Finally, a news story she could sink her teeth into. Kerry could almost hear her panting at the thought of getting an exclusive. "We were told that there was something carved on the victim's chest. Can you tell us exactly what it was?" Denise asked again, as if Kerry hadn't heard her.

"If you'll excuse me, I have work to do," Kerry said,

her hand on the door's handle. She pulled it open, looked back and frowned. "Please don't report news you haven't yet gotten corroborated."

"But, Chief!" Denise cried, trying to shove her foot in the door.

Paul Robertson stepped around Kerry as she came into the station and put his body between hers and Denise Capshaw's. "Did you get my good side?" he asked with a charming smile.

"Stop tape," Denise hissed at the cameraman. Cutting her eyes at Paul, she said, "I don't understand you people. The public has the right to know what's going on in their community."

Paul gave her an almost intimate perusal. If she weren't such a prickly gal, she might be cute. That "you people" comment rankled, though. He didn't like it when Northerners came down here and disdainfully regarded Southerners as hicks simply because people in the South had a certain way of doing things.

"Apparently you haven't lived in the area long, Miss Capshaw. Believe me, the citizens of Damascus have a communication system that's much swifter than WJXK. It's called the grapevine." With that, he closed the door and strode back into the police station.

Denise Capshaw angrily spun on her heels and began walking back to the WJXK News van. Terry Young, the cameraman, walking alongside her, smiled to himself. He'd enjoyed that. Denise kept forgetting that he was a hometown boy, and her disparaging remarks about the locals didn't exactly inspire loyalty in him.

"Come on," Denise grumbled. "Let's go to the county morgue and see what we can learn there. Maybe Dr. Soto will toss us a bone."

Terry almost shook his head in sympathy for her plight. She definitely wouldn't get anything out of the coroner, Dr. Lisa Soto. Dr. Soto and Chief Everett had attended the University of Florida together. He knew because he'd been in their graduating class six years ago. Kerry Everett had majored in criminal justice, Terry in journalism and mass communications, and Dr. Soto in biology. She'd gone on to medical school. Rumor had it Kerry and Lisa were still close friends.

But, he thought as he turned the key in the ignition and glanced at Denise Capshaw, sitting on his right and still fuming over the treatment she'd received from the chief, *let her find out for herself.*

One day she'd come around and realize she sometimes needed to use charm and finesse in order to get a story and leave the strong arm tactics at home. You couldn't shove a microphone under a Damascan's nose and *will* him to speak. Damascans were stubborn cusses, and guarded their privacy with their lives.

Kerry's stomach growled. She was sitting at her desk making up the duty roster for the month of August. With a total of ten men and women on the force, she staggered their schedules so that none of them would have to excessively pull night duty. Most of her people had families, and she was the type of boss who encouraged them to spend as much time with them as possible. Her own family had taught her the importance of strong familial ties, to one's emotional well-being.

The phone rang and she quickly picked up. "Hello, Chief Everett."

"Kerry, Lisa here." Lisa Soto, thirty-three, had a slight Spanish accent. Mexican-American, she'd come to the United States with her family when she was three.

"Hey, Lisa, what have you got for me?"

"I just threw Denise Capshaw out on her can. That oughta make you smile," Lisa returned. "It was a .22-caliber bullet that did Haywood in. That was the only gunshot wound on the body. The carving on his chest was done after death as evidenced by the lack of bleeding following the deed. There's something peculiar about his blood work. I'll get back to you on that, but from his temp, I'd say he'd been dead about six hours by the time the Carr kid found him. And I believe he had sex before he was killed. I don't want to imagine how else semen wound up on his . . . you know."

Kerry laughed shortly. "Me either. Listen to you, sounding squeamish when you deal with death on a daily basis."

"Nah, my job is different. It's clinical. I don't discover the bodies, I just find out what they died of. It's science, and therefore I can remain detached in a way you, for example, can't. You're in the thick of it. Speaking of you: This is your first murder in three years. How are you handling the stress?" Lisa asked, a humorous note to her voice.

Kerry knew what she was getting at. Lisa had been happily married for five years. Kerry had never been married and regarded sex as special. She made love to a man only when she was *in* love with him. Lisa had often joked that Kerry's water bill must be skyhigh, what with all that pent up sexual heat that needed cooling off.

"Don't you worry about me," Kerry said. "I'm handling it just fine, thank you."

"Mmm-huh," Lisa said, doubtful. "I *am* a doctor, you know. I know the horrible toll lack of sex can take on the human body. We're talking stress, hair loss, sleeplessness, unexplained weight gain . . ."

"I think Ben & Jerry's can be blamed for that," Kerry commented dryly.

"You're going to bed with Ben & Jerry's? I reserve that for *after* sex with Jon."

"Being celibate has its pluses." Kerry defended her lifestyle. "I don't have to worry about getting pregnant or any number of sexually transmitted diseases. Men have all the advantages in a sexual relationship. If a woman gets pregnant, he can claim it isn't his, but she can't claim it isn't hers. He can skip out on her, and she's left making the decision whether to keep the child or not."

"True, true," Lisa readily agreed. She sighed. "Occasionally, you do meet a guy who's worth risking it all for."

Kerry could think of a couple of men who fit that description. The first, she'd let slip through her fingers because she'd lacked the self-confidence to pursue him. The second was Dale Preston.

Dera stuck her head in the door. "Chief, the street fair committee is here."

"Lisa, I've got to run. Thanks for the rundown of your findings. If anything else turns up . . ."

"You'll be the first to know," Lisa assured her.

After hanging up, Kerry rose to greet the five members of the committee. Mrs. Mary Whitten, retired principal of Damascus Springs High School, age seventy-eight, strode in. As the sole female she got first dibs on the most comfortable chair in the room, a leather wing chair in front of the desk. The others, all males, jockeyed for space on the leather couch. They ranged in age from thirty-nine-year-old Dave Medeiros who owned a burger joint on Main Street, to seventy-five-year-old Donald Brown who owned the only hardware store in town. The other two members were Clyde Rice and Dale Preston Sr.

Hellos were said all around, after which Kerry went around and sat on the corner of her desk in an effort to keep the tone of the meeting casual. Last year, the meeting had turned into a name-calling free-for-all. Since the businesses sponsored the event, the business owners all wanted to make certain their businesses were prominently advertised and that they themselves were given proper credit for their generosity. If one businessman thought another was getting more free publicity than he was, it was cause for vociferous complaining.

Kerry knew she was in for a bumpy ride when the

first words out of the prim Mrs. Whitten's mouth were, "I *knew* Johnny Haywood would end up either dead or in prison."

Suppressing a sigh, Kerry gave her former principal a rueful look. "We're not here to discuss that, Mrs. Whitten."

"We should be," Donald Brown said, turning in his seat. His pale skin was so thin the veins could clearly be seen beneath it. "It's a question of safety, Miss Everett."

Kerry resisted reminding him that she should be addressed as Chief. The man routinely refused to acknowledge her position. At seventy-five, she wasn't about to change him. "I assure you, we're doing everything within our power to find Mr. Haywood's killer."

"I'm convinced you are," Donald Brown hastened to agree. "I don't doubt your desire to do your job, Miss Everett. I simply doubt your abilities to do it. It's not as if you've had very much practice hunting down a cold-blooded killer. We need someone in here who has solid experience."

Kerry knew Donald Brown had been a devout supporter of the former chief, Mike O'Hara. O'Hara had held the position for more than fifteen years. "It's true that since I was hired there have been no killings in Damascus," Kerry calmly said. "That doesn't mean I have no experience with violent suspects. I personally apprehended two males who were later convicted of murder when I was an officer in Miami. I think, Mr. Brown, that you should at least have the decency to wait for me to fall on my face before lodging a complaint."

Dale Preston Sr., tall, tanned, his dark brown hair graying at the temples, rose. He possessed a natural-born grace men envied and women found very attractive. "It's unfair to pounce on Chief Everett like this. The topic of the meeting is the street fair. I, for one, don't have time to discuss the Haywood case on top of that. I have to be some place in under an hour, and if we haven't discussed business within the allotted time period, I'll have to excuse myself."

"I second the motion." Dave Medeiros spoke up. "Let's get down to business."

Kerry could have kissed both men.

The second shift came on duty at six that evening. The deputies and office staff left, but Kerry stayed behind to speak with Jason Rivers, the watch commander for the evening. As chief of police, Kerry was always on call and was never without her beeper.

Jason, a tall African-American with dark brown skin and warm brown eyes, knocked on Kerry's door before walking in. He was the only officer on staff who routinely pulled night duty, which was his choice. His wife, Lucia, also worked nights as a nurse at North Florida Regional Hospital in Gainesville. They had two grown children, both of whom were on their own. They enjoyed having an empty nest.

Jason was fifty-six, and planned to retire in two years. Then he and Lucia, who was also retiring, would spend their twilight years pursuing second careers. Jason had always wanted to teach. And Lucia wanted to go to art school and refine her painting style. For the next four years they would live off their pensions, social security, and savings. They figured if they could send two children to college, they could also send themselves. Kerry admired them for that.

"Hey, Jake," Kerry said, looking up from last night's officer reports. She paused while Jason sat down. He groaned a little. Kerry knew that with the recent rainy weather his arthritic knee must be giving him hell. Though an older cop, Jason cut a fine figure in his uniform. And being athletic wasn't a requirement of his job.

What was needed was intelligence and a cool head. Jason possessed both.

"It says here that Abby Franklin was asked to stop hanging out on Maple Avenue last night. I suppose that means we didn't catch her actually soliciting business?"

Jason nodded. "That's right. But she's definitely on the street. We just haven't caught her in the act yet." An embarrassed expression fleetingly crossed his face. "That's not what I meant. I meant in the act of soliciting."

Kerry smiled. "I know, Jake. What I'm getting at is the fact that Johnny Haywood's street runs into Maple Avenue. He might have passed her when he left his house last night." She scanned the report again. "This says Abby was asked to move on at around midnight. Nicole Haywood says Johnny must have left their house at around ten-fifteen. That gives him plenty of time to have hooked up with Abby before she returned to her corner." She met Jason's eyes. "Dr. Soto says Johnny had sex with someone last night. But the way Nicole describes her interaction with Johnny, they argued, he struck her several times, and then he left her unconscious on the floor."

"What a prince," Jason said, his voice rich with sarcasm.

"Yeah," Kerry agreed. "At any rate, I'd like either you or one of your officers to ask Abby a few questions. See if she and Johnny got together last night."

"Will do," Jason said, a smile playing across his full lips.

Kerry rose, barely stifling a yawn she was so weary after the day's goings on. "Then I'm outta here."

It was dusk when Kerry left the station. The muggy air smelled of wild jasmine which grew in abundance all over Damascus, climbing fences and giving off its delightful odor more readily, it seemed, at night. Kerry liked to drive through the streets with her windows down, listening to the sounds of the settling town and breathing in that delightful fragrance.

She drove down Main Street, stopping at the sole red light. Traffic was heavier tonight than on weeknights. Couples were on dates. High school boys were cruising in their freshly washed cars, hoping to entice pretty girls strolling the sidewalks in groups to go for a ride with them. Kerry looked to the right. Dave Medeiros's Burger Palace was doing good business. The parking lot was full, and even the drive through was hopping.

The light turned green and she eased up on the brakes and gave the Explorer some gas. She had her radio tuned to a local R & B station. Destiny's Child was singing *Charlie's Angels'* praises again. Kerry hadn't seen the film, but if women cops all over the world looked like that, she was sure male cops would be much more welcoming to their sisters instead of giving them grief at every turn, as she'd been greeted with when she'd joined the Miami police force. After a while, though, she'd stopped trying to prove herself to her short-sighted male colleagues and just concentrated on doing her job. That was enough to shut up most of her detractors. The rest she didn't care about. A woman in law enforcement would always be seen as an oddity to some people, male *and* female. She just had to live with it.

Kerry had an attack of loneliness each evening when she entered the foyer. She supposed if she had someone to come home to, it would feel more welcoming. But even though she was happy to see her modest bungalow after a day like today, she was nonetheless gripped by loneliness the first few minutes upon crossing the threshold.

Lately, she was beginning to wonder if she'd ever find someone to share her life with. The last relationship she'd been in was short-lived at best. A few stolen kisses with Chuck Reeves, a sheriff's deputy whom she'd found momentarily irresistible. Then, with both their jobs on the line, she had found him eminently easy to let go of.

No, she wasn't another casualty of love. No man had ever gotten the chance to treat her badly, thereby leaving her bitter and unresponsive to whoever came along next. That wasn't her story. The fact was she'd been in love once, a long time ago. That experience had left her optimistic that she'd one day find that kind of love again. Of course, that could be a hindrance when you tended to compare every man you met to your one true love. None had even come close. Except Dale. Dale had potential.

Maybe she should give his proposal serious thought, she mused as she headed for the bathroom to take a quick shower. As she lathered her body beneath the warm spray of water, she allowed her mind to contemplate the urgency she'd sensed in Dale this morning. What had possessed him to spring a proposal on her? Could he have missed her that much while he was in Washington, D.C.?

Dale had put his cards on the table years ago, telling her he loved her and wanted more than friendship from her. He'd been patient, biding his time, being the friend she wanted. He'd, in essence, lulled her into a sense of complacency. She was very comfortable with their morning banter, his outrageous flirting without touching, and his intermittent declarations of intent: to get her into bed. But marriage? That was a tactic he'd never tried before.

Kerry stepped out of the shower stall onto a plush white towel. She languidly dried off with another and wrapped it around her body, tucking it in at her breasts. Going into her adjacent bedroom, she quickly glanced at the clock radio's dial on the nightstand: six forty-three. She was cutting it close. Kiana was expecting her at seven.

She momentarily felt sorry for herself. Why was she always the one who could be counted on to babysit? Not that she didn't thoroughly enjoy being with Courtney. It was just that she was only thirty-two, and she should be out on a date on Saturday night, just like every other young woman within a hundred mile radius.

It's all your fault, she thought as she sat on the edge of the bed to rub lotion onto her warm-from-the-shower body. *I'm sure Dale would be more than happy to show you a good time tonight.*

FOUR

"Don't you dare say a word," Kiana warned Gabriel, her golden-brown eyes fierce. She finished tying his tie and tiptoed to briefly kiss his mouth. Her husband was not content with a quick buss and pulled her firmly into his arms. "If you expect me to keep my mouth shut about this, you'll have to find something more enjoyable I can do with it." His dark eyes gleamed with mischief.

With that, he bent his head and met her mouth with intensity and purpose. Kiana was determined to keep her lips together; they had been late for more than *one* appointment because they'd gotten carried away while getting dressed. Etta James didn't do concert dates often, especially not this close to home, and Kiana didn't want to miss the blues diva.

The moment she felt his soft, pliable lips touch hers, though, then his tongue flick out to taste her, she knew it was a lost cause. "Oh, damn," she breathlessly murmured, and returned his kiss with gusto. If he broke the speed limit getting to Gainesville, they would arrive at The House of Blues just in time for the first set.

" 'Damn' is right, woman," Gabriel said, coming up for air. He buried his nose in the side of her neck. "I think you're even sexier now that you're pregnant." He gently cupped her breasts. "These are surely masterpieces." The look he gave her was smoldering.

Kiana was glad they'd locked their bedroom door. She

didn't want Courtney walking in on them while her uncle was feeling up her aunt. She smiled at him. "We both know how much you're enjoying 'the girls' lately, professor." She reached up and removed his hands from her breasts and stepped away. "Now, put on your pants if you can get them on over that." Her eyes were on the bulge in his boxers.

The doorbell rang. Kiana walked over to the door and pulled it open. Looking back at her husband, she said, "That's Kerry. Remember, not a word about Dale's proposal."

"She can do better," Gabriel said, picking up his trousers from the bed and sticking one muscular leg in them.

Kiana rolled her eyes and left the room.

Courtney, age five, was standing at the front door impatiently tapping her foot on the floor. Kiana had to smile at the picture she made. Courtney was the spitting image of her older sister, Dionne. She had her father Kevin's rich dark brown skintone, but the thick mass of black hair, golden-brown eyes, petulant nose and full heart-shaped mouth all came from her mother, Dionne.

She was itching to open the door. "I waited, Auntie Kiki. But it wasn't easy."

Kiana glanced through the peephole and saw an equally impatient Kerry standing on the other side of the door. "Go ahead and let your auntie in."

Grinning, Courtney made short work of unlocking the door and pulling it open; then she wrapped her arms around Kerry's waist. "Hey, sweet pea," Kerry said, laughing. She knelt on a jeans-clad knee to hug Courtney tightly. Her niece smelled like peaches. Must have been the body wash. Her braids were held on the top of her head by a purple scrunchie, and she wore a short yellow nightgown with Tweety Bird blazoned across the chest. "I see you're wearing the proper attire to watch *The Emperor's New Groove* and gorge yourself on junk food."

Kiana gave her younger sister a censuring look. "Not too much junk," she admonished.

Kiana was the disciplinarian, and Kerry was the aunt who spoiled Courtney rotten. The sisters tried to reach a happy medium, but Kerry was incorrigible and was always breaking Kiana's rules. "Okay, I'll be good," Kerry promised. She patted Courtney's cheek. "Why don't you go on into the den and put the disk in the DVD player while I scare up some treats."

"Okay!" Courtney said, excitedly. She loved it when she was allowed to act independently of the adults. Besides, she had an affinity for electronics. She'd been using a computer since she was four.

Kiana closed and locked the door and began walking toward the kitchen. Kerry followed. In the kitchen, Kerry leaned against one of the bright yellow-and-white counters, admiring her sister in her finery. She had to admit, pregnancy suited Kiana. Six months along, her belly appeared perfectly round. Kerry had heard about pregnant women glowing, but she'd never seen it with her own eyes before. Kiana's brown skin seemed to have some inner spiritual light that illuminated her soul for all the world to see. Kerry supposed that's what came with being in love, really in love, with the father of your child.

Kiana withdrew a small bottle of orange juice from the refrigerator and held it against her forehead. "Boy, it's hot." Her eyes met Kerry's. "I told Gabriel about you and Dale. Don't be surprised if he has a comment or two about it. You know him."

Kerry smiled. "Nobody's going to make up my mind for me. I'll take my time deciding. Right now I'm definitely leaning toward no. I don't know Dale well enough."

"You've known him all your life," Kiana disagreed.

"I've known *of* him all my life," Kerry countered reasonably. "He was the privileged golden boy whom everyone expected to go places."

"And he has," Kiana said, watching Kerry's face for some reaction. Kerry was silent.

Kiana opened the lid on the orange juice and drank deeply. The juice was rich in folic acid, and she planned on giving her child every good thing she could provide for him.

Some of the juice dribbled onto the tunic of her sleeveless silk pantsuit. "Oh, damn."

As luck would have it, Gabriel appeared just in time to hear the expletive. "Is that my cue to kiss you again?" He went to her. He was handsome in his black slacks, white shirt, and colorful tie Courtney had given him for Father's Day last June. It had frolicking bunnies all over it. She'd insisted he wear it tonight, and he hadn't wanted to disappoint her. Who cared if he'd get weird looks from every adult he came in contact with tonight?

Like all the Everett women, Kiana kept a box of baby wipes under the kitchen sink. They removed just about every stain known to man—and beast. Kerry went and got one for her sister, handing it to her. Kiana quickly swabbed the area.

"Shouldn't you two be getting out of here? Miss Etta isn't going to be pleased if you dis her by showing up late."

"Dis," Gabriel said, smoothly adopting his English professor persona. "Does that word appear in any of the accepted dictionaries?"

"Yeah," Kerry said. *"The Ebonics Dictionary.* It's right next to *The Homegirls' Guide to Finding Mr. Right* now in your favorite bookstore."

She walked them to the door and held it open for them. "If Miss Etta takes requests, ask her to sing 'At Last' for me."

Kiana stepped onto the front porch, but Gabriel lingered. He ran a big hand through his dreads and regarded Kerry with a serious expression on his dark-skinned face. "Hold out for a brother, Kerry."

Kiana yanked him onto the porch and pushed him down the steps. She tossed an apologetic look over her shoulder at Kerry. "I told you he wouldn't be able to resist."

Kerry laughed and stepped onto the porch to watch them as Gabriel held the Ford Expedition's door open for his wife, then trotted around to the driver's side. "Your African prince will arrive soon, Kerry. Be patient," he called before opening the car door and sliding behind the wheel.

Kerry heard them engaged in a lively argument as they sped off into the night.

Shaking her head, she laughed again, sighed and went back inside.

In the kitchen, Kerry went to the pantry adjacent to the back door and perused the goods. Kiana kept the special treats, or things she infrequently parceled out to Courtney, on the top shelf. Kerry, of course, went straight for the top shelf.

When she entered the den, she was carrying a tray laden with potato chips and onion dip, chocolate chip cookies and chocolate milk, and two kinds of popcorn, buttered and caramel. Both she and Courtney were headed for carbohydrate heaven.

Courtney had made herself comfortable on the couch right in front of the big screen TV. Her eyes lit up when she saw Kerry. "Good googalamoogala," she cried, using an expression she'd recently heard her cousin, E. J., use. "Is all that for *us*, Auntie?"

"Well, we don't have to eat it all in one sitting," Kerry said as she set the tray on the coffee table before them. She looked at the TV screen. Trailers were still running. She didn't know why they had to put previews on home movies. She glanced down at Courtney. "You know what to do."

Courtney picked up the DVD programmer and quickly

chose the program whereby the previews would be skipped and they'd get right to the movie.

"That's my girl," Kerry said with a big grin.

She sat down and handed Courtney the small carton of chocolate milk she'd brought for her. "So, you've never seen this one before, huh?"

"Oh, yeah," Courtney replied, screwing up her face as she found the place in the top of the carton where she could shove the miniature straw through. "But not much."

Kerry knew what that meant. She asked anyway. "Not much? How many times have you seen it already?"

"About five or six times. But I still don't know it by heart."

Kerry smiled and pulled her niece into the crook of her arm, sat back on the couch and got comfortable. It wasn't unusual for Courtney to watch a video ten to twenty times before she tired of it. Kerry supposed the familiar comforted small children. She knew that if *she* saw a Disney movie twenty times, she'd be about ready to commit hari-kari. But who was she to complain if it gave her niece pleasure?

She momentarily buried her face in Courtney's hair, breathing in her essence. The stresses of the day began to melt away.

A few minutes later, she was so into the animated film about a lackadaisical royal who was turned into a llama by the evil sorceress whom he'd dismissed, that she didn't even notice Courtney quietly snoring in the crook of her arm. Eartha Kitt was wonderful as the voice of the sorceress.

Easing Courtney into her arms, Kerry slowly rose and carried the child to her bedroom. Once in the bedroom, she placed Courtney on the already turned down bed (Kiana thought of everything), and drew the sheet up to her chin. She stood a moment, simply watching Courtney. Then she switched off the bedside lamp and left the room, leaving the door open a smidgen. She wanted to be able to hear Courtney should she cry out for her in her sleep.

Just as Kerry rounded the corner, she heard a tiny voice cry, "Auntie! I'm ready for my story now."

Grinning, Kerry spun on her heels and went back into Courtney's bedroom. She didn't think she was going to get off *that* easily, did she?

Courtney had switched on the bedside lamp and was sitting up in bed with an expectant expression in her dark eyes. "Would you read—"

"Let me guess," Kerry said, going over to the bookshelf by the window and choosing a thin, well-read book with brightly colored illustrations. "*The Girl Who Loved Butterflies*?"

Courtney nodded happily and scooted over to make room in bed for her aunt.

"All right," Kerry bargained. "But you have to lie down, hug your pillow tight, and close your eyes."

Smiling, Courtney did as she was told. And Kerry began: "Once upon a time, in an African land strange and wonderful and hence long forgotten by modern man, there lived a young woman who loved butterflies. Her name was Lirah, and she lived in a small village with her mother and father who were tailors. In those times there existed a great gulf between the rich and the poor. The king of this land tried to be fair; however, he was much removed from the masses and did not know how his people, especially the poor, were living from day to day.

"One fine spring day there came riding through the village the young Prince Deocles, scion of the royal family. Deocles was unhappy with his life. He could attend only so many feasts, court only so many princesses without becoming bored out of his royal skull. So, for a change of pace, he instructed his coachman to ride through the village and the adjoining countryside. He appeased his conscience by throwing gold coins to the children and beggars in the street. It seemed their numbers were increasing instead of decreasing. This troubled him because he thought of his father as a good king. A ruler who cared for all of his people.

"As they were leaving the village, they came upon a field of flowers and in the middle of this field they spied a beautiful maiden chasing a lone butterfly. 'Stop the carriage!' Deocles ordered his coachman. Deocles had never seen a princess as fair as this maiden in her plain sari. Her skin was the color of cinnamon, and her blue-black hair cascaded down her back in heavy braids. He was at once taken with her. In a flash of insight, he realized that if he caught the butterfly for the maiden, she might look upon him favorably.

" 'Coachman, I wish to step outside for a moment.'

"The coachman moved quickly to do his master's bidding, opening the door for Deocles and giving him a hand down.

" 'Your hat!' Deocles ordered, holding his hand out for the requested item.

"In those days coachmen wore big, floppy hats that looked rather like nets. Being without a net, Deocles figured the coachman's hat would suffice.

"Hat in hand, Deocles, a tall, powerfully built young nobleman, ran toward the field.

" 'Allow me to help you, maiden,' he called as he loped nearer.

"In one fell swoop, he had captured the frolicking butterfly. A triumphant smile on his handsome face, he offered the prize to the maiden. She took one look at the butterfly, laying stunned in the makeshift net, and let out a scream that would have curled the prince's hair had he not already been the proud wearer of an awesome 'fro.

" 'You've killed it, you brutish dolt!' Lirah cried, horrified. She angrily glared at him.

"Deocles was confused. Hadn't it been her objective to capture the creature? And brutish dolt . . . That wasn't a very nice manner in which to address your sovereign lord. Why, he could have her flogged for that comment. He would have, too, if he hadn't taken one look into her big, brown eyes and fallen deeply and unequivocally in love with her. . . ."

Courtney rolled over in bed and looked at her aunt at that point. "What does that word mean again, auntie?"

"It means he had no doubt in his mind that he was in love with her," Kerry answered with a warm smile. She liked the story almost as much as her niece did.

"Deocles held the hat open, shaking it a little. The dazed butterfly flew out of its temporary prison and into the nearby woods," she continued reading. " 'He lives,' Lirah said, relieved. Her smile was brilliant.

" 'Yes, I suppose he was only resting,' Deocles said. 'Did you not want him for your collection?'

" 'I did not!' Lirah informed him, dark eyes flashing angrily. 'He deserves to be free, just as all living creatures. Who are *you* to capture him?'

"Deocles pulled himself up to his full, rather formidable, height. 'I am Prince Deocles, son of the king, heir to the throne.'

" 'Then you should know better,' Lirah told him, not missing a beat. Then, she turned to leave.

"Deocles was not used to being dismissed.

"He reached out and grasped her by the arm, preventing her departure. 'You're not only insolent, but you appear to revel in it. What do you have against me?'

" 'It's your class,' Lirah explained, tossing her braids across her right shoulder with a little neck action. 'You think you own everything. Not just your material possessions, but that butterfly as well.' She looked down at the hand that firmly held her. 'Now, you hold me against my will. Do you also think you own me?'

"Deocles released her. 'You misunderstand me. I captured the butterfly only to offer it to you as a token of my admiration for your beauty.'

" 'Beauty is only on the surface, your majesty. I suppose if you hadn't thought me attractive you wouldn't have stopped. You're not only materialistic, but superficial.'

"Deocles could only stare at this young woman, totally aghast at every word that issued from her mouth. 'You are unfair, maiden. Am I to be judged so harshly simply because of the happenstance of my birth?'

" 'Am I to fall at your feet, smitten by you, because of the happenstance of your birth?' Lirah countered.

" 'I would not have you at my feet, but at my side. What can I do to prove to you that I am not unkind and selfish as you would paint me?'

" 'Have you one friend who is not of your class?'

" 'I have many!' Deocles confidently boasted.

" 'Name one,' she challenged him."

"He can't name one!" Courtney piped in. Kerry could tell, by the sound of her voice, that sleep was slowly claiming her.

"Be quiet, you!" Kerry admonished. "And close your eyes."

"He could not," she continued reading. "The coachman worked for him but they were not friends. The stable boy took care of his prized stallion, but they had little to say to each other. The cook made his favorite dishes daily but he didn't even know her name. He simply called her Cook.

"Lirah gave him a sad look as he stood there struggling to come up with the name of one friend who was not of his station in life. She sighed softly when he still did not answer the question. 'I am not for you, my lord,' she called as she turned and fled. 'Perhaps an empty-headed princess would be more suitable.'

" 'At least leave me your name,' Deocles called desperately after her.

" 'Lirah, daughter of Israh and Lili, tailors.' With that, she disappeared. Presumably out of his life forever.

"The next morning, Deocles went to his father, King Ketemba, and told him he wished to work for a living. He was tired of being idle. He wanted a purpose in life.

" 'Your purpose is to replace me when I die,' his father said. 'That is the normal routine.'

" 'Yes, father, but what do I do until that fateful day? Besides, you look extremely fit to me, thank Allah. I'd like to keep busy in the meantime.'

"King Ketemba saw the sincerity in his beloved son's eyes and granted him his request. From that day forth, Deocles would be his father's liaison between the common man and the monarchy.

"Deocles spent the next few months learning his new role, and excelled at it. Soon, the numbers of the poor began to decrease. Still, Lirah was never far from his thoughts. He longed for her. Not able to stay away any longer, he went to the shop of Israh and Lili. Their brown faces beamed with pleasure at having him patronize their little shop.

" 'What can we do for you, Prince Deocles?' Israh asked, already measuring the width of his shoulders with his practiced eyes. He envisioned the prince in the most expensive kente cloth and leather.

" 'I ask only for a bit of information,' Deocles began pleasantly. 'Would you be Israh and Lili, who have a daughter by the name of Lirah?'

"Now, this was a horse of a different color as far as Israh and Lili were concerned. A nobleman coming into their shop wanting new apparel was one thing, but a nobleman coming into their shop wanting their daughter, their reason for living, was quite another.

"Israh and Lili feigned ignorance. 'Lirah?' they asked. They had never heard of a child called Lirah. What kind of name was that anyway? It sounded like what one would call a musical instrument, not a child. And their names were Akil and Yasmin, not Israh and Lili. They had heard of such a couple in the next village perhaps and, come to think of it, maybe *they* had a daughter called Lina or Lida or something!

"Just then, Lirah entered the shop.

" 'Mother, Father, you must not work late again tonight. Old Nadir can do without his leather breeches one more day. I hear from his maid, Shahira, that you will probably have to let out the seat anyway. He eats like there is no tomorrow.'

"This was how Lirah entered a room, talking. This habit was nurtured by her parents who encouraged her to fully express herself. In fact, this was what tipped her off that all was not well with her parents. Instead of smiling at her as they usually did, they were frowning and vigorously indicating with an awkward twitching of their heads and the rolling of their eyes that she should leave the room at once, if not sooner.

"Walking farther into the room, Lirah spotted Deocles. For a long moment they drank each other in with their eyes. She could not believe he was there in her parents' humble shop. For his part, Deocles could not believe his good fortune at finally finding her.

" 'It's really you!' Deocles exclaimed, hurrying across the room.

" 'What are you doing here?' Lirah asked, her voice soft with wonder.

" 'I've found you,' Deocles said, finally standing in front of her. His face was bright with the light of his love for her.

" 'I wasn't lost,' Lirah returned, smiling at him, her features likewise illuminated.

" 'It took me days to locate your parents' shop after I finally got up the nerve to come looking for you. Then they told me they were not your parents and denied knowing you.'

" 'That's because you frightened them. Rich people

rarely ask after your kin with anything good in mind. Perhaps they thought you wished me harm.'

" 'Never!' Deocles disavowed. "I want us to be wed and live happily together."

" 'Then you should know a few things about me. I cannot marry a man who does not know what it's like to work for a living. Who cannot sympathize with those who have less than he has. Are you such a man?'

" 'Yes, and no,' Deocles said, truthfully. 'I do not have to work but I have recently taken a position whereby I'm able to help those who are less fortunate. And with you at my side, I'm sure that I'll be able to do an even better job.'

" 'He has a point, daughter,' Lili put in.

" 'And it will be a joy to make your wedding robes,' her father added proudly.

" 'Very well, I'll marry you,' Lirah said. 'If only to make my parents happy.'

"But her smile was only for him.

"King Deocles lived to a ripe old age, and Queen Lirah lived a day longer. They had many children and grandchildren who were always kind to butterflies, and people too. The end."

Kerry rose, planted a kiss on her sleeping niece's forehead, and returned the book to the shelf. *Princes and sassy maidens who fall in love at the drop of a hat,* she thought as she left the room. *Only in storybooks.*

Returning to the den, Kerry began collecting the leftovers from their movie feast. A few kernels of popcorn had fallen to the floor. She picked them up and placed them on the tray before taking the tray into the kitchen.

"Another successful pig-out," she said jokingly. It was a good thing she'd missed dinner. She'd devoured enough calories to cover dinner *and* a midnight snack. "All for a worthy cause," she added, thinking of Courtney's delightful giggles during the movie.

She washed the popcorn bowls at the sink and put

everything away. Glancing at the clock on the microwave as she walked out of the kitchen, she saw that it was nine thirty-nine. Kiana and Gabriel weren't expected back until midnight, or later. That left her a lot of quiet time during which to ponder her day.

Yeah, right.

She was asleep the moment her head hit the pillow on the couch in the den.

Beep, beep, beep.

Kerry awakened abruptly and went in her purse for her beeper. The small green-tinted screen displayed Jason Rivers's number at the station. She groaned and got up to use the phone in the kitchen.

Jason picked up after two rings. "Officer Jake Rivers."

"Jake, it's me. What's up?" Kerry said, her voice still groggy.

"I just got through questioning Abby Franklin," he began, his tone weary. Jake had a daughter about Abby's age. Kerry knew it must not have been easy for him to witness, first-hand, the degradation of a child that young. "She swears she didn't see Haywood last night, or any other night for that matter."

"Do you believe her?"

"Yeah, I do," Jake replied.

Kerry was quiet. Jake was extremely good at reading people. If he believed Abby's story, more than likely she was telling the truth. Okay, so whom did Johnny Haywood have sex with before his death?

"Okay, Jake. Thank you. Oh, listen, I don't know why I didn't think of this before but, Haywood's car. When I went to see his widow there were two cars in the driveway, a late-model Lexus and an older Cherokee. Not that I think we'll turn up much, but please check with the DMV to find out how many cars Haywood had registered in his name. He didn't *walk* away from his house after knocking his wife out."

"As many times as I followed the punk around, trying to catch him red-handed, I can provide the answer to that, Chief. Besides the Lexus and the Cherokee, he owned a black Benz. I hear he tried to give the Benz to Miss Bess for her birthday and she threw the keys in his face and told him to get away from her house."

"Then we're looking for a black Mercedes Benz," Kerry said. "Put an APB out on it, will you? Good night, Jake."

" 'Night, Chief."

Kerry hung up the phone and peered at the clock on the microwave. It was eleven-thirty. She'd been asleep nearly two hours. Yawning, she went into the fridge for a Diet Coke. Taking a big swallow, she wondered if they would ever find Haywood's Benz. She'd be willing to bet good money it was at the bottom of a local lake by now. As was the murder weapon, and every other piece of evidence that could link the killer to the crime. Unless they really *were* dealing with a serial killer. Sometimes they kept trophies from their murders in order to reminisce about a lovely time had by all—except for the victims, of course. A chill came over her as she recalled the case of Jeffrey Dahmer and the horrible evidence the FBI had discovered in his home upon his arrest. He'd been sentenced to death, but a fellow inmate had killed him before the state could do its job.

She hadn't been sitting on the couch in the den two minutes before her cell phone rang, startling her after the morbid thoughts that had been going through her mind.

It had to be a personal call because the station only contacted her via her beeper.

"Hey, this had better be good, 'cuz I was just about to go back to sleep. And you know how I prize my sleep!" she began jokingly.

Dale laughed. "I'm well aware of that, seeing as how

you've cussed me out more than once when I woke you up."

"Don't exaggerate. Calling you an ass doesn't qualify."

"I won't keep you from your beauty rest. I wanted to hear your voice before I fell asleep. And ask you if you've given any thought to my suggestions?" he said with a hopeful note to his baritone. "You *have* been distracted by a murder, no less. So if you haven't had the chance to consider my proposal, I'll understand."

"What is this? You're trying to take it back?" Kerry accused, laughter bubbling up.

"Are you actually saying you'll take what I said seriously, and not ignore me like you usually do?" he countered seriously.

"A woman my age takes every proposal seriously, Dale," Kerry said, her voice husky. What was happening to her? There she was sitting on the couch, embarrassment rendering her cheeks hot. She had to uncross her legs to squelch a decidedly warm sensation from invading her lower regions. *You're sick, girl,* she thought. *Allowing a man to turn you on over the telephone.*

"All right, then have breakfast with me tomorrow morning and tell me all about it," Dale said, his voice matching hers in sensual intensity. "I'll cook for you."

"But that means . . ."

"Exactly. Come to my place after you leave Kiana's and Gabriel's—that man doesn't like me for some reason—I'll leave the porch light on for you. I would come to your place, but you have nosy neighbors and my house is off by itself."

"Dale, Dale," Kerry said, sighing softly. "What happened to you in D.C.? You came back with both barrels blazing."

"I missed you more than I ever missed anyone in my life. That's what happened."

His sincerity made Kerry's heartbeat accelerate. She

imagined his full lips close to the phone's receiver and actually wished he was there so she could kiss him. Kiss him until their ears rang. *Must be this heat,* she thought. It wasn't the heat. The house was comfortably air-conditioned. Earlier it had been Kiana's hormones that were making her warm. Now it was Kerry's libido that was the culprit.

"Kerry, I want you," Dale said. His voice was like a siren, calling to her, bending her to his will. "I can't make it plainer than that. I want to make love to you. Right now. I want to undress you and kiss every inch of your beautiful body. I want to revel in you. Exult in you. Fulfill every fantasy you have, as long as it involves you and me, naked."

Kerry was tingling all over.

She was saved by the sound of keys jingling in the front door.

"My God," she breathed, "they're back home."

"Good, you can come right over," Dale said.

"I can't, Dale. Really, I can't," Kerry hurriedly replied.

"Damn it, Kerry. Then I'm coming over to your place."

"Not tonight, Dale," Kerry answered. "Good night!"

She pressed the OFF button on the cell phone. Another minute, and she would've given in. She knew it!

When Kiana and Gabriel came through the door, all mellow from their night out on the town, Kerry rushed to them and kissed Kiana's cheek. "Hey, you guys. Have a good time?"

"Miss Etta was in top form," Gabriel said, smiling, his gaze on his wife.

"She ended with 'At Last,' " Kiana told her. She did look at Kerry while she was speaking to her, but soon her bedroom eyes were on her husband, and Kerry knew when she wasn't wanted around. Gabriel pulled Kiana into his arms and they began to slow dance.

Kerry grabbed her shoulder bag. "Wonderful, wonderful! I'm going to make myself scarce, since it's obvious Miss Etta's music has once again worked its magic on her listeners. See y'all later."

"I'll walk you to the door," Kiana offered, turning out of Gabriel's embrace.

"I can find my way out," Kerry said with a smile. "Dance with your husband, girl, while you two still can." Her gaze lowered to Kiana's stomach.

"Oh, you!" Kiana cried, laughing. "Okay. Thanks for watching Coco. She always loves it when you come over for your pig-out parties."

Kerry went and kissed her sister's cheek again. "It was my pleasure."

She left them, quickly moving down the hallway to the foyer, then the front door.

Her car keys were in her hand by the time she stepped onto the porch. The air was a bit cooler than earlier in the evening, and, in the distance, lightning could be seen behind smoky gray clouds in the night sky. Maybe the weather service was right and they were in for stormy weather.

Kerry sat in the car a few moments with the doors locked before putting the key in the ignition. She couldn't help it. Seeing Kiana and Gabriel together made her ecstatic and sad all at once. Ecstatic because Kiana and Gabriel deserved happiness after everything they'd been through to find each other. And sad because she wanted that kind of love in her life. Sad also because she knew she could have it if only she'd let down her guard with Dale. Some part of her was aware of her limitations, though. She didn't love Dale Preston. Understanding why she didn't love him taxed her. Vexed her. Was she a racist? Was there something in her makeup that precluded falling in love with a white man? Had she lived in the South so long, hearing stories of blatant racial injustice, seeing it, *living* it, that the prospect of lov-

ing a man who didn't belong to her cultural background
was impossible?

Because when she considered Dale's qualities, his
kindness, his work ethic, his honesty, these were all
things that would recommend him as a lover, a husband,
a mate, a friend. What exactly was it that was making
her hesitate?

The question woke her up, and she felt alert as she
drove through the abandoned streets of Damascus. At
this hour, the red light became a flashing yellow warning
light. Drivers went through it at their discretion.

When she turned onto her street, she noticed her porch
light wasn't on. It was on an automatic timer. During
the early morning hours it came on every two hours. She
also had placed solar-powered lights two feet apart along
the walk. In daylight hours they absorbed solar light,
stored it, and at night gave off light for up to six hours.
These were burning, though not exceptionally brightly.

Getting out of the Explorer, she looked all around her
as she hurried up the walk. When she stepped onto the
porch, she heard the swing creak. Looking to the right
where the swing hung, she made out the shape of a large,
hulking figure rising from it. Her first impulse was to
reach for her gun, but she wasn't carrying her gun. It
was safely locked in her bureau drawer. Adrenaline shot
through her, and the next thing she knew she'd launched
herself at the figure. They both fell against the swing,
off the porch, and onto the lawn below.

Whoosh! She heard the air rush from the man's lungs.
She'd landed on top of him. He didn't move. Scrambling
to her feet, she took the opportunity to run. It was senseless to use hand-to-hand combat if you didn't have to.
Besides, he must weigh at least eighty pounds more than
she did. It wouldn't be a fair fight.

"Kerry?" a deep male voice inquired.

She paused and looked back.

"Kerry Everett, who went to boot camp at Parris Island, South Carolina?" He slowly got to his feet, his hands out at his sides to show her he had nothing in them.

"Who are you?" Kerry asked firmly. His voice sounded vaguely familiar. She was certain she'd heard it before. Someone she'd arrested? Some guy she'd sent to prison? He was tall, at least six-foot-three. And solid. She didn't think she could subdue him without the element of surprise on her side.

"You're not talking fast enough!" she nervously, loudly prodded him.

"It's Mac, Kerry," he said, laughing. "Maceo Kent."

Shock raced through Kerry like an electric current. *Mac?*

She stepped onto the illuminated walk. "I need to see you," she said.

He moved out of the shadows and joined her on the walk, no more than five feet away from her. Kerry's breath caught at the sight of his face. It was Mac all right. Perhaps a bit more mileage on his face. His hair was cut closer to his well-shaped head. The same high cheekbones that ran into widely spaced, dark brown eyes. That square-chinned face was the same, too. Kerry remembered how his wide, full-lipped mouth was given to smiling. Unless, of course, it was issuing orders with a voice like a foghorn. Mac had been her drill instructor in the Marine Corps. By the time she'd left the corps three years later, he'd become much, much more than that.

In an instant all the images of their past came flooding back. Inundating her mind with emotions she hadn't experienced in years. Sights, sounds, odors. Dear God! The Crucible. That final field exercise that every marine recruit had to undergo before being declared a genuine marine. More than a physical challenge, it was a rite of passage. She knew that if not for Mac, she would never have survived those grueling fifty-four hours. But Mac had been there, daring her to give up. Egging her on. They had marched forty miles during those fifty-four hours, through rain, through hell and back. Allowed only eight hours of sleep, some of them had felt as if they were losing their minds near the end, but they were a team. Nobody gave up because they knew if they could make it to the end, there was nothing, *nothing,* they couldn't do for the rest of their lives.

"You're looking good, Marine," Mac said, bringing Kerry back to the present.

Kerry walked into his open arms, and they embraced. Mac held her tightly against him, squeezing her and lifting her off the ground. Kerry laughed when her feet touched the walk again. His arms were around her waist now, their bodies pressed together. She tilted her face toward his. "Mac, you haven't changed a bit!"

"Sure I have," he said, dimples appearing in both clean-shaven cheeks. His eyes searched hers. "And so have you. Look at you. You're even more beautiful than you were ten years ago."

There were those emotions again. Kerry's stomach muscles constricted painfully, remembering their last night together. They'd parted amicably, it was true. Still, some part of her was hurt by his seeming willingness to give her up so easily. Without a fight. Without so much as an attempt to change her mind. Because she had been the one to break it off. Knowing they were of two different minds. Mac had been accepted into the FBI Academy at Quantico, and he'd wanted Kerry to apply, too. She had an exemplary record with the corps. He wanted her to stay with him and complete her BA and then apply for the program. The FBI was looking for minority recruits. Mac thought they would be lucky to get her. Kerry, however, opted to get her degree at UF, and go to the police academy in Miami. She felt she could do more good, serve more people as an urban police officer. That was then. Today, she wondered if Mac wasn't right and she should have gone to Quantico instead. After three years on the Miami police force, she was experiencing burnout. Just another cop who gave too much, who fought the good fight and lost. After she'd been shot in the shoulder with a 9mm brandished by a seventeen-year-old drug runner, frightened out of his wits when she'd pulled him over for a minor traffic violation, she decided to call it quits. She would be dead, and the streets of Miami would be status quo. If that made her a quitter, then so be it.

She came back home because home was where she actually felt she was making a difference. Police work was not about patrolling the streets for drug dealers, hookers, armed robbers, or any other ilk of criminal. It was about getting involved with the community and promoting crime prevention. Working from within. Not trying to clean up the mess when it was much too late.

It was then that it dawned on Kerry the reason why Mac had shown up on her doorstep. He was FBI. He'd come because of Johnny Haywood's murder.

She didn't know why she felt so disappointed upon realizing that. Why else would he have come? To pick up where they'd left off?

Extricating herself from his grasp, she laughed. "So you guys think we have a serial killer in Damascus?"

She didn't wait for his reply.

Walking toward the porch, she said, "We'd better finish this conversation inside. Voices carry in the dead of night."

Mac followed. He had sensed the change in her. Had felt it in her body. She'd tensed up just before she began talking about the reason he'd come. How could he explain the joy he'd felt deep inside upon seeing her again? Holding her in his arms. Inhaling the sweet fragrance of her warm skin. He wished he'd acted on his impulses a long time ago. Instead he'd assumed his getting in contact with her would have been an intrusion. She was probably married with children.

Kerry picked up her shoulder bag where she'd dropped it on the porch when she'd thrown herself at Mac a few minutes ago. She momentarily rummaged in her bag for the house key, her hand trembling a little she was still so surprised to see him. Wasn't this some kind of a miracle, even if he was solely here because of his job? The FBI could have sent someone else. Anyone besides Mac. Didn't that make it a minor miracle that he was here in the flesh, at her side, about to enter her home? She tried not to think in those terms. She had to suppress such thoughts because this was work, and if Mac went away with only one impression of her, it would be that she was a professional and did her job well.

In the foyer, she switched on the light and when they were both in, she shut and locked the door. Mac moved farther into the house, pausing when he reached the living room.

"Nice place."

"It's comfortable," Kerry said. She looked at him. Civilian clothing. Didn't they usually wear suits? Mac wore his jeans and muscle shirt well. The blue color of the shirt went well with his medium brown skin. Her perusal ended at the scar that ran along the left side of his face. Three inches long and faint. She resisted going to him and touching him there.

Golden-brown eyes met darker ones across the room. Kerry lowered hers and continued through the house. "Let's talk in the kitchen. I'll get you a sandwich or something. I'm sure you're tired and famished after traveling all the way from . . ."

"D.C."

"You're at headquarters now?"

"I was assigned there more than five years ago."

Kerry switched on the overhead lights. Her kitchen was ultramodern. Though the house was thirty years old, she'd remodeled practically every corner of it. Last summer, the kitchen had been her pet project. Four-inch-square sand-colored tiles gave it a wide, open appearance. The glass-fronted cabinets were in a light shade of pine, and the appliances were all done in almond.

"Sit," she said to Mac, pointing to the cushioned stools at the breakfast nook. Mac sat down and watched her. How her jeans fit her shapely hips. The crop top that afforded a glimpse of her flat belly when she moved in just the right way. She was wearing snow white athletic shoes. Probably the ones she wore only when she wasn't going to work out, he figured. Where had she been returning from when he had surprised her? From her lover's arms?

He checked his emotions. He had no right whatsoever to be wondering what Kerry did in her spare moments. Still, he wanted to walk over to her, remove that clasp from her wavy hair, allowing it to spill down her back, and then kiss her breath away, she looked so good to him. He remembered everything. From the first day they met. She was a raw recruit. He was a sergeant. Seven years older. Years wiser—or so he'd thought. Turned out, she'd taught him many things. Among them, how to love.

And he'd given that up!

Kerry went to the sink and washed her hands. As she was drying them with a paper towel, she regarded him. "You still partial to turkey sandwiches with tomato, lettuce, and mayo?"

"I am," he confirmed with a smile.

Kerry's heart thudded. This was unreal. Mac in her kitchen on a Saturday night. She went to the refrigerator and began pulling out the makings for the sandwich. When they were piled in her arms, she transferred everything to the counter next to the stove and reached on top of the fridge for the loaf of brown bread.

"The FBI works fast. I just sent in the info this morning," she told him as she spread mayonnaise on two slices of bread.

"The guy we're looking for leaves behind very little evidence. Just those words he carves on the chests of all his victims. We want him badly."

"The victims are all African-American males?"

"No, but they're all drug dealers. They come from varied backgrounds. However they've all been killed with a single shot to the head."

"So, if we have a copycat killer, he knows your boy's MO like the back of his hand."

"Definitely."

She presented him with the sandwich. "Want a beer? I keep them for friends."

"Still a teetotaler?" His eyes raked over her face.

"Yeah," she responded, blushing.

"Sure, I'll take a cold one."

Kerry was happy to get out from under his scrutiny.

Returning with the beer, she sat two stools away from him. She simply watched him eat, willing to wait to continue their conversation. It would give her time to compose herself. After a few moments of silence, he said, "You're not having anything?"

"I've already eaten."

"Oh, hot date tonight?"

"Something like that." He didn't need to know her hot date had been a pig-out with her five-and-a-half-year-old niece.

His eyes were on her hands. "You're not married or engaged. Have you been?"

"Married? No. Engaged? Yes. It didn't work out. You?"

Mac took a swig of his beer before answering. "I came close, too, about three years ago. But then our bicoastal relationship began crumbling, and we both thought better of it. She's married to a doctor now and lives in California."

"Sorry it didn't work out."

"I'm not. I wasn't ready to make the commitment marriage requires. I was still too into the job then. I was relieved when Tamara called it off. She deserved someone who would give her the attention she needed." He looked her straight in the eyes. "Are you involved with anyone right now?"

Kerry hesitated. How could she answer that? Okay. Dale had proposed to her, but she'd been blindsided . . . *Dale!* He'd threatened to come over tonight. What if he showed up and found Mac here innocently eating a sandwich in her kitchen?

"Are you?" she countered. Who said he had to be the one to ask the tough questions? She, also, had a few pertinent questions she wanted answers to. Such as, "Why didn't you ever phone or write, Mac?"

"I figured it was best for you if it was a clean cut," he said truthfully. "Your mind seemed made up. I did follow your career for a long time afterward. I only stopped checking up on you around four years ago when I thought my preoccupation with your movements was beginning to border on stalking." He was smiling, but she could see in his eyes the seriousness of the statement. He'd given up on tracking her for his own mental health. His admission made Kerry want to cry. She bit down hard on her bottom lip and blinked furiously. Looking away, she said, "Yeah, well, I wondered about you a lot, too." She didn't tell him he'd been on her mind earlier that day. Too scary.

Mac was about to say something else when the doorbell rang.

Kerry nearly jumped out of her skin. Good Lord! Dale had actually followed through with his threat. Wasn't *this* night stacking up to being a memorable one?

"If that's your boyfriend, tell him I'm your old buddy from the corps," Mac said, amusement dancing in his mellow brown eyes. "That's my cover."

Kerry had forgotten how Mac liked to rib her. She shot him an annoyed look before going to answer the door. Actually, if she had *her* way, Dale wouldn't even find out she had anyone in the house.

FIVE

Let him wait, Kerry thought as she swiftly removed her top and jeans in the bathroom, and put on her pink terry cloth bathrobe. She picked up her toothbrush, hastily spread Colgate on it and frantically brushed, then rinsed and spat. If it was going to look like she was preparing for bed, she had to use realistic touches. Next, the cold cream.

She wrapped her hair in a towel before slathering on the Oil of Olay. Glancing in the mirror, she thought she was adequately repulsive. This getup would cool any man's ardor. She hoped. Dale had been waiting a *long* time. He might consider a woman with cold cream on her face the height of sensuality! Barefoot, she hurried through the house to the front door. When she passed the hallway, she saw Mac standing there, out of sight. Apparently his curiosity had gotten the best of him.

Dale had a bottle of chilled wine in one hand and a single long-stemmed red rose in the other. She wondered where he'd gotten the rose at this hour. He'd probably pilfered it from his dad's yard. Dale Sr.'s roses took first prize in the local flower show every spring.

Her right hand primly held the bathrobe closed at the neck. "Dale, what are you doing here?" She looked nervously out at the darkened homes nearby, as if she expected the neighbors to be spying on them from behind curtains right now.

Dale, being no fool, stepped forward, his right foot already in the door, and pressed forward until his entire body was through the opening Kerry had left in the door-way.

"Don't be coy, Chief. You know why I'm here. I spelled it out for you over the phone not thirty minutes ago." He grinned at her, showing straight, white teeth in his tanned face. His dark blue eyes narrowed as he took in her appearance. "What is that you have on your face?"

"None of your business!" Kerry said, turning to go into the living room, which was right off the foyer and would allow Mac time to slink back into the kitchen undetected.

Damn, Dale smelled good. He was wearing a pair of loose-fitting Levi's and a gray pullover shirt that displayed his pectorals to perfection. Not allowing the Oil of Olay to deter him, he pulled her into his arms once he had put the bottle of wine on the coffee table. "We're getting married, I think it is my business." He handed her the rose. "Is this something you leave on all night, or did I interrupt you in the middle of your toilette?"

Kerry sputtered with laughter. "Toilette? I'm not some Southern belle, you know! I don't do toilettes, I get ready for bed. And, no, I don't sleep with it on. I cleanse my face with it. How was I to know you were going to come tearing in here in the middle of the night?" She held the rose behind her as Dale pressed her closer to him.

"I *told* you I was coming."

"And I distinctly recall telling you, 'not tonight'!" She wriggled in his embrace.

"Kerry, Kerry," Dale cajoled, his tone husky, "quite contrary. Afraid of what her neighbors will think when they find out she's a normal woman with normal needs, and a man has actually invaded her territory past midnight." He released her, walked over to the big picture window and opened the draperies. Standing in front of the window, he exclaimed, "Look at me, Dale Preston, Esquire, here to seduce your chief of police!"

Kerry blew air between her lips and went to pull Dale away from the window. He went quietly. After closing the draperies, she faced him. "I'm not ready for this, Dale." She glanced pointedly at the bottle of wine he had deposited on the coffee table. "You started the party without me?"

"Nonalcoholic. I know you don't drink," Dale said, his voice tight. Sighing, he added, "What's going on? You're giving me mixed signals. This morning, after that kiss, I thought you and I were on the same wavelength."

"Stay here, I'm going to wash this off," Kerry told him. He deserved an explanation, and as long as Mac remained as quiet as a mouse, there was no reason why Dale should discover another man was in the house.

A few minutes later, she returned with a freshly washed face and her hair spilling down her back. She hadn't taken the time to apply any makeup, but Dale had seen her many times without it.

Dale was sitting on the couch when she came into the room. He rose and went to her. "This doesn't feel right, Kerry. I sense you're about to tell me something I don't want to hear." His eyes bored into hers. "Am I going to be yet another casualty of the Everett women?"

Kerry frowned. "I'm not clear on what you mean by that."

"Oh, come on. You know what I mean. Your mother, Evelyn, was dating Tad Armstrong before your father, Edward, came to town, a complete stranger, and stole her right out from under Tad's nose. Tad joined the army after that. Unfortunately, it was during the Vietnam War, and when he returned, he was never the same."

"That isn't fair!" Kerry protested. She knew the story, of course. But where had *he* heard it? "Who told you that?"

"My dad is Tad's lawyer. Tad told him all about it once in a fit of despair."

"Why did your dad tell *you?*"

"Oh, he told me about it a couple of years ago after I confessed I was in love with you. He thought I should be forewarned about, and this is how he put it, the 'fickle-hearted Everett women.' "

Shocked, Kerry stared at him. He'd told his father about them? And what was this about her mother and sisters having fickle hearts? "I suppose you're going to tell me my grandmother broke some poor sap's heart, too!"

"No, but your sisters did. Dionne threw Bill Phillips over for Kevin. Bill never recovered. He had a prosperous trucking business, owning twelve trucks. Now he's down to four trucks and two employees."

"You can't blame Dionne for Bill's bad business sense!"

Dale was on a roll. "Then there's Kiana who kicked poor Coach—"

"Carter cheated on Kiana! She had every right to kick his ass to the curb. He's lucky I didn't get my hands around his scrawny neck." Actually Carter had a bull neck, but Kerry was too upset to be accurate at this juncture. She had her mother and sisters' honor to think about. "You're saying all of this because?" she asked, her brows arched.

"Because I think you Everett women love it when two men are vying for your attention. And since I got here first, I should be on the lookout for number two. He'll be the one whose time I'll have to beat."

"Your argument is completely without substantiation," Kerry vehemently said, coining a term he could wrap his lawyer mind around. "For one thing, if my mother and Dionne had been in love with Tad and Bill, no one would have been able to come between them. And as for Kiana, she did love Carter, but how many times must a woman forgive a man for infidelity without losing some of her self-respect?"

"Okay," Dale relented. He closed his eyes for a second or two, as if he was weary. "I admit, I got a bit defensive, especially since you didn't seem very excited to see me." He sounded hurt by her lack of interest. Moving closer he reached out and gently caressed her cheek, his hand moving up into her thick, black hair. He bent his head, his mouth mere inches from hers. "I *do* have an ego," he began.

"A mile wide," Kerry said, a smile turning up the corners of her mouth.

"A healthy ego," Dale reiterated. "And when I'm turned down, it begins to eat away at my confidence."

"Poor baby, you're not used to being turned down," Kerry cooed.

Dale's reply to that was to cover her mouth with his. He tasted clean and faintly of peppermint. Or was that her Colgate? Kerry didn't know. All she knew was that she couldn't get into his kiss this time. Not with Mac less than thirty feet away, possibly listening to everything that transpired. Of course, Dale wasn't aware of the hindrance to her enjoyment of his kisses. He simply thought she'd cooled toward him since that morning. He released her and took a step backward, his hooded eyes on her face.

"What did I do wrong?" he plaintively asked, frowning. "Just tell me, and I'll correct it. I knew I surprised you just now, but it has to be more than that that's making you behave this way toward me."

Kerry tried to stroke his cheek with her right hand, but he stepped out of her reach. "Dale, this morning when you came out of the blue with a proposal, I was rocked to the core. You must have known how shocked I was."

"Just say it, Kerry!" Dale impatiently ground out, eyes narrowed.

"I'm attracted to you, Dale." Her tone was soft. "But I'm not in love with you. I can't explain it. I've turned it over and over in my mind, trying to figure out why I'm not. You're everything a woman looks for in a man."

"But I don't do it for you," Dale intoned with a deflated sigh.

He turned his back to her, preparing to leave. Kerry went and put her arms around him from behind. "Dale, please, I don't want our friendship to end over this."

She felt his body relax somewhat.

He turned and they embraced. They stood there for a long time, just holding each other. He spoke first. "Then your answer is no."

"I'm sorry."

"I suppose a pity roll in the hay would be out of the question?"

Kerry looked deeply into his eyes. For a while, she wasn't able to discern whether he was joking or not. Then he slowly smiled. "Because a pity roll in the hay would go a long way toward healing my heart. Although *two* pity rolls in the hay would be even better. I have a big heart, and it's going to take a lot of tender loving care to help heal it. Now if you *really* wanted to show your sympathy, you would simply marry me and forget all this nonsense about not loving me. Love is a highly overrated emotion. It's better to respect your mate rather than love him. That way, when the blush of love has worn off, you will still leave him some dignity when you drag his ass through divorce court. I ought to know, because Carla didn't leave me with any love or respect!"

Kerry felt tears moisten her cheeks for the second time that day. She hadn't meant to hurt Dale, but she had. By allowing him to have hope the entire day. Hope that she would accept his proposal. Instead of telling him right away how she really felt, she'd allowed hope to sprout and grow. She'd taken his proposal and regarded it as if it were some trophy. Evidence of her ability to still snag a man. How she'd bragged to Kiana! And boldly admitted that she didn't love Dale, but she was still considering his proposal.

Why? Because she was afraid she'd never be asked again?

She had a lot of soul-searching to do.

But first, she owed Dale an apology. "My vanity got in the way," she said, looking him in the eyes. "It's not every day a gorgeous, successful lawyer asks me to marry him. It went straight to my head. I couldn't wait to tell Kiana about it. It took a while for it all to sink in. Then I realized I had to tell you the truth. You deserve someone who's going to love you wholly for who you are inside, Dale, which is a wonderful man with a good heart. You deserve someone who can fully appreciate you. Someone who can get lost in you. Lap up everything you have to offer and still be hungry for more. That's how much I care about you, Dale. I want you to have the best."

"You are the best," he said, his voice intense, his eyes watery with emotion.

"But not for you," she said sadly. Sniffing, she kissed him high on his cheek. "You'll never know how much having you in my life has meant to me these past three years. There were times I never thought I'd make it as chief in a town that's more than sixty percent white, and where half the citizens are just waiting for me to trip up. But you, you welcomed me with open arms, made me laugh at them, and at myself. You made me feel as if I could do this with very little effort at all. For that I thank you, Dale."

"Now, don't lay it on too thick," Dale said with that crooked grin he was so well-known for. "I didn't tell you anything you didn't already know yourself. You're a bright, capable woman who can do anything she sets her mind to."

He bent and touched her forehead with his. "Okay,

so you don't love me enough to marry me." He kissed
the tip of her nose. "I'll tell you what, if you're not
married by the time you're forty, and I'm not married,
we'll get hitched, love or no love. I may not be your first
choice, but hell, I can be your last resort!"

Kerry giggled and threw her arms around his neck.
"All right. All right, it's a deal."

Dale left soon after that, and Kerry joined Mac in the
kitchen.

She caught him going through her cabinets looking
for ground coffee. He'd found the coffeemaker on the
counter and had prepared it to receive the grounds.

Kerry cleared her throat. "Can I help you find something?"

Mac turned to respond, but when he saw her standing
there in that robe, her long hair in disarray, with that
telltale look of having been kissed on her flushed face,
he lost his train of thought. "Ah . . ."

Kerry spied the coffeemaker then. Mac had pulled it
slightly forward on the countertop. "I keep the grounds
in the refrigerator. My mom says it lasts longer. I'm not
a regular coffee drinker and one package lasts me
months."

"Not a regular coffee drinker?" Mac said with a guf-
faw. "What kind of cop *are* you?"

"One without a caffeine buzz," Kerry responded
lightly. It had been a forced lightness. She worried about
how much Mac had overheard. How much of her personal life he had witnessed in the space of an hour? She
felt curiously exposed. Naked.

"I'll do it," she announced, crossing the room.

But Mac was already in front of the refrigerator and
pulling the door open. They both reached in and grabbed
the vacuum-packed container of Folger's at the same
time.

Mac let go of it and rose to his full height, allowing
Kerry to retrieve the package of coffee. He stepped back

and leaned against the counter, watching her. His eyes lowered to her feet, which were bare. He could see she still enjoyed pampering her feet. The heels were smooth, the nails manicured and painted pink. Brown and pink. There was something extremely sexy about the contrast of brown skin and pink toenails.

Kerry was busy clipping the top of the foil package with kitchen shears. "How many cups do you think you'll be drinking?"

"A couple will do. I should try and get some sleep tonight."

"I'd never get to sleep if I drank even one cup," Kerry said, making inane conversation.

Mac pushed away from the counter and paced the kitchen floor. "Listen, Kerry, I suppose, after ten years, we can expect to feel uncomfortable around each other."

Kerry poured grounds into the filter Mac had earlier put in the coffeemaker. "That's an understatement. You feel like a stranger to me, Mac."

"I know. I feel like I don't know you anymore either."

Kerry checked to see if Mac had put water in the coffeemaker. He had. She switched it on and placed it back in its normal spot on the counter. Turning to face Mac, she said, "It would be weird if we simply took up where we left off ten years ago. We're not the same people we were back then." She absentmindedly ran her hand up beneath her heavy hair, momentarily lifting it off her neck and allowing it to fall back in place. A nervous habit she had whenever she wore it down and suddenly got too warm. To Mac, however, it was as seductive an act as a striptease.

He might not know her anymore, but it was obvious he was still physically attracted to her. Big time. That meant he had to watch his emotions. He'd seen how she'd eagerly gone into that guy's arms. She must love him. He hadn't stuck around for an encore.

Kerry looked up to find Mac watching her. "I hope

you won't take this the wrong way, Mac, but may I see some ID?"

That threw cold water on his libido. There he was in the midst of a fantasy about her posing for his benefit, when her calculating mind was wondering about his authority to be here. He didn't argue though. He bent and lifted his left pants leg. Strapped to his leg was his wallet with his badge inside. He handed it to her.

Kerry perused it. Carefully read the information on his FBI picture ID. Special Agent, Maceo Kent, it read. She gave it back to him. "All right, thanks. I hated to think you might be a nutcase ex-boyfriend stalking me."

Mac laughed. "It pays to be careful. But, how do you explain my showing up here so soon after the murder?"

"Oh, come on, Mac, the story has been in the news. A resourceful stalker could use the media to his advantage."

"All right, I'll give you that."

Kerry gestured to the kitchen nook. "Shall we try this again?"

Once they were seated, she crossed her legs and leaned toward him. "Okay, I want to hear everything you know about the guy you're looking for. Don't leave anything out."

"I'll tell you what I can," Mac hedged.

Kerry sniffed derisively. "Don't give me that bull, Mac. This is my town. I'm responsible for the safety of every soul in it, and I want to know what we're up against. I need to know why the FBI thinks he may still be here after killing Haywood. I knew the victim. I didn't like him, but I'm fond of his mother and I *want* his killer, Mac. If only for closure for his mother."

Mac instinctively knew that wasn't the only reason Kerry wanted the killer. It was also the idea that someone had had the temerity to commit such an act in her territory. Law officers were notoriously territorial. They guarded their home ground like a bull dog, taking it personally when someone encroached. Murder was encroachment of the worst sort. "Okay," he began. "Our guy is an above-average thirty- to forty-five-year-old white male."

"That profile could fit practically every serial killer out there," Kerry said, dissatisfied. "Tell me, does he usually work alone, or in tandem with another killer like the Hillside Strangler—Stranglers—as it turned out?"

"He usually works alone, but as you noted, that doesn't preclude his changing up his modus operandi. He's smart. He's left a trail of ten bodies throughout the Southeast. The last was in a suburb of Washington, D.C., around three months ago."

"Where are your hard files on him, in your car? Where is it parked anyway, down the street? And how long were you waiting on my porch swing?"

"Slow down," Mac said, smiling at her. "Nah, I have a laptop in the rental car's trunk. I'll access the files for you in the morning. Yes, I parked down the street. And I've already booked a room online at your local inn for the duration. Though I haven't checked in." He glanced at the clock on the wall. "I hope they don't mind being awakened at one in the morning around here."

The coffeemaker gurgled and Kerry got up to get Mac his first cup of coffee. Returning with it, she set it before him then pushed the swivel coffee caddie with sugar, sweetener and Coffee-mate packets on it toward him. Mac added sweetener only.

"You'll have to spend the night here," Kerry told him matter-of-factly. "The Moores, the couple who own the inn, are elderly. Mr. Moore is sickly and it's best if you don't get them up tonight." She met his gaze. "My couch is comfortable."

"Are you sure your boyfriend won't mind?"

Kerry cocked her head to the side and grinned at him. So, he hadn't eavesdropped, after all. Kerry saw no guile in his brown depths. Although, the Mac before her now might be an accomplished liar. The old Mac was brutally honest.

Let's see if the old Mac is still in there somewhere, she thought. "What did you think of him?" she asked. "I saw you in the hallway. I figured you wanted a look at him."

"I can't judge on just appearance. He seems very fond of you," Mac said, taking the middle road. "What does he do for a living?"

"He's a defense attorney."

"Successful?"

"Yes, he's sought after in his field."

"Well, as successful defense attorneys go, I'd say he's right up there in the top echelon of boyfriends. I just never expected it of you." He met her eyes over the rim of his cup.

"What?" She hoped she'd kept the defensiveness out of her tone, but doubted it.

"Either that was a very light-skinned brother, or you're dating a white guy."

There, he'd said it. Let her deal with it. She wanted to have a civilized conversation about another man? Hoping to get his seal of approval? Didn't she realize he'd never approve of anyone she dated? Brother, white guy, Asian, Native American. It didn't matter. He'd played the race card only because her innocent parading of her lover in front of him had irritated him. He could kick himself for *letting* it irritate him.

Miffed, Kerry rose. "Maybe I got tired of waiting for my African prince to get up the courage to phone!" She turned and headed for the exit. "I'm going to get you some linen and pillows for the sofa; then I'm going to bed."

Mac watched her go, wondering what he'd gotten himself into. Raw emotions were already coming to the surface. Anger for having waited so long to see her again. Resentment because she hadn't once sought him out all these years. It worked both ways, you know. She could have phoned *him*.

When Kerry rose the next morning, ready to do battle, she discovered that Mac had folded the linens, washed the coffee carafe and his cup, and taken off. She imagined he'd departed before daylight, not wanting the neighbors to see him leaving her house.

She didn't have time to ponder the reason behind his rude comments last night. Let him think what he wanted to think about her. He made her feel like she was a traitor to her race because she'd kissed Dale Preston. As if Mac confined his dating to sisters only. He had some nerve!

Kerry didn't have to worry about finding a seat when she arrived at St. John A.M.E. Church later that morning. Her mother, Evelyn, always reserved a spot right next to her. Kerry slid onto the seat and rubbed her cheek against her mother's. "Morning, Momma." Evelyn was wearing a navy blue boater over her short, dark brown hair. She'd started cutting it when she turned fifty. Her daughters got their hair length and texture from her. The black, sooty color they got from their father, Edward "Buddy" Everett.

"Good morning, dear," Evelyn said in a whisper. She smoothed the skirt of her navy blue suit and picked up her Brown's Funeral Home fan from her lap and fanned her face. The services hadn't begun. Folks were milling about visiting, gossiping about this and that, and generally catching up on one another's lives.

Kerry saw Bess Haywood sitting in her pew, Harold next to her, a morose expression on his face. Bess had probably insisted he come. Crossing her legs, Kerry got comfortable. Her mother glanced down at her stocking-covered legs. "Light colored shoes, light colored hose," she said in a sing songy voice.

When Kerry had looked in her underwear drawer that

morning, she had discovered she was fresh out of light colored hose. And she didn't want to traipse down to the Winn-Dixie to buy a pair. The hose she had on suited her fine.

Her suit was pale blue, as were her shoes. A summery outfit. No one would notice the disparity between the hose and the shoes, except her mother.

"We went by Nicole Haywood's yesterday as you suggested," Evelyn said close to Kerry's ear. "But she turned us away, saying she was too upset for company just then. She asked us to come back today."

"What time today?"

"After noon, she said."

"Mmm," Kerry mused. "Okay." She wondered why Nicole had done that. But it was her prerogative whether or not she allowed anyone in her home.

The pianist took her seat and began to play. That was the cue for everyone to officially settle down. Parishioners returned to their seats, mothers shushed their children. The rustle of pages being turned in hymnals was now the only sound in the edifice. As one, the assemblage began to sing the words of a well-loved spiritual.

One of the deacons rose to give the invocation, and shortly after the prayer, Reverend Benjamin Darton took the pulpit. For the next forty-five minutes everyone sat rapt as he expounded upon the sorrow caused in today's society when young people chose a life of crime over a more godly life, just for the privilege of living fast and dying young.

A chorus of amens was heard throughout the church, often accompanied by sympathetic glances in the direction of the Haywood pew. Kerry knew this was Reverend Darton's way of offering his support to Bess. The congregation grieved with her. Would stand by her. Even if they didn't approve of her son's lifestyle. They would be her strength in this coming storm. If only she'd lean on them.

Kerry hoped she would. No one should have to go through the stress of losing a loved one alone.

After Reverend Darton took his seat, the choir sang, "Precious Lord, take my hand." The reverand's impassioned sermon had left them all emotionally spent.

Tears were streaming down Bess Haywood's face. Kerry imagined the outpouring of love had touched her greatly. She felt a little misty-eyed herself.

As they filed out of the church and gathered on the lawn, Kerry looked up and saw Mac walking toward her. He was attired in a summer-weight suit in dark blue. A white shirt was under the coat, and a striped silk tie in light blue accentuated it all nicely. She glanced down at his highly polished dress shoes. He definitely cleaned up well. She felt proud. In a crowd of two hundred, Mac stood out. "Excuse me, excuse me," she heard him say as he approached her. She waited to see what his next move would be. He hadn't even told her he'd be showing up here this morning.

Evelyn was nearby chatting with the pastor's wife, June Darton. The two were as different as night and day. June was petite and rather quiet. Evelyn, tall, stately and gregarious. They had been best friends for over thirty years.

"Kerry!" Mac called, loud enough to be heard by those around them. "Kerry Anne Everett!" Nobody ever used her middle name. That did, however, single him out as someone who knew her personally. Which, she supposed, was his intention.

He grabbed her in a bear hug, lifting her clear off the ground. "Hey, Marine. Don't you have a hello for your old"—*Dear God, don't say boyfriend,* Kerry fretted—"drill instructor?"

"Mac, what are you doing here?" She didn't have to fake her astonishment.

"I told you, in my last e-mail, I was coming. What, you didn't believe me?" His rich brown eyes were dancing, and she knew he was enjoying this. He set her back down, but wasn't willing to let go of her just yet. His arm remained draped around her waist. *Oh,* Kerry thought with a smirk, *so you're going to be my Internet sweetie.*

At this point Evelyn stepped forward, interested in this big man who was reducing her daughter to mush right before her eyes. And on church grounds!

"Well, who is this?" she asked, her tone pleasant but demanding all at once. She actually went into her purse for her glasses, and put them on for a better look.

"Momma," Kerry said, her smile set. "This is Maceo Kent. As he so eloquently put it a minute ago, he was my drill instructor in the corps."

"Ma'am," Mac said, bowing his head in Evelyn's direction in a gentlemanly gesture. He let go of Kerry in order to grasp Evelyn's hand in his. He didn't shake it; instead he placed his other hand on top and peered down into her upturned face. "It's a real pleasure to meet you. Kerry has told me so much about you."

Evelyn smiled warmly, patting the hand that sat atop hers. "Our Kerry has been holding out on us, young man, because she has never mentioned you to me." Evelyn was a lot of things, but subtle wasn't one of them. She intended to get to the bottom of this surprise appearance. "However, just because my daughter has been remiss, that doesn't mean you are not more than welcome." She turned her eyes on her chastened daughter. "Bring him to dinner, *Kerry Anne.*" She didn't wait for Kerry's reply. It was, after all, an order, not a request. Come to dinner, he would. Turning back to Mac, she said, "The whole family will be there. And I'm sure they will be as delighted to meet you as I am."

With that she took her leave. She had to coordinate the cleaning of Nicole Haywood's house with the other church mothers.

Alone, Mac and Kerry looked at each other and burst

out laughing. Kerry began walking down the grassy slope toward the parking area. Mac ambled alongside her, smiling contentedly. He liked her mother. He liked this town. He liked that startled, yet warm look in Kerry's eyes when she'd first spotted him coming toward her.

When they reached the Explorer, Kerry leaned against it and looked up at him. She squinted in the bright sunlight. "I guess you're in like Flynn, as they say. Once my Mom gets through spreading the news, everyone in Damascus will know you're in town to see me, and then minds will start wondering about our relationship."

Mac's thick brows drew together in a frown. "I hope I didn't cause trouble for you with your boyfriend." He sighed, and leaned against the Explorer, too. "Look, Kerry, I owe you an apology. I had no right to say the things I said to you last night."

"No, you didn't." She was still hurt by his callousness. However, she had to be fair about it. It was difficult to look him in the eyes when she said, "To be honest, though, I was baiting you. I wanted to see if you were as forthright as you used to be, Mac. And I figured the best way to get a reaction out of you was by asking you about Dale, who is, by the way, *not* my boyfriend. He's just a friend."

Mac was nonplussed. He bit his bottom lip, thinking. "You kiss friends like that?"

"You spied on us?"

"You knew I was in the hallway," he reminded her.

"Yeah, but I didn't think you would wait around. You said you only wanted a glimpse of him."

"He grabbed you so fast, I didn't have the chance to get out of there before you two were in a liplock."

"That wasn't a liplock. He kissed *me!* And you had plenty of time to leave. I went and washed my face and came back before he kissed me."

"Okay, so curiosity killed the cat! Your body language

said it all. You couldn't keep your hands off each other. Every few seconds you were in a clinch."

"How long did you spy on us?" Kerry asked, her voice rising with indignation.

"Believe me, I didn't stick around after that kiss to see what else *friends* do with each other! I'd seen enough."

"Well, if you had you would have heard me turn down his marriage proposal." Kerry relished the look of utter disbelief on Mac's face.

"Marriage proposal? You said you were just friends."

"I don't know what I was thinking," Kerry explained in low tones. "Being friends with a man who'd told me he loved me and wanted more? But I enjoyed Dale's friendship. I kept seeing him. We'd jog together. Go to movies. Have meals together. He'd flirt, and I'd ignore him. We'd never even kissed until recently. Then, right after he kissed me, he asked me to marry him. I was shocked. So shocked that, for half a day, I even thought of taking him up on his offer. But last night, I realized I had to tell him the truth: I don't love him. I don't think I could ever love him. It just so happened your arrival coincided with that revelation."

Mac didn't miss the meaning behind her last statement. "Don't worry, I won't think that seeing *me* again had anything to do with your decision."

Kerry narrowed her eyes at him. "Good, because it didn't. You're here to do a job, Mac, and I intend to cooperate fully. But I don't want you getting any ideas."

Mac pursed his lips. "Such as?"

"That I'm going to sleep with you, for one. Because it isn't going to happen."

Mac leaned close to her. So close she could feel his clean breath on her cheek. Butterflies suddenly alighted in Kerry's stomach. Bravado aside, the man still made her ache to touch him. She closed her eyes, steeling herself for a biting comment.

"It's a woman's prerogative to change her mind. And you will," he confidently said.

He straightened and smiled down at her. Suddenly, he was all business. "We still need to discuss the particulars of the case. Shall I follow you home?"

Kerry didn't know if she could find her voice. "All right," she softly croaked.

After sandwiches and coffee for Mac, caffeine-free Diet Coke for her, Kerry and Mac got down to business in her den. Mac had his laptop on the desk Kerry had cleared off for him. As he sat behind the desk on a swivel chair, Kerry stood looking over his shoulder. He accessed the file on the unidentified serial killer he suspected had struck in Damascus Friday night.

Kerry studied the grisly photographs of his victims. They had been positioned just as Johnny had been: on their backs, arms splayed at their sides, wearing only slacks, barefoot, with the same words carved in their chests.

"You never told me why you think he may still be here," Kerry said in a toneless voice. Studying those photographs had left her with a feeling of lethargy. A sense of hopelessness. Where was the justice in the world when animals like this existed?

"Because he likes to play cat and mouse with the cops. He has rarely moved on without committing another murder, sometimes three, in the same location. In Baltimore—"

"Your hometown!"

Mac nodded. "In Baltimore, he murdered three men in quick succession. Only days apart. One of the men wasn't even a dealer. He slipped up on that one. And guess what he did? He wrote a note to the man's mother, apologizing for his screwup, but saying it was an honest mistake, her son associated with known drug dealers."

"So, he sees himself as a savior."

"Yes, he sees himself as someone who's cleaning up the streets. Doing what the cops can't or won't do."

"He's unique, isn't he? Vigilante killings aren't usually associated with serial killers. Aren't serial killers mostly sexual deviants, sociopaths? And aren't they driven by the desire for personal gratification? This guy sounds like he's on a mission. As if he had suffered at the hands of a drug dealer. Maybe his mother, his wife, someone close to him was hooked on drugs, died of an overdose. And now he's trying to rid the world of the parasites."

"Your assessment jibes with the profilers'." Mac rose so Kerry could sit at the desk and read the case file. He went to the kitchen to get another cup of coffee while she read more than she ever wanted to know about the method, the mind, and the motives of the man they had dubbed "The Sharpshooter" for his excellent marksmanship. One bullet between the eyes for every victim. Kerry had earned the title of sharpshooter when she was in the corps. She knew how difficult it was to shoot a man right between the eyes.

Thinking of this gave her an idea. When Mac returned, she told him what was on her mind, but they would have to wait until Monday to follow up on her hunch.

Therefore they spent the rest of the afternoon in her office at the police station where Mac went over the officer reports pertaining to the Haywood case.

When it was nearing five P.M., the usual time the Everett family got together for Sunday dinner, Kerry said to Mac from her perch on the leather couch, "If you want to beg off, I'll understand. Dinner in the Everett house is never less than a production, and if you're tired, I'm sure I can come up with a believable excuse for you."

Mac got right to the point: "You don't want me to go?"

Kerry sat up on the couch, staring at him with wide

eyes. Why would he say that? "Yes, I'd like you to meet everyone. I was just giving you an out."

"I'll have to meet everyone, eventually, if this case lasts a while."

Kerry hadn't thought about that. She knew that the longer it took to apprehend a perp, the colder the trail got. If they didn't come up with a clue soon, they might never find him. She'd assumed things would move swiftly, and Mac would be out of her life again. That's why she wanted to remain emotionally aloof. If she had no romantic notions about Mac, she wouldn't get hurt when he left.

Closing the file folder on the desk before him, Mac pushed his chair back and rose. "Come on, Marine, I survived The Crucible. I can survive a meal with your family, for God's sake."

Famous last words, Kerry thought with a knowing smile.

"All right," she reluctantly agreed, rising too. "But if you're going to go into the lion's den, you should at least have the proper weapons with which to defend yourself."

Then, as they walked through the semiabandoned police station, she told him every salient bit of information about her family she could think of, especially about her sister, Kiana, who might resent him on sight.

SIX

The Ichetucknee River, a tributary of the Santa Fe River, is a wondrous place of crystal clear springs. Because of the clarity of the water, the Ichetucknee is known for attracting tubers, those hearty souls who inflate the inner tubes of tires and use them as flotation devices while drifting down a lazy river.

Not many tubers were on the water today. The cloudy weather had deterred some, and talk of Hurricane Sonia changing direction had convinced others to wait for a sunny day. Hal Taylor had brought his two kids, Donnie and Britney, down to the river to give their mother a break. Hal was a used car salesman. His wife, Lucy, was a cashier at the Winn Dixie in Damascus. Winn-Dixie was one of the largest supermarket chains in the state.

It was a little after five, and since the day had started out overcast it was already getting dark. Hal sat on the river's bank on a towel, keeping his eyes on Donnie and Britney. Donnie, seven, had a tendency to try to hold his sister's head under the water too long if their father didn't stay vigilant. Britney, five, adored her big brother and trusted that he wouldn't let her drown for real. It was only make-believe.

Donnie grabbed her now and pushed her head under the water. Britney tightly shut her eyes; she was terrified something would get in them and blind her. After several long seconds, she realized her brother wasn't going to let her up any time soon, so she started struggling. She grabbed the wrist of the offending hand and tried to pry it loose. He was too strong for her. Images of her own drowned body flashed through her mind. Her big, blue eyes wide open with a horrified expression in them. Her blond hair bobbing in the buoyancy of the river like the tentacles of an octopus.

Then she remembered what her best friend had once told her during recess at school. She stopped trying to pry Donnie's hand from the top of her head, reached down, grabbed his privates and squeezed with all her might. Donnie shrieked and let her go. Britney swam out of his reach, arm over arm, quick, smooth, and strong. She knew Donnie would retaliate as soon as he got his breath back. She gulped air and tried to slow her racing heart. Her daddy was jumping into the water calling, "Britney, Britney, you all right? Don't worry, baby, Daddy's coming. Donnie, you're gonna get it, buddy!"

In the meantime, Donnie was going under. A teen floating near him, his butt sticking through the hole in his inner tube, the rest of him trying to soak up whatever sun the clouds allowed to break through, saw him and began using his hands as paddles to reach him before his head went under. "Gotcha," he cried, grabbing Donnie by the left arm. Donnie gratefully took hold of the inner tube and held on.

Hal was swimming toward Britney as fast as his flabby body could carry him. He didn't know how Britney was staying afloat. He didn't see her arms or legs flailing in the water. She was perfectly still, yet she wasn't sinking. The water came up to her neck, but she didn't appear to be in any distress.

"Daddy, I'm standin' on somethin'," Britney said excitedly.

* * *

Since the Everett dinner was a casual affair, Kerry who'd changed into jeans and a T-shirt after church, was now waiting outside The Inn, a Victorian home that had been converted into an inn by the Moores, while Mac was inside doing the same. He'd asked her to come in. She'd declined.

While her fingers tapped the Explorer's steering wheel, her mind was on Nicole Haywood and her description of the last time she'd seen her husband alive. Johnny had definitely had sex with someone. Could it have been Nicole? And if so, why had she lied about it? Or perhaps it had been an honest omission. She was upset when she was recounting the last few hours. Maybe she'd just slipped up. Then again, the rule was, when someone was killed, you looked first at the people closest to him. She'd been easy on Nicole because it appeared that learning of her husband's death had devastated her. That hadn't gotten Nicole off the hook, though. She was a suspect, as was everyone he'd come in contact with Friday night. The thing was, you didn't go around announcing to suspects that they *were* suspects. That just made them watch their movements. Kerry wanted whoever had killed Johnny Haywood to believe he'd gotten away with it.

"Let me get this straight," Mac said as he slid onto the seat next to her. He looked her in the eyes as he shut the door. "You told your sisters about me, but you didn't tell anyone else in your family about me?"

Uh-oh, here it comes, Kerry thought as she started the engine and put the car in drive. "That's right." She pulled onto Main Street, glad to have to turn her gaze elsewhere.

"What am I, a footnote in your life?" Mac asked, incredulous. He fastened his seat belt, his eyes never leaving her profile. "We were together for nearly a year. I didn't rate a mention to your parents?"

"It was over between us, Mac. What kind of fool

would I have sounded like coming back home raving about the man who got away? I told Dionne and Kiana. We always discussed 'man problems.' Traded horror stories."

"Damn. I'm a footnote, then I'm a *horror* story?"

Kerry smiled. Men. Egomaniacs, all of them. "Did it ever occur to you that it wasn't about you?" she asked. "I was hurting, and I needed the consolation of my sisters to help me get over you. So, I made you sound a bit . . . well, like the heavy."

Mac expressed an exasperated sigh between full lips and fumed. He crossed his arms over his chest and suddenly became interested in the passing scenery. They rode in silence until he finally could hold his anger in no longer. "You have selective memory." His voice was cold and hard. "I wanted you to stay. I would have gone to any lengths for that outcome. But every suggestion I made was unacceptable. You had this idea that you weren't your own woman if you depended on a man for anything. And in order for us to stay together while you pursued a degree, you would have to depend on me for room and board. Try to remember: That was fine with me!" He stopped and took a deep breath. A cleansing breath that would calm him. "Face it, Kerry, you are the reason why we're not married with three or four children by now!" Okay, so he wasn't exactly the Dalai Lama when it came to controlling his anger.

He was so in the moment that he hadn't noticed that Kerry was in the process of pulling the car over to the side of the road. She parked and unbuckled her seat belt. Turning to him, she slapped his face so quickly and with such force that Mac was seeing double for the next few seconds. "Don't you *ever* blame me for what happened, Mac! I loved you."

Furious tears sprang to her eyes. Mac was instantly out of his restraints. He grabbed her by both wrists, and pulled her toward him. Kerry squirmed to no avail. He held her fast. He pressed her so tightly to his chest, her nipples felt abraded.

"Damn, woman, that hurt like hell."

Kerry's eyes were so full of pain that Mac wanted to look away, but he didn't. From this moment on he would do no less than go the distance. If, after ten years, her emotions matched his own in intensity, he had to know where this epiphany would lead them. "I loved you, too, Kerry. I'd never loved a woman before you, and I haven't loved another since. What does that make me? An obsessive, looking for someone just like you to take your place, or simply unlucky in love?"

Kerry was speechless. She felt the tears rolling down her cheeks, her nose stopping up. She felt Mac's grip on her wrists loosen, and then his big hands were gently moving up and down her back. She heard him sigh with relief. With her right ear pressed against his chest she could feel the steady rhythm of his heart. Anger fled, and a warmth suffused her, filling her with a peace she hadn't known in a very long time.

She sat up and gently caressed Mac's face with her right hand, allowing her fingers to lightly touch his scar. "You're the only man I've ever loved. Seeing you again hasn't been easy for me. Your sweet face, Mac. Your sweet face brings back all the things I regret in life. Not staying with you. Not following you to the academy. Not making a life with you. If I had been confident enough back then, I would have never let you go. But that's all water under the bridge, we're two different people now, and we can't go back in time. You have your life, I have mine."

"And never the twain shall meet?" Mac said with a slow smile. "Well, meet this."

His mouth came down on hers, catching her in midbreath. Kerry exhaled and fell into him. His hand moved up to hold her at the base of her skull as the kiss deepened, their tongues playing, testing, tasting. Letting go, his fingers were now in her hair. Kerry moaned deep in her throat and turned her face to the side, temporarily breaking off the kiss. "Mac, is this wise? What about the case?" She sucked on his bottom lip.

"If you're still thinking about the case, I must be doing something wrong," Mac said, his voice thick with desire. Cocking one eyebrow, he bent his head and redoubled his efforts. He first touched his mouth to hers. Gently, deliberately. And when he felt her relaxing and her breath mingling with his, he let his tongue move between her slightly parted lips. Kerry took his tongue into her mouth and circled it with her own. How many times had she dreamed of this? Literally dreamed of Mac kissing her, touching her, making her senses sing, manipulating them, and bending them to his will? Giving her exactly what she craved, what she desired more than anything else? This was *real*.

Mac was back.

"Your lips look like you've had collagen treatments," Kiana said to Kerry once she was able to extricate her from the dinner table. The sisters had gone to the kitchen to get the dessert, Evelyn's pineapple layer cake. It was a yellow cake with crushed pineapple filling, and topped with vanilla icing. It couldn't be found in any recipe book since it was Evelyn's own creation, and a family favorite.

Kiana was coolly elegant in a white sleeveless pant-suit. Her hair done up on the top of her head. Kerry thought her sister had never looked lovelier. Next to her, she felt like a tomboy. Which, growing up, she had been. When Kiana had finally hung up her boy-butt-kicking boots, she'd been deemed the beauty in the family. Dionne, the brain, and Kerry, the one to worry about whether she'd ever wear a dress properly or not.

Their mother's kitchen was large with an island in the

middle that served as the nook. It was also the place where Evelyn watched her soaps on a nine-inch color TV, and paid the household bills. Kerry stood at the island now cutting the cake and putting slices on dessert plates. She'd lick her fingers with every slice cut. She was ignoring her sister's comments, which irritated Kiana, no end.

"And don't think I don't know who he is," Kiana continued. "Maceo Kent. Just a friend visiting to catch up on old times? Ha! He's the only man you ever let break your heart." Her dark eyes zeroed in on her sister's. "Out with it, Kerry. Why is he *really* here?"

Their mother came through the double swinging doors, her daughter-in-law Jorga in tow, an air of complacency with her.

Evelyn was always happy when her family was all under one roof. Since Dionne and Kevin's deaths, it had become her mission to make certain her family didn't miss an opportunity to gather together. Life was short and unpredictable. Best to live it to the fullest while you can, and let the small things go. It was love that mattered, above all else. And if you loved someone, you'd better let them know today because tomorrow wasn't promised to you.

She walked up to Kerry and kissed her on the cheek. "Yes! I like me some Mac Kent. I hope we're going to be seeing a lot more of him."

Kiana laughed. "Watch out, Kerry. She practically *pushed* me into Gabriel's arms."

"And look who's happily married," Evelyn pointed out. She'd come to the kitchen to tease Kerry and get the coffee. Crossing the room, she went to the cabinet above the sink and retrieved several coffee cups and saucers. "Let's see, who'll be having coffee?" she wondered aloud. "Your father doesn't drink it, Eddie will have a cup, Gabriel, too." She glanced in Kerry's direction. "How about your Mac, will he be having coffee?"

"Yes," Kerry said calmly, not giving her mother the satisfaction of rising to the bait.

Evelyn prepared the tray, all the while talking: "With so many bad things happening in the world, this awful time Bess is going through, it's important for us to count our blessings." She turned with the tray in her hands and looked Kerry directly in the eyes. "When we get another chance at love, we must not spoil it with petty hurts, wondering what might have been, things of that sort. That's all in the past."

Kerry cocked her head to the side, staring at her mother. "You *know*, don't you?"

Evelyn set the tray on the island and went to clasp her daughter's hands in hers. She smiled warmly at her. "If you're asking whether I know Mac was your first love, the answer is yes."

Kerry turned accusing eyes on Kiana.

Kiana threw her hands up. *"I* didn't tell her!"

"It was Dionne," their mother confessed, remembering her eldest daughter. "One day we were discussing you, Kerry. I was fretting over the fact that you'd never brought a man home. Not once since coming back from the corps, or returning from Miami. I told her I was afraid you'd joined the other team."

"Momma!" Kerry cried, horrified.

Kiana and Jorja nearly burst their sides laughing.

"It happens," Evelyn insisted. "I wouldn't have loved you any less. Many families have to deal with homo-sexuality at one time or another."

"But I dated men," Kerry reminded her. "Not a lot, but I did date."

"Yes, but we never met any of them. You rarely went out with them long enough to know what their favorite colors were, let alone long enough to develop a meaningful relationship." Evelyn moistened her red-tinted lips. "I was beginning to worry."

"She has a point," Kiana put in. She'd managed to cease laughing, but her entire demeanor bespoke amusement. Kerry on the hot seat. That didn't happen very often. Usually, it was her butt roasting over the fire.

"Well, you'll all be happy to hear I'm still on the home team, and I've never even done any pinch-hitting for the other guys," Kerry said, laughter threatening to bubble up. "To think my own mother thought that of me. Not that I have anything against lesbians, but I'm just not made that way."

"Made what way?" Buddy asked as he came through the door. "I was wondering what was keeping that cake." His gaze took in the faces of all present, then settled on Kerry.

At six feet, he was only a few inches taller than Evelyn. He stood beside her, his thick brows arched in an askance expression. "Is anyone going to tell me what's going on?"

"No," Evelyn replied, picking up the tray and heading for the exit. "No more than you're going to tell us what you roosters were talking about while we hens were in here."

Kerry, Kiana, and Jorja got busy gathering the cake on plates, and followed their fearless leader, Evelyn, through the swinging doors.

Shaking his head, Buddy laughed and brought up the rear. One of these days he was going to get the last word in with that woman. He guessed it wasn't going to be today, though.

Kerry caught the gist of the conversation the men had been engaged in when she reentered the dining room. Canoeing. Her brother-in-law, Gabriel, was wild about sculling. He'd even gotten her out on the lake a couple of times. Though rowing was a great form of exercise, building up arm, chest, and leg muscles, she found it a

bit slow for her tastes. Kiana had become somewhat of
an enthusiast since marrying Gabriel. She'd given it up
after learning she was pregnant, and promised her husband she'd resume after the baby came.

The women, naturally, set slices of cake in front of
their respective men. "Thank you, Kerry," Mac said as
Kerry placed his on the table. His appreciative eyes
swept over her face. Blushing, Kerry murmured, "You're
welcome."

Evelyn witnessed this exchange and approved heartily.

She served the coffee and, soon, everyone was throwing more questions at Mac who had told them he was a
telephone lineman from Baltimore. He hadn't been out
to impress anyone. Since being in these folks' presence,
though, he'd learned they didn't put on airs and a telephone lineman was good enough for Kerry, if that was
whom she wanted. He and Kerry weren't fooling anyone.
Friends? Yes. But not just friends. He didn't care if they
knew. But, as he turned his head to look at Kerry again,
at the way she grinned so easily, that dimple in her chin
so cute, he wondered if it bothered her that her family
was making assumptions about them.

It fit perfectly as far as his cover was concerned. No
one would suspect he was FBI if he was thought to be
courting the chief.

Courtney appeared in the doorway. She and her cous-
ins, E. J. and Deja, had gone into the den, adjacent to
the foyer, to watch the children's network, Nickelodeon,
right after dinner. Their grandmother had promised to
give them ice cream and cake if they behaved. She was
carrying Kerry's shoulder bag. "Auntie, your beeper's
going off." She went and handed the bag to Kerry.
"Thank you, sweet pea," Kerry said, her love for her
niece shining in her eyes.

This done, Courtney looked at her grandmother: "That
cake sure looks good."

Taking the hint, Evelyn rose to go to the kitchen and get the children their treats.

Kerry sat at the table and used her cellular phone to call the station.

"Dispatch," came Miranda Acosta's deep southern drawl. Miranda was one of the part-time dispatchers.

"Chief Everett," Kerry said.

"Oh, Chief, a man said there's a car in the Ichetucknee, about ten yards from the beach where that Peterson boy nearly drowned last summer."

"I know the spot. I'll get out there right away. Please get Paul and ask him to meet me there. Tell him to bring his diving gear."

"Will do, Chief," Miranda said.

"Thanks," Kerry said, and quickly rang off.

She looked up to find all eyes on her. "I've got to go," she said, pushing her chair back and getting to her feet. Her family knew not to question her about her job, no matter how curious they got. They'd always left it up to her whether or not she wanted to volunteer, but knew the nature of her work required discretion.

Evelyn stuck her head through the swinging doors. "What? That's the job, baby?"

"Yes, Momma. Thanks for dinner, it was delicious." Kerry went to touch her cheek to her mother's. "You be careful," Evelyn admonished.

Mac rose, too. "Thank you all for making me feel so welcome." He smiled at Evelyn. "I haven't had a meal that good since I sat at my own mother's table."

"Well, come on back tomorrow night for leftovers," Evelyn joked. She came through the doors, an ice cream scoop with melting vanilla ice cream on it in one hand and a slice of cake on a dessert plate in the other. She handed both to Kiana. "Would you please finish fixing the children's desserts while I walk Kerry and Mac to the door?"

Kiana was happy to oblige.

Gabriel, Buddy, and Eddie all rose to shake Mac's hand, telling him how good it had been to meet him. Evelyn then commandeered Kerry and Mac, taking each by an arm and walking them through the house to the front door.

"I know this probably has something to do with Bess's boy's death," she said to Kerry. "Like I said, you be real careful." She didn't say more, but Kerry could practically hear her unspoken words: *I couldn't bear to lose another child.*

Kerry hugged her mother tightly at the door. "Don't worry, Momma."

"I can't help that," her mother said. "But I know you're good at what you do. That's some consolation."

Darkness had fallen while they were inside. A breeze stirred the muggy air about, though it didn't lower the temperature one iota. Kerry walked swiftly across the lawn, eager to get out to the Ichetucknee and investigate. She hoped Paul would be there by the time she and Mac arrived. "A car's been found in a local river. It may be Haywood's. One of my deputies is a certified diver, and he's going to go down and see if he can identify it," she told him once they were in the Explorer. She backed the Explorer out of the driveway and headed east. "Of course that's all we can do tonight, but I'm curious to know if it's Haywood's vehicle."

"How far away is it?" Mac asked, wondering how easy it would have been for the killer to ditch the car out there.

"It's only about five miles," Kerry replied. "From Mason's Auto Parts, it's even closer. Three miles, tops."

Mac could hear the excitement in her voice. "Don't be disappointed if it isn't Haywood's car. It's a long shot at best. Car thieves ditch them in this fashion all the time. Nine times out of ten, it's a vehicle some teen took on a joy ride."

"I know. But if it is, maybe we'll finally catch a lead."

* * *

As Kerry suspected, the only vehicle she saw upon turning down the poorly maintained road and driving through a grove of willow trees was Paul's black Toyota 4Runner. There were no streetlights out there, but Kerry and Paul were both prepared for that. When Paul saw her Explorer pull up, he got out of the 4Runner, already in his diving suit whose legs ended a couple inches above the knees.

"You up to this tonight, Paul? Because if you aren't we can wait until morning."

"Nah," Paul said, eager to use his expertise, which he hadn't been called on to use in some time. "I'm looking forward to it, Chief. Piece of cake. Shouldn't take long to check out the make and model. Besides, you saved me from a boring evening of listening to my grandfather recount Iwo Jima for the nth time."

"All right," Kerry said, satisfied. Remembering Mac, she said, "Paul Robertson, meet Mac Kent. Mac was my drill instructor in the corps."

The two men shook. "Pleased to meet you," Paul said amiably.

"Same here," Mac returned.

A mosquito buzzed around Kerry's ear. She and Mac walked with Paul to the water's edge, sand getting in their shoes. Paul put on his goggles and held the torch in his right hand. He would be free-diving. The water wasn't deep, and he wouldn't require oxygen for the length of time he'd be under. After he'd walked out until the water was up to his chest, he sucked air into his lungs and dived in.

Kerry and Mac stood watching, Kerry following Paul's movements. His torch was quite visible beneath the surface. She was thankful the water was so clear. At least his vision wouldn't be obscured. Only a few miles downriver, it became deep and slow and the water was a brown, murky color.

Paul surfaced for air and went back down. He swam farther out. Kerry worried that this might not have been a good idea after all. Paul surfaced and went back under four more times. Each time Kerry's nerves became even more frayed.

She started prancing, slapping at mosquitoes, trying to follow Paul's movements, always aware of Mac's presence.

Funny how the mosquitoes weren't biting *him*. "If it is Haywood's car, do you think your people will be able to lift prints?" she asked him, nervous by the silence between them.

"You'd be surprised," Mac said, "by how much forensics can find in a submerged vehicle. If it's the car."

"It's the car," Kerry said, willing it to be.

"Let's make a wager on it."

"You're on."

"Okay, if it's the car I'll give you a pedicure."

"And if it isn't?"

"You'll give me a full body massage."

"Greedy man. Yet, I'm hoping I lose," she said with a laugh.

Anyone looking on would have seen two people standing two feet apart, side by side, their body language not even hinting at the level of intimacy their conversation had reached. "I'm counting on it," Mac said, his deep voice sincere.

Paul surfaced again and began swimming toward shore. Kerry didn't bother asking him if he'd found anything. He had to reserve his air. She was fairly jumping up and down in anticipation when he finally reached them, breathing hard, but smiling broadly.

"Vanity plates," he informed them. "D-R-F-L-G-D."

Kerry and Paul gave each other high fives. "You're indispensable, Robertson!"

Confused, Mac asked, "D-R-F-L-G-D?"

"Dr. Feelgood," Kerry supplied the answer. "The car's Haywood's."

Monday morning. Kerry felt energized. Atta Girl hadn't even gotten her goat. She actually made kissing noises at the cantankerous pooch and kept jogging. They would find evidence in Haywood's car, she felt it in her bones. Some slipup by the killer that would lead them to him. Plus, she had a few hunches she needed to follow up on today. One: Was there the possibility that Nicole had had sex with her husband the night he'd died? And two: Who, in this area, was a good enough marksman to have shot Haywood between the eyes? This being the South, there were a lot of gun enthusiasts. From the country club set, to the pickup-driving, tobacco-chewing set. She knew where they practiced. It wouldn't be easy getting information out of either set. They were all suspicious, especially of a black girl with a badge and a gun of her own on her hip. She wouldn't let that stop her, though.

Kerry heard another jogger approaching her from the rear. She glanced back and saw Mac closing the space between them. He wore hunter-green jogging shorts that clung to his muscular thighs, Adidas shoes, and a T-shirt with the Marine Corps emblem blazoned across the chest. He was perspiring, so she figured he'd been at it a while. She jogged in place until he was beside her, and then continued running. "Hey, sleep well?"

"Like a baby," Mac said. "This town is so quiet, I woke up in the middle of the night and thought I'd gone deaf."

Kerry laughed. "You get used to it. The slower pace, I mean. You say you've been based in D.C. for over five years? You must be experiencing culture shock down here."

"Actually, I feel pretty much at home anywhere," Mac said, putting her mind at ease. She was always trying to find differences between them. Why wasn't she trying to find a common link between them? Yesterday she'd listed the reasons why they couldn't stay together. He wanted to hear some suggestions as to how they *could*. He was finished wishing he'd done things differently ten years ago. He was ready to do something about it. It was not too late for them.

"That's your marine training," Kerry said. "For a long time that's what I told myself, too. No matter where I was, I was perfectly in tune with my surroundings. I learned that wasn't the case, though. I feel more alive here than anywhere else."

"How could you not?" Mac asked. They were passing the kudzu jungle now. "You have everyone who loves you right here. They provide you with the cushion you need to fall back on. You have a great family, Kerry. But could you be using them as a crutch that keeps you from achieving your full potential?"

Kerry knew what he was getting at. Mac believed she could be more than a small-town chief of police. He was preparing to campaign for her to join the bureau.

She surprised him by saying, "I've often wondered about that myself, Mac. So, don't worry that you've offended me."

"I'm not worried about offending you, Kerry. I plan to say whatever's on my mind from now on. There will be no holding my tongue, or being sheepish about revealing my true feelings. If I leave this time, it will not be because I didn't give you everything I had to give. It will be because you asked me to leave. But this time, I won't go without a fight."

He had her attention, and he knew it.

"When I saw you with your family yesterday, I realized I wanted that, too, Kerry. Your father looks at your mother with nothing but love in his eyes. Your brother-in-law, Gabriel, absolutely adores your sister, Kiana. And your brother, Eddie, feels the same way about Jorja. I'm a stranger, and I could see that. How could you not thrive around those kinds of examples?"

"But, what about you? All those couples have been through the fire together. They have been tested, and because of their level of devotion, were able to come through it. What I'm asking you is, do you have it within you to go the distance with the man you love? Now, I'm not suggesting that I'm that man, because that has yet to be seen. You made it clear, yesterday, that there's a lot of water under the bridge and we're not the same people we were. But, unlike you, I do believe we have a chance. If we're both willing to take it."

He suddenly began jogging in place, and looking all around them. "I thought I heard something over there." He pointed in the woods across Highway 441.

Kerry followed his lead and jogged in place. It wasn't anyone but, "Dale? If you're out there please show yourself."

They heard the rustling of bushes, and Dale stepped out from behind a large, old oak tree. He jogged over to Kerry, his eyes on Mac. "I didn't know we'd have company this morning."

"Sorry to horn in," Mac lied, eyes narrowed. "You must be the fiancé."

"You must be number two," Dale said coolly.

"Dale Preston, Mac Kent." Kerry made the introductions. "Mac and I knew each other in the corps. He's visiting for a few days."

She continued jogging, halfway hoping they'd give up and go home. The testosterone was flying, and she expected a macho battle of one-upmanship to commence any minute now. They flanked her: Dale on the right, Mac on the left.

"When did he get here?" Dale asked.

"Does he pester you like this every morning?" Mac

wanted to know. "And what did that 'number two' comment mean, anyway?"

"I'd be glad to explain it," Dale came back, looking over Kerry's head at Mac.

"I wish you wouldn't," Kerry said irritably. "That theory's a load of crock."

"What theory?" Mac asked, looking over her head at Dale.

Kerry was getting tired of being looked over. "Listen, if you two want to be alone, I'll run ahead and let you talk." She picked up her pace, but they easily matched it.

"I came to Damascus to be with you," Mac said. "Not him."

"I need to speak with the chief about a legal matter. Why don't you get lost?"

"Why don't you make an appointment?" Mac countered. "The chief isn't in yet. This is her personal time."

"Speaking of time, you're not making any, big boy."

"Boy?" Mac asked, taking offense. "I'm not anybody's 'boy'."

"I was alluding to your size, not your race, as you well know," Dale replied, refusing to get pulled into an argument based on race. Mac was around two inches taller and fifty pounds heavier than Dale. He regarded Kerry. "Honestly, Kerry, I need to speak with you privately. My client wants to know when her husband's body is going to be released for burial. She has to make arrangements, notify family who live out of town . . ."

Kerry stopped in her tracks and stared at Dale. "Nicole Haywood is your client? When did you start representing widows who're afraid their possessions are going to be seized because their husbands were drug dealers?"

Dale had a lawyer's mug. His expression remained neutral. "How did you know she was concerned about that?"

"She told me after she'd recovered from the shock of

her husband's death. Which took all of about ten minutes."

Mac stood apart, listening.

"I don't like what you're suggesting," Dale said. "Nicole is devastated by Johnny's death. She's absolutely beside herself."

Kerry sighed and stood with her legs slightly parted, one hand on her hip. "Did she kill him, Dale? Is that why she was so quick to retain a defense attorney? Did she kill him and is working up the nerve to confess? Because if she did, she'd better do it soon. The longer she takes, the harder it's going to be on her."

"I assure you, if that were so, I would advise Nicole to turn herself in. I'm just trying to find out when she can bury her husband. Is that so much to ask for?"

Kerry felt sweat trickling down her back. She didn't know why she was so annoyed to learn Dale was representing Nicole Haywood. Something stank to high heaven, but she just couldn't put her finger on it. "All right. I'll get that information to you by noon. Now, if you don't mind, I'd like to continue my workout."

She began jogging again. Mac and Dale also began jogging right alongside her.

Kerry stopped abruptly and glared at both men. "Alone!"

Mac and Dale stood still while Kerry jogged ahead of them.

When she was out of earshot, Mac said, "Okay, buddy. Now, you can tell me what this theory of yours is."

"I'd be delighted," Dale said with a self-satisfied smile. "It goes back to her mother, Evelyn . . ."

SEVEN

"Chief! I wasn't expecting to see you again so soon," Nicole Haywood said, backing away from the door to allow Kerry entrance. Kerry could smell the Pine-Sol before she got one foot in the door good. The ladies of St. John A.M.E. had been busy.

Nicole's appearance was much improved, too. The swelling on her left jaw had gone down. In keeping with her status as a widow she was dressed in a dark, sleeveless sheath that fell two inches above her knees. Black pumps completed the outfit. Her short hair was in a neat bob, and makeup helped cover the bruises her husband had given her.

The house was immaculate. The expensive gray carpeting had obviously been shampooed because it was a shade lighter. Everything in the room appeared lighter somehow, including the owner herself. She was all smiles.

"I want to thank you for sending the church ladies over," Nicole said after she'd closed the door. She motioned for Kerry to go into the living room. "I don't think I would've been up to do all that cleaning. I wasn't myself for a long time after you told me about Johnny's death."

"That's to be expected," Kerry told her, a smile turning up the corners of her mouth. She cocked an ear, wondering if Jack were somewhere around. She'd been in the house a whole minute, and he hadn't toddled into the room yet. "Where's Jack? He's such a cute guy I was hoping to say hello to him."

"Oh, he's in Gainesville. My parents are looking after him. I had so much to do, what with arranging the funeral and all, that my mom suggested it."

"Well, that was sweet of her," Kerry said.

They sat on the couch facing each other. "I just need to ask you a few things I figured you were too upset to answer when I was here last."

"Oh, go right ahead."

"Johnny's friends. Can you tell me whom he hung out with? There's a possibility he saw them Friday night."

Nicole shook her head in the negative. "I wish I could, but like I told you, Johnny kept everything he did a secret. Oh, he and his brother, Harold, used to kick it every now and then. But I think Harold would have to sneak around and do that because Miss Bess didn't want him associating with Johnny." She paused, apparently thinking. "There was Mr. Tad. Johnny used to call him an old fool, but I think he must have been kinda fond of him because Johnny didn't suffer fools gladly, and he allowed Mr. Tad to talk to him any kinda way."

"What do you mean?" Kerry asked.

"Oh, sometimes Johnny and Jack and I would go down to the Burger Palace and get a burger and eat it right there in the car. You know how they have those waitresses who serve you on a little tray right in your car?"

"Yeah, that's cool."

"Mmm-huh. Anyway, Mr. Tad would ride up on his bicycle and just start in on Johnny. 'When are you going to do something worthwhile with your life, boy?' he'd ask. 'You've got a beautiful family to see after. You shouldn't be doing what you're doing.' And Johnny would say something like, 'Keep your voice down, Tad, and get away from my car, you're dirtying it.' Oh, he'd be real mean to Mr. Tad. But Mr. Tad wouldn't pay him no never mind. He'd leave when he got good and ready." She looked Kerry in the eyes, her own sad. "I believe, in some way, Johnny appreciated Mr. Tad getting on his case like that. He used to say his own daddy never took any time with them at all, he was always in and out of prison."

"That's true, I knew his father," Kerry told her.

"That's sad," Nicole said, sighing. "I sure don't want Jack growing up in that kind of environment. As soon as this is all over, we're moving back to Gainesville."

"Well," Kerry said, rising, "I hope you and Jack will be happy there."

Anticipating walking Kerry to the door, Nicole sprang to her feet, too. "Thank you, Chief. I'm so sorry I couldn't help you more."

"Oh, don't worry about that," Kerry told her. "But there's one more thing: When you described your last night with Johnny, you said your conversation was no longer than fifteen minutes. You argued. He knocked you out and left. Nothing else happened? That's exactly how it went?"

"That's exactly how it went, Chief."

"The reason I ask," Kerry said slowly, measuring her words, "is that there's evidence that Johnny had sex just before he died. I don't mean to be crass, Nicole, but if he didn't have sex with you, whom did he have sex with? This opens up a whole new line of questions."

Kerry had to admit, Nicole was cool. She frowned when Kerry revealed her husband had had sex before death, but showed no surprise. "I suspected he was cheating on me," she said, her voice dispassionate. "Now I have proof."

Kerry reached out and gave her arm a sympathetic squeeze. "I'm sorry to be the bearer of even more bad news."

"Don't apologize, Chief. I'm glad I know. I should be

tested for AIDS. There's no telling how many women he slept with."

"Yeah, you take care of yourself," Kerry said, heading for the front door. At the door, she turned once more and smiled at Nicole. "I'm told Johnny's body will be released by the coroner tomorrow morning. You can have the mortuary you've chosen phone them."

"All right, I'll do that, Chief," Nicole promised, reaching for the door's handle. "Thank you."

Kerry left, feeling that Nicole had been less than forthcoming. She didn't know any of her husband's cronies? Not one, save his own brother and a man old enough to have been his father? It all didn't compute.

God grumbled as she hurried to the Explorer. Distant thunder told her she'd better get out to the Willow Bend Country Club before the downpour. She was taking the lesser of the two evils first. Even if she got a cold shoulder from the country club crowd, the surroundings would be nice to look at. Going to Shaggy's Bar down by the Santa Fe River was something she'd rather put off as long as possible. Those were the two places in the area gun enthusiasts went to practice their aim.

Willow Bend Country Club sat on two hundred acres of verdant farmland. The property had once belonged to an African-American family, the Cades. They'd sold it in 1981 when developers offered them what was then a fortune, five hundred thousand dollars. When the family was done splitting up the cash, the principal owner, Fred Cade, was left with just enough money to buy a tract home on two acres. Today he led a modest life with his wife and was said to think he'd been hoodwinked. Which, Kerry thought as she drove up the majestic oak tree-lined road that led to the country club, he probably had been.

The Willow Bend Country Club had become a cottage industry. Not only was it an exclusive club that boasted two eighteen-hole golf courses, two pools, one indoor and one outdoor, tennis courts, a clubhouse with a stage for dancing and a full bar, and a four-star restaurant on the premises, but the owners had also started buying up property around the club. Now, upscale homes were on the perimeter. Some of them close enough to the golf courses so that an owner could awaken in the morning, walk out of his front door and go play a round of golf.

Kerry loved the looks she got from the chic members, all of them attired in expensive athletic gear, as she walked through the foyer to the reception desk.

It even smells like money up in here, Kerry thought, as she smiled at the curious club members who'd followed her progress across the room. "Good afternoon, folks."

"Good afternoon," one woman said and hurried off as if Kerry were there to arrest her.

The receptionist, a tall, well-preserved brunette who had to be pushing fifty, but thanks to plastic surgery could pass for forty, gave Kerry a rapid once-over before asking, "Is there something I can help you with . . ." Her eyes quickly scanned the name on Kerry's uniform front. ". . . Chief Everett?"

"I'd like to speak with the person in charge," Kerry told her.

"That would be Mrs. Crichton," the woman said, a hand at her throat in a nervous gesture. What to do, what to do? "Ah, umm, Mrs. Crichton is usually busy this time of day."

Kerry's brows raised in surprise at the woman's attitude. She wasn't going to be allowed an audience with the vaunted Mrs. Crichton? *Well, we'll see about that.* "If Mrs. Crichton is too busy to see me alone, I can return with ten deputies and see if she's more amenable to seeing me then. Her choice."

The receptionist's eyes grew a size larger. "I'm sure that won't be necessary. I'll go see if Mrs. Crichton can see you now."

"Thank you very much," Kerry said with a smile.

The receptionist hurried down the hall.

Not five minutes later a door opened directly behind the reception desk. A petite woman in a charcoal-gray suit walked through it. Her short, snow-white hair was combed back from a sharp-chinned, though attractive, face. Laughing green eyes looked up at Kerry. "We finally meet," she said. "I've heard so much about you."

She offered Kerry a hand. They shook. Her handshake was firm and no-nonsense.

"From your receptionist?"

"Yes, but Meredith can pack a whole lot in two minutes." She laughed, and Meredith, who was reclaiming her spot at the reception desk, laughed with her.

"Step around the desk, Chief Everett," Mrs. Crichton instructed. "My office is some distance down the hall."

Kerry followed her through the door behind the reception desk. Once the door was closed behind them, Kerry thought she was in a private home. A well-appointed home, but a home nonetheless. The hardwood floor gleamed, and the wallpaper was a tasteful golden color that was calming to one's senses.

"Call me Fiona," Mrs. Crichton said as they continued down the corridor. "I only kept the name Crichton because it belongs to an old-money family. I divorced Scotty, but his name comes in handy when you associate with people of this sort."

Since Fiona seemed the talkative type, Kerry obliged her. "People of this sort? You are not of this sort?"

"Heavens, no," Fiona said with a chuckle. "My people are Tennessee mountain folk. Took me years to lose the accent. Don't get me wrong, I'm not ashamed of my background, it was just the poor part I didn't care for."

"I hear you," Kerry commiserated.

"So, I married a rich guy. But found out being rich didn't necessarily make you nice. Divorced him, kept the name and the kids. Found out I liked working for a living. Came down here to visit a dear-loved aunt and stumbled upon this gig. I've been managing the club for ten years now. Put two children through college. I'm happy."

They arrived at a mahogany door. Fiona opened it and allowed Kerry to precede her into a large office with antique furnishings.

Fiona closed the door behind them, invited Kerry to be seated with a gesture, and went around the desk to sit down herself. "Tell me how I can help you, Chief."

"I take it you've heard of the recent murder in Damascus?"

"Of course, I read the *Damascus Herald*. I prefer it to watching the local news."

"The victim was shot between the eyes. You have a shooting range here. I'd like to know if you retain the scores of your members."

"You do realize that that's privileged information? It's one of the bylaws of this club, that what's done here will not be subject to public record. Our lawyers can, and have, defended that right."

"I don't want to have to ask for a subpoena in order to see the records, Fiona," Kerry said. She leaned forward. "This is a long shot, at best, but I need to know in order to start eliminating suspects."

"I can't do it, Chief," Fiona obstinately refused. She frowned. "But there's something I can do. You can go down to the shooting range and ask the members, themselves, about their scores. They're free to disclose any information they like. But our hands are tied. Unless you'd like to untie them in court."

"Like I said, I don't want to have to do that," Kerry said regrettably.

Fiona rose. "Then may I escort you to the shooting range? In your uniform, you'll look as if you belong there. I know you're not supposed to use your service revolver for practice shooting, so I'll loan you one of mine."

You could have knocked Kerry over with a feather. "You own a gun?"

"Honey," Fiona said, "I own three. Haven't you heard? According to the NRA, the fastest-growing segment of the gun-toting population is women."

Kerry had heard all right. And the news was disturbing. She didn't think the solution to violence was to own more guns. But how could you tell that to a single mother who worked double shifts, got off the bus five blocks from home at midnight and had to walk through a tough neighborhood?

"Excuse me a moment," Fiona said and disappeared into a back room. When she returned she was carrying a 9mm gun. She handed it to Kerry. "It's unloaded. They'll supply you with ammunition at the range. Come on, I'll sign you in and tell them to provide you with anything you need."

Fiona was as good as her word.

Kerry spent the next few minutes shooting at a cardboard figure with a bull's-eye on its forehead. After a certain number of rounds, the attendant would call to her to stop so that the hits she'd made on the figure could be counted, and the figure replaced with a fresh one. She rarely missed her target.

Before long, she had an audience, and those around her started wagering on how many hits she'd get. Because of the noise level it was necessary to wear protection for the ears. Because the sounds around her were somewhat muffled Kerry couldn't hear what was being said by the onlookers.

When the second target was being replaced, a woman walked up to her and tapped her on the shoulder. Kerry turned, pulling out her earplugs. She grinned when she saw who it was. "Jenna, what are you doing here?"

Jenna, dark-haired, blue-eyed, just like her brother, grinned back at her. "A girl has to know how to protect herself," she said. "I didn't know you practiced here."

"I don't," Kerry told her.

"She doesn't need to practice," a middle-aged man called, which elicited laughter from the other ten or so people standing around.

"How would you like to make this interesting?" Jenna asked. "Me against you. See if you crumble under the competition."

"Yeah," someone said excitedly. "Let's see how you do against the club champ."

"Club champ, huh?" Kerry said, impressed. "All right, you're on."

Jenna was soon set up in the booth next to Kerry's, and the attendant called the game.

"It's a tie!" the attendant announced after it was over. The audience, which had grown by then, cheered.

While the targets were being replaced, Jenna stepped over into Kerry's booth. Working her neck, she said only for Kerry's ears, "You're bad, girlfriend. But I'm inspired by my brother's broken heart to whup your butt!" She smiled mischievously.

"Broken heart?" Kerry said in equally low tones, getting into the rhythm of their banter. "The women around here breathed a collective sigh of relief when I turned him down."

The targets were ready and each woman went back into her own booth and began shooting. Minutes later, the attendant called, "Miss Preston was off by one hit."

"Yikes," Jenna said. "Best two out of three?"

The attendant moaned. He was understandably getting tired of running back and forth replacing targets.

"Okay," Kerry said. "Last time. I have to be going."

The attendant set up again and dragged himself to the sidelines.

Kerry concentrated. She definitely didn't want to be beat by Dale's little sister!

"Chief wins!" the attendant announced, happy it was over.

Jenna joined Kerry in her booth and gave her a warm hug. "Ah well, Dale'll have to defend his own honor." She met Kerry's eyes, a roguish grin on her lips. "Sorry I missed having you for a sister-in-law."

Kerry didn't know what to make of that. She returned Jenna's hug and accepted the accolades and the pats on the back from the other club members, then handed the gun to the attendant for cleaning before she personally returned it to Fiona.

To her thinking, short of getting a court order, this was as close as she was going to get to finding out who among them were crack shots. Dale's own sister was the club champion. She couldn't imagine connecting Jenna Preston to Johnny Haywood. It was true Jenna had had her wild moments. But as far as Kerry knew, Jenna had never been connected with drugs.

Ten minutes later, she was in the club bar drinking an orange juice with Fiona, who'd insisted she have a drink before departing.

One side of the room was a glass wall that afforded a spectacular view of the grounds.

"Find out anything interesting?" Fiona asked as she raised her Virgin Mary to her lips.

"I found out how fruitless my search will be after engaging in a competition with your club champion." She sighed.

"Oh, Jenna," Fiona said. "I've seen her in action many times. She definitely puts me to shame. The woman she brings with her sometimes is pretty good though."

"What woman?" Kerry asked. "Oh, sorry, I forgot that was strictly taboo."

Fiona smiled. "She isn't a member. Her name's Nicole Haywood."

"You devil!" Kerry said, laughing. "You made me go through all that, when you knew all along what I was looking for?"

Fiona shook her head in the negative. "I honestly

didn't remember until you mentioned the club champion. Then it dawned on me: Johnny Haywood, Nicole Haywood. I hope this proves to be a help to you."

"A help?" Kerry said. "I could kiss you, Fiona."

"Don't you dare," Fiona said. She looked around at the sedate club members enjoying their first drinks of the day. "I'd never live it down."

Kerry drove away from Willow Bend Country Club on cloud nine. A real clue. At least she hoped so. There could be other reasons Jenna and Nicole practiced shooting together. The fact that she'd had no idea the two women were friends didn't mean anything. In a town of more than five thousand, she couldn't possibly know everything that was going on.

She definitely had some questions for those two ladies, though. And they'd better have good answers.

Later that afternoon, she was at her desk wolfing down a sandwich she should have had at lunchtime and simultaneously reading last night's officer reports. She saw that a drunk driver had been arrested, two speeding tickets issued, and there had been one domestic violence call. It brought her back to Nicole Haywood. Nicole had said Johnny beat her Friday night. Had he made it a practice, or had it been an isolated incident? And why hadn't she ever reported it to the police if it was an ongoing behavior on Johnny's part?

Kerry knew there were many victims of domestic violence who were suffering in silence. Afraid their husbands would retaliate. Willing to take the beatings in order to keep a roof over their children's heads.

Her phone buzzed. She picked up. "Yeah?"

"You sound tired," Mac said.

"I am tired. But I have good news. Nicole Haywood, the widow of Johnny Haywood, is a crack shot. She's been known to practice at the local country club. The club's manager remembered her."

"That is good news," Mac said, sounding impressed. "I have some good news for you. The guys from the local field office say the car's trunk contained Haywood's shirt, shoes, and cell phone. After a closer inspection, they found the murder weapon stashed under the seat."

"Any info on whom it might belong to?"

"It's sad, really," Mac said. "I'm told that the owner is a local man. A Vietnam vet. I couldn't even find a speeding ticket on him. He's an upstanding citizen, Kerry. What would make him do something like this?"

"Mac!" Kerry cried, frustrated. "Tell me his name already."

"Tad Armstrong. The gun's registered to Tad Armstrong, Kerry. Your mother's old boyfriend."

Kerry could tell he'd been talking to Dale. She made no comment about that right then though. "I don't believe it," she said. "Tad Armstrong is not capable of killing anyone."

"You can believe it or not," Mac said. "But since this is your town, and it now appears that it doesn't come under the jurisdiction of the government, you're going to have to make the arrest."

"Damn," Kerry muttered. "Damn, damn, damn!"

"It's cut and dried, Kerry," Mac said.

"All right," Kerry said. "I'll go pick him up. But, I'm not going to enjoy it."

"I'm sorry, Kerry," Mac told her. "I know this didn't turn out the way you expected it to."

"Something's fishy, Mac. I swear."

"All we can do is follow procedure and see where it leads us," Mac said, offering comfort. From where, Kerry didn't know.

"You're still in town?"

"Of course, I'm still in town. I told you, I'm not going anywhere until you tell me to go. Believe that, Kerry."

Kerry smiled in spite of the recent bad news. "I might need a whole lot of consoling tonight." She knew she was issuing an invitation that she had vowed would never be forthcoming, but she didn't care. She needed Mac's arms around her. This was too sad. Tad Armstrong, a murderer?

"Just let me know what you want to do, and I'm there," Mac promised.

"Meet me at the house at seven?"

"I'll bring dinner."

"Thanks, I don't think I'm gonna feel up to cooking."

Tad Armstrong had been home from the boat factory a little under an hour when the doorbell rang. His mother, Annie, an invalid who spent her days sitting in a wheelchair, doing the best she could with the housework and cooking, had retired for the night. It was barely six o'clock, but she went to bed early and rose early. Many nights she read her Bible until her eyes got grainy, then fell asleep with it in her arms.

Tad, sixty-four, had never married. He'd had some close calls. But, the woman he truly loved had belonged to someone else and he didn't think it was fair to another woman to marry a man who couldn't love her with his whole heart.

He'd worked at the boat factory since coming back from 'Nam. What he did to the wood siding of a sailboat was considered an art form by his grateful bosses. He was among a handful of living artisans who could shape a wooden sailboat from conception to the finished product. Tad was proud to be good at something. When he returned from the war, shell-shocked, folks around here figured he'd never amount to much.

He did have the love and support of a select few. Among them, Evelyn Everett. She'd been a good friend over the years. As was her husband, Buddy.

So, it was with a confused expression that he stood in the door looking at Kerry Everett flanked by two deputies, one black, one white. And it was even more surreal when she said, "I'm sorry, Mr. Armstrong, but you're under arrest for the murder of Johnny Haywood."

Tad laughed, sure Kerry was pulling some kind of trick on him. "Kerry Everett, what is this? It's much too late for April Fool's Day."

Kerry stepped across the threshold, followed by her deputies.

Tad hadn't even changed out of his work clothes, a dark blue jumpsuit and a pair of steel-toed work boots. He was a man of average height and weight. His black hair had gray at the temples, but his dark brown face was mostly unlined.

Dark brown eyes held Kerry's gaze. "You aren't joking, are you?"

Kerry reached out to grasp Tad by the shoulders and began reading him his rights.

"I don't need the Miranda read to me, Kerry. I haven't done anything."

Kerry continued until she was finished.

"Please don't say anything right now, Mr. Armstrong. Wait until you've consulted with your lawyer."

"I understand my rights, Kerry. And I waive them. I haven't done anything. I couldn't kill that boy." Tears sprang to his eyes. He went to say something but apparently thought better of it. Holding both wrists out to Kerry, he said, "All right, cuff me but, y'all please, don't make a lot of noise. My mother's sleeping and I don't want her to know about this until morning. She sleeps fitfully as it is and she needs her rest."

"Paul, go ahead and cuff Mr. Armstrong," Kerry ordered, and Paul stepped forward and cuffed Tad's hands behind his back. Kerry led the way as Paul escorted Tad to the waiting black and white. The other deputy closed the door behind them, making sure it was locked.

Kerry told Tad: "If you'd like, we can get someone over here tonight to stay with your mother."

"No, she'll be fine until tomorrow morning. She usually rises at six. If you could have someone come over around then, I'd appreciate it."

"Very well, then," Kerry agreed.

She left him in Paul Robertson's care, going down the street to her Explorer. The other deputy rode with Paul to the station, and Kerry followed.

At the station, Kerry had Tad brought to her office where she advised him of the charges against him. Tad sat across from her slowly shaking his head in disbelief.

"My gun was found in Johnny's car? But I haven't used that gun in years. It's kept in my gun case in the den at the house."

Kerry looked up at Paul who stood sentinel next to the door. "Paul, would you go to the evidence room and get the weapon, please?"

Paul left the room, and Kerry reached across the desk to grasp Tad by the arm, squeezing it reassuringly. "I know I'm not supposed to state an opinion here, Mr. Armstrong, but I believe you. And I *will* get to the bottom of this."

Tad's eyes were glassy. "Who would want to frame me? I've never intentionally hurt anyone in my life."

"I don't know for certain, but I have a hunch and I'm going to play it out. You just sit tight."

Paul returned with the .22-caliber pistol in a clear plastic evidence bag. He handed it to Kerry. Kerry put on surgical gloves before reaching into the bag and lifting the pistol. She held it out for Tad to get a good look. "Don't touch it," she instructed. She read the serial number from it. Tad's face collapsed. "That's my gun. But how did it get out of my gun case? The only people who are allowed in the house are the ladies who bring Momma her midday meal, and the visiting nurses who come in once every two weeks to give her physical therapy and take her vital signs. She had a stroke about six months ago."

Kerry had heard. Before the stroke Annie Armstrong had been a vibrant woman, active in the community and her church. The friends she'd made before her illness were now supporting her in her time of need.

Kerry didn't say it out loud, but that's where she would start, with the ladies and the visiting nurses who visited Annie Armstrong on a regular basis. She'd find the person who'd ripped off Tad's weapon, and used it to kill Johnny and frame Tad.

"When was the last time you actually saw the gun in the gun case, Mr. Armstrong?" Kerry asked, eyes narrowed in concentration.

"I can't remember, Chief," Tad said, mindful of Paul Robertson's presence, and how it would appear if he continued to call the deputy's superior by her first name. It may look as if Kerry were guilty of favoritism. He was convinced she was on his side and would do everything within her power to clear him of the charges.

"Do you take the guns out of the case to clean them periodically?"

"Yeah," Tad said, the first glimmer of hope in his eyes. "I cleaned them about two months ago."

"Two months. That's a long time to work back from," Kerry said regrettably. She sat up straighter on her chair. "All right, Deputy Robertson will get you fingerprinted and allow you to make your phone call."

She stood while Paul escorted Tad out of the room. Then she walked over to the door and closed it behind them. Leaning against it, she wondered if it was proper for a chief of police to bawl like a baby in her private office. She certainly *felt* like crying. But she was mad, too. Unbearably angry at the murderer for trying to ruin a good man like Tad Armstrong.

* * *

Kerry's cellular phone rang while she was en route to home later that night.

"Chief Everett."

"I don't know why you have an answering machine at home since you never bother to check your messages," Kiana began. "I've figured it out. And it's been wracking my brain all day long. Why is an FBI man masquerading as a telephone lineman? He's undercover, right?"

"You're too smart for your own good. Now, I'll have to deputize you or something."

Kiana laughed. "Don't worry, your secret's safe with me. How goes the murder investigation?"

"Tad Armstrong has just been arrested for the murder."

"What? That man wouldn't hurt a fly let alone a snake like Johnny Haywood."

"Tell Momma. She can tell Miss Bess. They're friends and I think if the news came from her it might go down easier."

"I can't believe it," Kiana intoned sadly.

"I can't either. That's why, as far as I'm concerned, I'm still looking for the killer."

"I guess you heard Ike Jr. hit town this afternoon." Kiana went on to the next subject on her list while she had her sister on the phone.

"No, I've been busy all day. Haven't had much time to stop and chat with the good citizens of Damascus."

"Yeah, blew into town on a Greyhound, went to his mother's house and proceeded to show his ass. Talking about catching his brother's killer, even if it means killing him some crackers."

"He *would* go straight there," Kerry said of Ike Jr.'s penchant for stirring up trouble, and laying the blame on the white man for all his ills. "I see no one phoned the police, so it must have been resolved peacefully."

"Yeah, Daddy, Gabriel, your guy, Mac, and three other men went over there and showed him what upsetting his mother would get him if he ever acted the fool again. Plus, Miss Bess firmly put her foot down. She told him if he continued to raise her blood pressure, he could live on the street for all she cared. His father had nearly killed her, and he wasn't going to come, fresh out of prison, and finish the job. Then Mac, who has an *amazing* knowledge of the law, reminded him that his behavior could land him back in prison, and it was only his mother's grace that was keeping him out, and preventing her neighbors from calling the law. We haven't heard a peep out of him since then."

"Well, thanks for the lowdown, sis," Kerry said, relaxing for the first time that day. "I can go home now, knowing the streets of Damascus are safe."

Kiana chuckled. "All right. Love you, girl."

"Love you, too."

They hung up, and Kerry turned down her street hoping to see Mac's car in her driveway. Out of consideration for her, he'd parked the rental on the street instead.

After she'd parked, she sat there a while, nervous all of a sudden. But Mac was having none of that, and before she realized it, he'd sneaked up on the driver's side and was pulling the door open. His smile set her heartbeat racing. The unconcealed longing in his warm, brown eyes when he reached for her hand made her forget her name. She was in his arms, her body pressed, full-length, against his. His warm breath was on her neck. "Hello, beautiful," he said in that lazy way he had. Searching lips nuzzled the side of her neck. Kissed her there. All the while, her insides were undergoing a metamorphosis. The tension she'd earlier been tearful from was slowly leaking out of her, leaving her with a sensual sensation that was causing chaos in places that hadn't been awakened like that in some time. A memory stirred. Images of her and Mac together. How good it had been between them.

Mac's big hands were on her back, going lower, caressing her bottom. His touch burned her. She closed her eyes and exhaled. That was when his mouth descended upon hers, and she was glad she'd taken the time to brush after that turkey sandwich. Mac plundered her mouth, giving no surcease. Relentlessly working her into a sexual frenzy. And she wanted more. His hand was in her hair. That bun had to go. He groaned against her mouth. Kerry turned her head to the side, breaking off the kiss. "House," she managed before his mouth found hers again.

"Mmm," was the only sound Mac made. He'd gotten the message, however, for he began walking her toward the house though he never once let her go. When they hit the lawn, he broke off the kiss and swept her up into his arms.

"I'm no lightweight," Kerry warned him with a giggle.

"I'm no weakling, either," Mac said, and groaned as if she weighed a ton.

He took the steps with no difficulty and deposited her on the porch. His impatience showed while she fumbled with the key. He took the key and opened the door himself.

"Excuse me a minute." Out of habit, Kerry went to her bedroom and put away her gun. It was good to shed its weight after a long day. Returning to the living room, she sniffed the air. "Is that roast chicken I smell?" She hurried to the kitchen and opened the oven door. A rotisserie chicken was warming inside. She saw the restaurant's name on boxes on the counter, but it was still sweet of him. There were also grilled vegetables and sourdough bread warming. She turned to stare at Mac who was standing in the doorway, a grin on his handsome face. "Some things never change. You still keep an extra house key under a rock down by the front steps. Unwise habit, my love."

"Some things might not have changed, but some

things have," Kerry said with a leer. "You'd better turn the oven off, I'm not hungry for food right now."

With that, she began to slowly back away from Mac. Mac cocked a brow. Things were certainly warming up. He paused long enough to turn off the stove as he passed it.

Kerry unbuttoned her shirt with agonizing deliberation. Mac licked his lips and moved with her, but stayed several feet away, his eyes riveted on her. The shirt was doffed. Underneath was a lacy white bra. She went to unsnap the clasps, but instead teased him by pulling down first the right strap, then the left. Her arms came through them. The bra was now being held up only by her full breasts, whose tips were quickly hardening.

Lowering her eyes to Mac's crotch, she saw her performance was well-appreciated.

Mac cleared his suddenly dry throat. She was more beautiful than he'd remembered. No longer a woman-child, she was a full-bodied woman with luscious curves that were making him wish he could mold her to him right now. Feel that warm golden-brown skin. Taste it. Inhale its scent. But then his eyes focused on a spot only a few inches from her right collar bone. A scar. More specifically, a bullet wound.

"What the hell." He crossed the room in a matter of seconds and firmly held Kerry by the shoulders. His intense gaze went from the scar, to her eyes. Kerry parted her lips to say something and Mac kissed her before she could get a word out.

When they parted, his eyes were misty. She felt the tension in his body. He was holding her so tightly, she could barely breathe.

"Mac, it's all right," Kerry said softly. "It was a nervous kid transporting drugs. He lost it after I pulled him over for running a red light during rush hour in Miami."

"I never wanted you to go to Miami," Mac said, his voice harsh.

He backed away from her, the pain in his heart mirrored on his face. His hands were balled into fists, as he tried to suppress the anger he'd felt upon learning she'd been shot in the line of duty. Shot. She could have been killed, and he would never have seen her sweet face again.

Kerry went to him and threw herself into his arms. "Love me, Mac. Love me *now*. We both made mistakes. But we're here now. I'm sorry I hurt you." She planted kisses all over his face. "I never stopped thinking of you, wishing I'd done things differently."

Mac kissed her forehead and gently pulled her more fully into his arms. "Once, I was at Quantico and an old friend of mine told me about a visiting cop who'd impressed him. She was there for a course in—"

"SWAT team management." Kerry finished his sentence. "That was my first year as chief. I've never had the chance to use my skills." She smiled into his eyes. "I felt your presence everywhere while I was there, Mac. I kept expecting to turn a corner and run into you." She had a story for him, too. "I was in Atlanta last year, at a conference, and one night as I was dressing for bed, I saw you on CNN." She was near tears now, remembering. But she pulled herself together, and went on. "You were escorting a prisoner out of a federal courthouse in Oklahoma City. Oh, Mac, when I saw you after so many years, a dam broke inside of me. I sat there, alone, in my hotel room crying my eyes out over what a fool I'd been."

"And still, you didn't call me," he said, his eyes sad.

"What would I have done if you'd been happily married with children?"

"You might have felt like a bigger fool, but at least you would have finally known."

"And what about you, Mac? Why didn't you call?" Her voice was rife with pain.

"I told you, it was because I thought you didn't want me. You'd made your choice."

Mac had backed her against the hallway wall. Kerry's hands were on the fly of his jeans. "Not want you, Mac? I've never stopped wanting you. I was too young and inexperienced to know exactly *what* I wanted. Sometimes, sometimes I wished you would have just taken me."

Mac knew she wasn't speaking in sexual terms, but the husky quality of her deep, low voice was turning him on in good fashion. He couldn't help kissing her between her lush, honeysuckle-scented breasts. "Take you? We weren't living in caveman times when a man simply grabbed a woman and pulled her, kicking and screaming, back to his cave."

Kerry decided there had been much too much talk. She reached out and grasped Mac's shirt and pulled it over his head. "Mac, I'm not going to pretend with you. I haven't been with anyone in a long time." Her hands were on his smooth, muscular chest.

"How do you manage?" He knew her pretty well in that department.

"Yeah, when we were together I did have a healthy appetite. And I still do, but I have an aversion to sleeping with someone just to be sleeping with him. It's been a while between committed relationships." Her dark, cinnamon-colored eyes regarded him. "I'm nearly in pain here. So, let's make this fast: I'm free of all sexually transmitted diseases. I know that isn't a very romantic thing to talk about at this stage, but, hey, this *is* the twenty-first century and you have to know."

"I've got a clean bill of health," Mac said with a smile.

"Got condoms?"

Mac laughed because she sounded so much like those "Got Milk?" commercials on TV.

"In my jeans pocket."

Kerry laughed, too. "Excellent. I'll wash your back if you'll wash mine."

Kerry was delighted to see Mac had invaded her bedroom as well. He had a Nina Simone CD playing in her CD player, and had spread rose petals on the turned-down bed. "You were confident," she said as she reached back and clasped his hand, pulling him toward the bathroom.

"Still am," he said.

In the large bathroom, Kerry immediately went and turned the water on warm in the shower. She selected two thick bath towels and washcloths from the shelf adjacent to the door and placed them on the towel rack within reaching distance of the shower stall. Then she began removing the rest of her clothing. Mac had gotten down to his briefs. A pair of gray Hanes. Kerry had to come out of her oxfords before pulling off her slacks.

After she removed the oxfords, she picked them up and set them in a corner of the bathroom, out of the way. Mac did the same with his athletic shoes and socks. Returning, he knelt on one knee before Kerry and began rolling down the leg of the sock on her right foot. He kissed the front of her thigh. Kerry trembled with anticipation. When both socks were pulled off, Mac handed them to her. He watched her hip action as she took them and put them with her oxfords.

Her white, lacy bikini panties matched the bra, and were very nearly transparent. He didn't think he could ever look at her in her uniform again without imagining what she had on under it.

Kerry's emotions were all there for him to see. In her eyes he saw her passion warring with her caution. She was taking a chance. But so was he. She was letting down her guard, risking her heart again. With the only man who had ever hurt her, if his guess was on the money. Well, she was the only woman who'd ever left him wounded, too.

"I've gained ten pounds since the last time we made love."

"You gained them in all the right places," he told her with an appreciative once-over.

They stood in the middle of the room, two people whose emotions were so raw, they were afraid to touch, and afraid not to. At last, she reached behind her with both hands and undid the clasp on the bra. Her heavy breasts had dark brown nipples that were already tumescent. Mac wanted to touch her, but restrained himself. Instead, he removed his briefs and stood before her equally exposed. Kerry held her breath momentarily, then let out a, hopefully, indiscernible sigh. Okay. That was definitely the Mac she remembered. After that, she couldn't get out of her panties fast enough. Mac smiled as he followed her into the shower stall.

She reached for the peach-scented bath gel. Mac reached for the Safeguard.

"You can smell like a fruit if you want to," he joked. "But I'd rather not."

Kerry laughed, and suddenly remembered she'd gotten into the shower without her shower cap. Her hair was long and thick, and she didn't relish having to wash it tonight, so she grabbed the shower cap hanging on the peg right next to the stall. It was Mac's turn to laugh. "Black women, and their hair."

"That's right, don't mess with a sister's hair," Kerry defended, and squeezed some bath gel onto her washcloth. She soaped her body, and enjoyed the view as Mac did the same.

"How was your day?" she asked.

"Oh, you mean after you left me with your boyfriend?"

"I see he couldn't wait to fill you in on that ridiculous notion he has that Everett women go around breaking unsuspecting men's hearts."

"From what I've seen of the Everett women, they're

passionate, smart, feisty, and gorgeous on top of all that. If a man can't handle them, he should step aside for a brother who can."

Kerry reached down and wrapped her hand around his semierect penis. "Well said."

EIGHT

"My baby don't care for shows. My baby don't care for clothes . . ." A Nina Simone CD was on the CD player when Kerry and Mac reentered the bedroom, both wrapped in warm, dry towels

Kerry had let her hair down and had secured her towel just above her breasts. Mac's hung low on his waist. Muscles flexed in his powerful thighs with each step. He pulled Kerry into his arms and they began a slow dance. Kerry's nose came to his collarbone. She breathed in the clean, masculine scent of him.

"I see you still love Nina," Mac said in her ear. "You must have every record she ever made in your collection."

"Can't help it, she speaks to me," Kerry said. "When she sings 'I Want a Little Sugar in My Bowl,' or 'My Baby Just Cares For Me,' I know exactly what she's talking about. Plus, I can admit now, her songs reminded me of you."

Mac dipped her. Bringing her slowly back up, he said, "Is *that* why my collection rivals yours?" Dark eyes looked deeply into hers.

Kerry's lips peeled back in a sexy grin, revealing straight, white teeth. Strands of wavy black hair fell into her face and she tossed them back behind her head with a little neck action. "Know what I dreamed of time and time again?"

"Tell me, and I'll make sure it comes true tonight."

"The topsy-turvy."

Mac threw his head back and laughed delightedly. "I was twenty-nine then. I might pull something if I attempted that today. I never tried it after you and I split up."

Kerry was flattered. "That was our thing, huh? It's good to know that there was some part of you that was mine, and mine alone." She kissed his chest, and then lay her head on it as they moved to the music, their bodies rubbing together, the tenuous holds of the knots in the towels working their way loose. Mac's was the first to fall away. Kerry smiled when she felt it drop. Through her towel she felt the tip of Mac's engorged penis pressing against her crotch.

Mac reached out and removed her towel. "Just helping gravity a little."

He didn't get any protests from Kerry whose pleasure points were a riot of sensual sensations at the moment. Mac ran his big hands up from her thighs, lingered a while on her wonderfully rounded bottom, pressing her closer to his erection.

Kerry closed her eyes and lazily arched her back, thrusting out full, peaked breasts.

Mac, unable to resist an offer like that, bent his head and gently pulled one hard nub into his mouth, running his firm tongue over it. Kerry's toes felt as if they were literally curling. Mac treated the other nipple to the same slow, deliberate near-torture.

When she was panting, he raised his head and looked into her dreamy eyes. "I'll be going lower now," he announced unnecessarily, for his right hand was already between her legs, his long fingers spreading her thighs. Kerry's feminine center throbbed, and she knew she was already moist, ready for him.

Mac went down on one knee and gently kissed her smooth, fragrant belly. His tongue left a wet trail from her belly button to the top of her mound. When his tongue went between the lips of her vagina, Kerry tensed. Mac didn't pause, though. He plunged in, his tongue rubbing against her clitoris then eagerly delving deeper into the velvety-soft folds of her passionflower. Kerry bloomed. Her entire golden-brown body flushed ever so slightly. Her scalp tingled. The bottoms of her feet got warm. "Ah . . ." she sighed, and fell into Mac's arms.

Mac carried her to the bed. Laying her on the bed of roses, he straightened back up and just gazed down at her, in the throes of her first orgasm of the night. He was so hard, he was almost in pain. Turning away, he went back into the bathroom where he'd left the condoms in his jeans pocket.

Kerry rose up on an elbow, her thick hair falling across a shoulder. Admiring the play of muscles in his back, buttocks, and legs, she smiled to herself. She could lie here all night just watching him. *But,* she thought, when he returned, condom in hand, his penis hard and stiff enough to hang a DO NOT DISTURB sign on, *sometimes participating is much more pleasurable than just observing.*

As Mac approached the bed, she held out her hand for the foil-wrapped condom. One of the bonuses of making love to Mac was touching him every chance she got. Mac was more than glad to relinquish the job. Kerry sat on the edge of the bed. Mac stood before her. She gently kissed his belly. His penis moved upward. Kerry smiled and kissed him there before rolling the latex condom onto him.

Mac playfully pushed her back onto the bed. Kerry moved backward, spreading her legs as she did so. Their eyes met as Mac knelt on the bed and came toward her. "I'm going to impale you to this bed."

"And you have just the sword to do it with, too, my lord," Kerry replied, licking her lips. She remembered how Mac used to like role-playing while making love.

In this scenario, he was a medieval lord about to ravish a kidnapped virgin. Unbeknownst to him, the virgin was ready, willing, and able. Kerry tried to look demure, but it was a hard act to pull off since she was fairly trembling with the need to have him inside of her right about now.

She primly closed her legs and inched toward the headboard as if she were afraid of Mac. Her hands covered her breasts. "Be gentle, my lord. I beg of you."

Mac pulled her none too gently against his chest and spread her legs. "Hell, Kerry, I tried to hold off by playing games, but all I want to do is make love to you until your eyes roll back in your head."

"Yes, my lord, yes, yes, yes!" Kerry cried, and arched her hips.

Mac slid right into her, she was so ready for him. Kerry sinuously moved her hips, but not too swiftly. They both liked it slow and rhythmic.

Mac sighed when he felt all of him inside of her. Kerry wasn't a small woman, so he didn't have to fear hurting her. She'd taken all of him every time, and wanted more. He'd never had a lover before or after her who was as equal to the task. He felt like he was home at last. He felt her muscles tightening around him. It felt so good to him, he thought he'd come right then and there. But she relaxed. He looked into her eyes, and saw a passion there that matched his own. Knew she was enjoying it as much as he was.

He pushed deeper, moving in and out with increasing frequency. Kerry's strong thighs closed tighter around his waist, but then she relaxed and held her legs open and thrust upward in a submissive gesture that said, *here, take your pleasure. Take me, I'm yours.* And he took her. He took her soaring to the peak, and then he fell with her back down to earth. Spent, but ever so satisfied, Mac lay on top of her a few minutes, not allowing his full weight to smother her. He rolled onto his side after a while, and they lovingly gazed into each other's eyes. They lay like that for a long time.

Then, suddenly, they burst into laughter. Rich, throaty laughter that came up from their bellies and spread to each corner of their bodies. Because, as it had been with them before, sex was contentment. Sex relaxed them. Sex made them glad to be alive. Sex was the embodiment of their love for each other.

Kerry rolled off the bed first, going to the bathroom. Looking back at Mac, who was right behind her and busy removing the spent condom, she said, "You should have seen your face when you came, Mac. Your eyes did that fluttery thing." She demonstrated, rapidly batting her eyelashes.

"My eyes?" Mac said with a sardonic lift of a brow. "All I could see were the whites of yours as you came down."

He deposited the condom in the wastebasket. Kerry slapped him on the behind as she stepped into the shower stall. "That's 'cause it was so damn good I was about to pass out," she joked.

Mac stepped into the shower with her. This time he put her shower cap on over her tresses. After he'd tucked any stray hairs underneath, he bent and kissed her. "I adore you, Kerry Anne. It will always be that good between us. We'll have love and laughter, because what's love without a little laughter?"

"Whatever happened to Bo Brookman," Kerry asked over dinner.

They were eating in the kitchen. She'd put on her robe, and Mac had had to put his jeans back on since he hadn't had the presence of mind to bring along a change of clothing. Kerry had piled her hair on top of her head in a jaunty do. Mac was enjoying the sight of her, so relaxed and animated. This case had been hard on her. Now, he knew she was trying to distance herself from it, if only for tonight.

"Bo Brookman left the corps soon after you left. He went into business with his dad who owns several car dealerships in Detroit."

"Bo, selling cars?" Kerry faked a tremble. "I always thought he'd go into the CIA or something. That boy loved him some war games."

"Yeah, he was a bit gung ho. But I think that was just a ruse to hide his more sensitive side. Turns out the corps was just his way to get the macho aggression out of his system, or so he says. He's married now, with four kids last I heard."

"Four kids. More power to him." She took a swallow of iced tea and met Mac's gaze. "Do you have any, Mac?"

Mac stared at her. "I just got through making love to you. Don't you think I would've told you if I did? Before doing the act that makes them with *you?*"

"Yeah, I suppose, but you've only been here two days. It isn't as if we've had time to really discuss what we've each been up to the last ten years."

"Children should be at the top of the list, Kerry. No, I don't have any children. I don't want any children until I'm ready to settle down."

Kerry didn't comment. Things were moving fast enough between them. Forty-eight hours together and she'd made love to him. Forty-eight more, and she'd be planning the wedding. Better not start talking about children.

"Tell me about your family. How are they?"

"Mom and Dad are both in good health, thank God. They're in their seventies now. My brothers and sisters all live pretty close. No one more than a two-hour drive away."

"And Baltimore's not very far from D.C."

"Right." He smiled at her. "It almost sounds like you

and your family, doesn't it? I never thought about it, but I suppose I chose to work in D.C. because it *is* so close to home."

"There's nothing wrong with that," Kerry said. She knew she enjoyed having the love and support of her family. But, if the man she loved asked her, she'd live anywhere on the planet, as long as she was with him.

"I feel like such a hypocrite," Mac insisted. "Telling you you used your family as a crutch that prevented you from reaching your full potential."

"That was the old Mac talking," Kerry said. "The one who wanted to dictate to me how I should build a career."

Mac was silent a moment. He placed his fork on his plate and met her eyes across the table. "I did, didn't I? I figured since I was older, I was also wiser. And you, Kerry, you had so much going for you. You could have done anything. Anything! Plus, I wanted you beside me. I didn't want to lose you." He bit his bottom lip. "But I still lost you. My pride got in the way. I should have told you that no matter what you decided to do, I'd be there for you. Instead, I went off like a big, dumb jerk who'd just got his feelings hurt."

"And I ventured forth like a liberated woman. 'I am woman, hear me roar!' " Kerry said with a laugh. "It was pride that got me, too, Mac."

She reached across the tiny, round table, grasped Mac's hand in hers and squeezed.

"I won't let pride get in my way any longer."

Mac brought her hand up and kissed the knuckles. His dark eyes caressed her face.

"Me, either."

The next morning, the sky was slate gray. Already rumblings could be heard in the distance. Kerry thought she could get in a couple of miles, at least, so she set out on her morning jog. She hoped Dale had gotten the hint and wouldn't be joining her.

Feeling mellow after a night of lovemaking, her usual alert senses were dulled. When she passed Deeks's place, it didn't occur to her that Atta Girl hadn't greeted her with her usual ferocious "good morning." Jogging past the fence, she was suddenly brought up short when she heard growling behind her. At once, she knew something was amiss since that sound was coming from outside the gate, rather than inside.

She froze in place. From the corner of her eye she saw Atta Girl racing toward her. Remembering her training, Kerry immediately called out in as forceful a voice as she could manage. "Heel!"

Atta Girl kept coming. "Heel!" Kerry tried more forcefully.

Seeing that the dog was intent on attacking, Kerry did the next best thing, she dropped to the ground and rolled into a ball, tucked her head in and covered it with her arms as best she could. If she allowed the dog to get to her throat, she'd be a goner in less than a minute.

Pain shot through her as the dog sank its teeth into the upper part of her right arm. Kerry dared not get out of the position. White light appeared at the backs of her eyes as the dog bit into her thigh.

"Atta Girl, heel!" came a masculine voice Kerry's frantic mind thought it recognized as belonging to Lewis Deeks. "Atta Girl, heel!"

Gunfire. Atta Girl slumped to the side with her teeth still sunk into Kerry's thigh.

Kerry lay there, afraid to move, with tears streaming down her face.

Lewis Deeks went over to her. Bending over her, he gingerly touched her shoulder.

"Chief Everett? You conscious?"

He lifted the dog's body off Kerry. Kerry was bleeding profusely from her arm and her leg. Deeks stumbled off as if nauseated by the sight of the blood. "I'll get help," he said.

Kerry watched him leave, a short, stubby man. Funny how she'd always assumed he was much larger. His legendary hatred for others had made him bigger than life. He was just a tiny man, really. That was the last conscious thought she had.

Bright lights were everywhere. And she was moving somehow. She was racing along a corridor on her back. Flying. Yes, flying. It was such a smooth ride, too, this flying. She felt weightless. No human body held her anchored to the earth.

"Kerry, Kerry! Can you hear me?" Was that Kiana's voice?

Kerry struggled to answer her, but she was being inexorably dragged down a dark tunnel. Peace could be found there. And rest. She was so tired.

". . . blood, but she's stable now. The puncture wounds were deep. With puncture wounds that deep, I'd be surprised if plastic surgery would do any good."

Kiana angrily glared at the young doctor. She went to him and boldly took the chart from his hand. "I'd like to see that if you don't mind." *And to hell with you if you do!* she mentally added. The size of the woman's two companions made the doctor reconsider the retort he had on the tip of his tongue.

One had dreads and the other had barely any hair at all, and he was the more menacing-looking one. Both were dark-skinned and stood with their arms akimbo, as if they were ready to kick somebody's butt, anybody's butt, with very little provocation.

Satisfied that Kerry was, indeed, on the road to recovery, Kiana handed the chart back to the doctor. "I would appreciate it if you wouldn't talk negatively around my sister. Your opinion about plastic surgery isn't needed since you're not a plastic surgeon."

The doctor blushed red, clear to his ears. "It wasn't my intention to upset anyone."

"Too late, we're already upset," the bigger guy said.

He walked over to the bed and peered down at Kerry. Unshed tears sat in his eyes.

Kerry turned her head and looked into his eyes. "Don't kill the messenger, Mac."

No one was more relieved than the doctor to see her awake and talking. He hurried to her bedside and grasped her wrist, taking her pulse. Nervously chewing on his top lip, he counted. Back to normal. She was strong. He managed a smile. "Glad to see you back, Miss Everett," he said.

"Thank you, Doctor," Kerry said. She felt sorry for the poor guy. Her family could be intimidating when anyone stood between them and a loved one. And Mac, Mac could freeze a timid heart with just a look when he wanted to.

"Don't stay too long," the doctor admonished as he left the room. "She needs her rest."

Kiana was the first to plant a kiss on her forehead. "Baby sis, you had me worried there, for a minute. Momma and Daddy came in here, saw you and had to go back out to the waiting room they were so upset. I'm going to tell them you're awake now." She kissed her again before going to do just that.

Gabriel went and kissed her cheek. "Get well quick, sis." He left the room, too.

Mac held her hand in his, lovingly rubbing it against his cheek, relishing the feel of her warm, alive hand on his skin. "God, Kerry."

Kerry had never seen Mac cry. The sight of his tears, shed because of her, was a humbling experience. "I'm going to be fine. Didn't you hear the doctor? Who cares about a few more scars?" Her voice had broken at the end, and tears rushed out of the corners of her eyes, spilled into her mouth. Delayed hysteria? That was life, wasn't it? When she'd gone through The Crucible, she thought there would never be anything that would challenge her more. And then she'd been shot. After she'd been shot, she was absolutely certain nothing could be scarier. Until a vicious dog sank its teeth into her.

She was literally trembling. Mac nearly got up in the bed with her in order to hold her close to him. He kissed her forehead, her cheek, her mouth. "You're safe now, baby. Let it go."

She tried to let it go. But she couldn't. So she tried thinking like a cop.

"Has Deeks been arrested?"

"He was taken in for questioning and released," Mac told her as he smoothed her hair back from her face. "He claimed someone had cut the lock on the gate, allowing the dog to get out. Paul Robertson went to investigate himself, and found that not only had someone cut the lock on the gate, but had spread ground meat on the lawn in order to lure the dog outside."

"But who would do something like that, knowing what a badass that dog was?"

"Someone who knows your routine. Someone who wanted you out of the picture because you're getting too close to the truth."

Kerry gazed up at him. "You believe me now? That Tad Armstrong's not guilty?"

"I believed you all along," Mac told her. He planted another kiss high on her cheek. "And you're not going anywhere without me from now on."

At that moment, Evelyn and Buddy came barreling into the room, all smiles.

"Baby!" Evelyn cried, her eyes already tearing up. Mac moved out of the way as Evelyn took his place on the bed. "I swear, the news that that dog had attacked you took ten years off my life." Kerry smiled up at her mother. "How anybody can say a pit bull is a docile animal is beyond me." She looked over at Mac. "The dog's dead, isn't it? Because, if it isn't, I'm going over there and personally shoot it myself. And I don't care about the ASPCA!"

"The dog's dead," Mac confirmed. "Deeks killed it himself."

Kerry was released from the hospital the next day with the understanding that she would take the rest of the week off from work. She knew her people could handle her absence for a few days, so she spent the next four days at home being coddled by her mother, Kiana, and Mac, who'd practically moved in.

She was sitting by the window in her bedroom, Thursday afternoon, looking at the rain, which had been constant the last sixteen hours. Hurricane Sonia was nearing Cuba, the Weather Channel reported, and South Florida might be next. Remembering Hurricane Andrew, many South Floridians had boarded up the windows of their homes, collected their insurance policies and headed north. Even North Floridians were getting nervous. The ladies of St. John A.M.E. were telling all church families to fill water bottles, clear any objects from their yards that would turn into a missile in windy weather, stock up on nonperishables, get batteries for flashlights and portable radios, and make sure the family boat was in good repair in case it was needed. There was a chance the Santa Fe River might overflow and they'd be flooded out.

Mac came into the room with a golden delicious apple and a coring knife on a tray.

He sat down on the chair next to her and began peeling the apple for her. Kerry watched. They'd become so used to each other's presence, so comfortable in it, that speaking wasn't always necessary. After Mac had finished peeling the apple, he expertly cored it and cut it into thin slices. Then he began feeding Kerry the apple, slice by slice. Kerry thought it was the most sensual thing a man had ever done for her.

Mac broke the silence with, "You think too much."

Kerry swallowed. "How do you know I'm thinking?"

"You're not only thinking, you're simmering. You're mad as hell. And who can blame you? Someone tried to kill you."

"We keep saying 'someone,' " Kerry said. "Let's call a duck a duck. Nicole Haywood killed her husband, framed Tad, and she tried to get me killed, too. And, somehow, Jenna Preston is involved. I haven't figured that one out yet. Maybe Nicole just used her for shooting lessons. But that doesn't explain the two sets of prints at the crime scene. Nor the fact that the culprits were two lightweights. Jenna must have helped her dispose of the body. But why? Why would she do something that stupid? She could go to prison for years for aiding and abetting a murderer."

"Who's to say Jenna didn't kill Haywood, and Nicole did the aiding and abetting?" Mac asked, being the devil's advocate.

Kerry considered it. "I don't know, Mac. We start with the person who has the most to gain. Nicole is the person who would be rid of an abusive, womanizing, drug-dealing husband. The drug dealing part, I'm convinced of. The other two, I'm not so certain of. That's the way she described him. But no one else has come forward accusing him of beating her or cheating on her."

"We'll just have to trip her up," Mac said.

"With what?"

"Something she overlooked. They always overlook something."

On Saturday, Hurricane Sonia changed course making Floridians, statewide, breath a collective sigh of relief. But her aftermath was devastating. Homes in Dade

County had roofs ripped off by hundred-mile-per-hour winds. Tornadoes laid waste to trailer parks from Dade County to Orange County. And in Alachua County, where Damascus sat, the Santa Fe River overflowed and flooded out over a hundred families who lived nearby. Damascus Springs High School and the Health Center, where Kiana volunteered her services as a nurse, were designated shelters for those who didn't have inland friends or relatives they could stay with.

Kerry and Mac were helping out at the shelter Saturday afternoon. Kerry was in the kitchen helping the ladies of St. John A.M.E. prepare dinner for the thirty-odd refugees. Mac was outside helping to unload supplies from the back of a semi that had come all the way from Memphis, Tennesee. The A.M.E. brethren up there had collected blankets, canned goods, clothes, and drinking water for those in need.

Courtney was running around the center playing with the children, trying her best to cheer up her new friends. Damascans came out to help; among them, Doreen Wilkins and her son, Jamie. Jamie and Courtney were friends from way back.

Doreen considered Kiana to be as much an angel as the ones God had created. Kiana had been helping her with her dialysis for years, and not once had she made her feel like a number, a person without a heart and a soul.

So, if peeling a few potatoes helped her out, she was right there!

The two women were at the sink now, rinsing already peeled potatoes. Kerry was stirring a pot of beef vegetable soup at the stove. Doreen was a gray-eyed blonde in her early thirties. A bit too slim due to her illness, she was nonetheless optimistic by nature.

"Who's that guy that's been hanging around Kerry lately?" she asked Kiana now.

"Kerry's got a boyfriend," Kiana said in a singsong

voice, making sure she could be heard by her sister six feet away.

Kerry smiled to herself. Kiana loved to mess with her about Mac about as much as she used to rib her about her and Gabriel when they first started seeing each other. She guessed payback was fair play.

"All right, knock it off, girls," she said to Kiana and Doreen. "It's all right if the chief finally gets lucky."

"How lucky are we talking?" Doreen asked. Her husband, Scott, was outside helping to unload the semi, too. They'd been married ten years and were deeply in love. Her condition had been harder on Scott than it had been on her. Scott *and* Jamie. Jamie deserved a mother who would be around to see him grow up.

Now she wanted to hear that her friend, Kerry, was finally finding the love that had, so far, eluded her. "Tell me all about it. I love a good romance."

"They met ten years ago when Kerry was in the Marine Corps," Kiana said, as excited for her sister as she'd be if she were telling her own story.

"A marine," Doreen said, her voice awe-filled. "He looks like a marine."

Kerry had to tell the story Mac had given her: "We hooked up again via e-mail," she said. "For months we wrote back and forth. He'd promise he would come see me, but I didn't believe him. And last Sunday he just showed up at church."

Doreen smiled at Kerry. "That is so sweet. It sounds like one of those romance novels I love to read on a rainy day. Only this is real life."

Being a demonstrative person, she had to give Kerry a hug. Kerry accepted it, not hugging her back too tightly for Doreen was frail even though she never wanted you to acknowledge it. She was strong that way.

Mac and several of the other men came through the kitchen door hauling crates of food supplies and piling them in a corner. When Mac looked at Kerry from across the room she blushed in spite of herself.

Three hours later, everyone had been fed, the kitchen cleaned, and mothers and fathers were getting their children ready for bed, taking turns using the center's two bathrooms. Kerry and Mac left for the day, running to his car through the persistent rain.

In the car, Mac pulled her into his arms. "Are you all right? I think you may have overdone it today." He rubbed her back.

"Mac, I would never have taken you for a mother hen," Kerry said. She felt fine. Her arm and leg were still a bit sore, but the soreness was lessening every day. There was no infection. And, thank God, Deeks had had the good sense to get the dog's shots as they were needed. There was no fear of rabies.

"You look a bit wan."

"It's because I feel for those folks. Their homes destroyed by flood waters. Some of them didn't have insurance. How're they going to rebuild?"

"Honey, the president will be declaring the Santa Fe River area a disaster area. The government will provide most of the funds, and charitable organizations will take up the slack. They'll be taken care of."

He kissed the top of her head. "Let's get you home. You need a hot shower and something to eat, then bed."

Kerry smiled at the mention of bed.

Mac must have read her mind. "Maybe, if you eat all your dinner."

"What is he doing here?" Kerry wondered aloud as Mac pulled the rental into the driveway. Ike Haywood Jr. was standing on her porch. Kerry squinted through the windshield, checking his body language, checking his hands for any weapons, his body for any telltale bulges underneath his clothes. She hated to admit it, but a residual of the dislike she'd had for Ike Jr. when they were kids had followed her into adulthood. Perhaps his having spent his life in and out of prison for crimes ranging from car theft to assault with a deadly weapon had something to do with it.

"He would be a fool to try anything," Mac said, his tone bordering on belligerent.

"I'll handle this," Kerry said, reaching for her door's handle.

"You can do all the talking," Mac said. "And I'll do the intimidating."

The rain had slacked up a bit on the drive across town. Kerry and Mac had the option of walking slowly instead of sprinting to the house. Ike Jr. watched them warily, rocking from one foot to the other. Kerry didn't like it when volatile people like Ike Jr. were nervous. You could never predict what they would do next.

Ike Jr. moved aside as first Mac, then Kerry stepped onto the porch. Mac put himself between Kerry and Ike Jr. his narrowed dark eyes sending warning signals to Ike Jr. to behave himself. "I ain't here to cause trouble," Ike Jr. said right away.

Ike Jr. reminded Kerry so much of Johnny, it was almost like seeing a ghost. The same pecan-tan skin, good-looking face, dark brown curly hair. Though Johnny had gone to a professional barber to get his haircut, whereas his brother's hair looked like a prison hack had gone at it with garden shears. It stood out at weird angles. A closer inspection revealed he'd begun twisting it, creating locks.

Six feet tall and around two hundred pounds of muscle, Ike Jr. had apparently taken advantage of the weight room at the state prison. "I know you don't have any reason to believe me, K . . . Chief, but I'm a changed man."

"Forgive me if I'm having trouble believing that, Ike, when the first thing you did when you got home was threaten to kill white folks to avenge Johnny's death. For your information, there is no evidence whatsoever that his killing was racially motivated. I believe he was killed by someone close to him."

"That's why I'm here," Ike said. He raised a hand to run it through his hair, but as soon as he raised it, Mac went into "defensive mode" and leaned toward him. Ike Jr. held his hands up. "Whoa, big fella, it was just a nervous gesture. Chill out."

He looked at Kerry with beseeching eyes.

Kerry said, "Why don't we all sit down? We're all a little tense standing here like this." She indicated he should sit on the swing on the south side of the porch. Ike went and sat down. Kerry took the rocker next to it, and Mac stood by her side.

"Okay," she said, giving Ike Jr. her full attention, "tell me why you're here."

"I'm here to speak on behalf of Mr. Tad," Ike Jr. said. He rubbed his chin, the muscles in his right arm bulging. "I've met some killers in my time, and Mr. Tad is not a killer. He is a friend of the family, a real friend. I have more memories of Mr. Tad in my life than I do of my own father." He met Kerry's eyes. "You knew my daddy, K . . . Chief."

"Oh, hell, call me Kerry. That way, you can get on with what you have to say."

"Mr. Tad used to do things with us boys. Things a father would do. He took us to ballgames. Taught us how to drive. Tried to teach us right from wrong." He looked sheepish. "When I was a kid, I would wonder why he would come around so much, but when I grew up, I realized he had a thing for Momma. Now, I'm not judging them. Because my dad was in prison so much, I know Momma must have gotten lonely. Besides, they kept things cool, you know? We boys never suspected anything when we were kids." He paused. "What I'm trying to say is, Mr. Tad loved Momma. And I believe he still loves her. I don't think he'd ever do anything to hurt her."

Kerry thought of something Nicole had told her about Johnny and Tad Armstrong.

"Ike, Johnny's wife told me that Johnny and Mr. Armstrong got into public arguments quite often. Mr. Armstrong was apparently trying to talk Johnny into changing his lifestyle. Did Johnny ever visit you in prison? Did he ever tell you about his relationship with Mr. Armstrong?"

Ike was nodding in the affirmative. "Yeah, he did. And it's true, Mr. Tad was always on his case to straighten up and fly right."

Kerry considered this. So, Nicole had told the truth that time. It probably furthered her purposes to do so. Kerry cleared her throat. "Before your parole you'd been in prison how long?"

"Seven years for robbery."

"Then that means you'd never met Nicole before you went in? I'm assuming since she and Johnny haven't been married that long."

"Oh, no," Ike contradicted her. "I knew Nicole before I went to prison. She was around eighteen the first time I met her. As a matter of fact, Johnny met her the same time I did. It was at a party for her brother, Nick. Back then Johnny and I were heavy into dealing in Gainesville, and not so much in this area. Nick Blanchard was considered the top Gainesville dealer. He wanted to check me and Johnny out, see what we were about, and threaten us, of course. We were so cocky back then, nothing scared us. We each flirted outrageously with little Nicky as everybody called her. You see, Nick was named after their father, and so was Nicole."

Kerry's face remained impassive. Nicole, caught in another lie. She'd said she didn't know anything about her husband's business. She'd said she hated it, and had begged him to get out of it. No mention of the fact that her own brother was a drug dealer.

"So, she was just the protected kid sister?" Kerry asked. "She was kept out of the business?"

"That's the impression I got," Ike said. "Nick would make her leave the room whenever we discussed business."

Kerry sighed. The Lord giveth and the Lord taketh away. Perhaps Nicole actually didn't know anything about the drug business. She could be the innocent battered wife she claimed to be. Okay, so maybe taking over her husband's business wasn't the main motive for his cold-blooded murder. The fact was, though, she'd planned his murder down to the last detail, from stealing Tad's gun to the actual executionstyle killing. She couldn't argue that she'd killed Johnny on the spur-of-the-moment.

Of course that made her more desperate than ever not to get caught.

"Does the rest of your family know she comes from a drug background?"

"Kerry, you know Momma wasn't gonna be hearing that," Ike said with a laugh. "No, nobody knew except for me and Johnny."

"That doesn't bode well for you," Mac put in with a rueful smile. "Because if she killed Johnny, and you're the only person in town who knows who she really is, it's going to be that much more difficult for her to disappear when the time comes."

"I'm sure she didn't figure on your getting paroled," Kerry said, picking up where Mac left off.

Ike had gone still. His eyes widened, and his mouth sat open in surprise.

Kerry snapped her fingers in front of his eyes. "Hey, Ike, you in there?"

"Someone tried to run me down when I was out walking yesterday," he said.

"Walking in the rain?" Kerry asked.

"I'm used to much worse," Ike said of his life in prison. "I had to get out of the house. Momma is in a state of depression right now, over Johnny's death and Mr. Tad's arrest. And Harold blames me for adding to her stress."

"Did you get a look at the vehicle?" Kerry wanted to know.

"I was too busy jumping into a ditch to avoid becoming roadkill," Ike said regrettably.

NINE

"Why don't we go over there and ask her why she was shooting targets at Willow Bend Country Club?" Kerry asked as she put a forkful of spinach salad in her mouth.

Mac sat across from her cutting into his steak. "Because we don't want to show our hand. Besides, it's all circumstantial evidence. Going to a shooting range isn't a crime. I'm sure she and Jenna Preston can come up with a reasonable explanation as to why they were there. Girlfriends looking out for each other?"

"Don't you think that's a strange pairing?" Kerry asked, frowning.

"No, not really. You said Jenna has been a bit wild all her life. They could have met anywhere, at a club, at the supermarket. Doesn't matter. We've got to catch her in something that has her name written all over it."

"Of course, the only prints on Tad's gun would belong to him," Kerry said with a weary sigh. She adjusted the cloth napkin on her lap, put her elbow on the table and her chin in her hand. Looking forlornly at Mac, she said, "But, it all goes back to the beginning, Mac. To the moment I saw Johnny's body. Those two sets of footprints. That has to mean something."

"Maybe it's time to lean on her," Mac said. "You can do your Columbo act. Nicely pester the hell out of her until she cries, 'uncle.' "

"Sounds like a plan," Kerry agreed. She smiled at him. The idea of making Nicole Haywood sweat appealed to her a great deal.

"Eat," Mac ordered, pointing at her untouched steak. Because of the amount of blood Kerry had lost, the doctor had put her on an iron-rich diet until her next checkup, at which time he'd let her know if it was safe to resume her regular diet.

Kerry wasn't a fan of beef. A fish person, she could eat fresh fish every day if she could get it. "A fisherman," she joked. "I should marry a fisherman; then I could have fish every day."

Mac laughed. "If that's all you want, I know someone I can get it from for wholesale. Book the church, you can marry me."

Kerry knew he was only kidding, but her heart skipped a beat anyway. Cutting the tender steak with the edge of her fork, she said, "Fish every day? You've got a deal."

"Okay," Mac said, inclining his head. "Though at the prices they get for seafood nowadays, I'll be poor inside of a year and you'll be looking for husband number two." He met her eyes across the table. "Oh, wait a minute, I *am* number two according to number one. I guess you'll have to be content with me."

Kerry threw her napkin at him. Dale and his tall tales.

Mac caught the napkin in midair and got up to walk around to her side of the table. He placed it in her lap, then bent and kissed the side of her neck. "Eat all of your dinner and I'll give you a massage you'll never forget," he said close to her ear.

He went and sat back down.

Kerry ate with gusto.

A few minutes later, they were sprawled on the sofa in front of the TV looking at the evening news. Mac sat close to the corner, his arm along the back of the sofa. Kerry's head was in the crook of his arm, and her legs were on the coffee table. They were both in jeans, T-shirts and white athletic socks. Except Kerry had a noticeable bulge on her right leg beneath her jeans; the bandage that covered the dog bite. The wound was throbbing, but she ignored it. Not used to taking drugs, the pain pills the doctor had prescribed put her to sleep. As long as Mac was around, she wanted to be alert so that she could recall every precious moment when he was gone.

Mac observed her while she was watching the news. He loved the baby-fine hair around her hairline. It curled into tiny ringlets when she perspired. He knew that if they ever had a little girl, she would have hair like that. The dimple in her chin was a favorite place to kiss. And the tip of her nose, which was slightly hooked, if the truth be told, was sexy to him. Her eyes could not lie. He had but to look in them to know what she was feeling. Which made her a poor poker player, but a real turn-on in the bedroom because she couldn't fake an orgasm to save her life.

The weather man was saying Hurricane Sonia had blown itself out over the Atlantic Ocean. Kerry switched the set off and turned to him. "Not that you were aware of what was going on, anyway," she said of his watching her, instead of the news.

Mac smiled slowly and didn't even try to deny it. Shrugging, he said, "Your bottom lip is fuller than your top lip. That space above your top lip that looks like a miniature ski slope has peach fuzz on it."

Kerry's right hand went to her face. "Oh, my God. I'm getting Aunt Eunice's mustache." She sprang to her feet and hurried from the living room, heading to the hall bathroom.

Mac groaned and followed. He'd put his foot in it, when he'd thought he was being romantic. "I love the peach fuzz," he called after her.

He found Kerry peering into the bathroom mirror, tweezers in her hand. "Where are they?" She was plucking at air because nothing was appearing between the pincers of the tweezers.

Mac caught her by the wrist and took the tweezers from her. Placing them on the sink, he pulled her into his arms and said, "Were you listening to me, woman? I was trying to be romantic, talking about the endearing parts of your body. Those little things about you that turn me on."

Kerry relaxed in his embrace. "My hairy upper lip?"

"You can't even see it without a magnifying glass."

"I'm not neurotic, you know. I mean, I really don't care if a man doesn't think I'm perfect. It's just that you make me nervous, Mac."

"I make you nervous?" His dark eyes danced. His wide, mobile mouth broke into a grin. "Me? I've seen you naked more than a hundred times, and I make you nervous?"

Kerry wriggled out of his embrace and entered the hallway. "You noticed the fuzz on my top lip, Mac. Soon, you'll be noticing that my breasts aren't as perky as they used to be and my butt not as taut, and it'll be just an excuse to not find me as desirable as you thought I was upon your arrival."

"You're doing it again," Mac said. "You're dreaming up reasons why we can't be together. Look at your sister and your brother-in-law. They live most of the year in Connecticut where he's a tenured professor. Your sister managed to build a career as a nurse in Bridgeport. Why? Because she loves her husband, and she wants to be with him. And then they spend summers here with you and your family to give Courtney the chance to know her mother's people, and to give Kiana what she no doubt craves those other months she spends in Bridgeport, a family who supports her unconditionally."

He stopped because Kerry was gazing up at him with such love in her beautiful eyes that he lost his train of thought. She walked into his open arms, there in the hallway, and laid her head on his chest. When she did that, his brain started functioning again, and he completed his spiel. "You and I can work something out, too. I like Florida, even though the heat and humidity can kill you."

"Wait until October," Kerry said. "Then we have the most beautiful weather you ever saw anywhere in the world. From October to April, our days are cool topped with blue skies, gentle breezes. You open your windows and breathe in the orangeblossom-scented air and thank God for heaven on earth." She peered up at him. "You caught us during our rainy season."

"In Washington it's cherry blossoms in springtime," Mac said. "You should see it, Kerry. It's a beautiful time of the year."

"I can't wait," she told him as she tiptoed to meet his mouth in a slow, deep kiss.

Kerry returned to work Monday morning and couldn't have been happier. The whole morning crew greeted her with a surprise "welcome back" party replete with doughnuts from the local Krispy Kreme doughnut shop, and balloons.

Dera got emotional and threw her arms around Kerry's waist. Kerry bent and gave her a warm hug. "Don't get mushy on me, Stephenson. There's no crying in a police station." Dera hugged her harder before turning away and returning to her computer.

"Oh, yes there is," Paul Robertson said as he dunked a glazed doughnut into his cup of coffee and bit into it. "We've had a couple of emotional days since you've been gone."

"Come to my office later, and fill me in," Kerry told him.

She was grateful her people cared enough about her to put together this celebratory respite, but it was time to get down to business, and she was raring to go. She met Royce Clemons' eyes as she turned to go to her office. He gave her a genuine smile, with no hidden contempt somewhere deep in his eyes. She didn't know exactly what to make of that. "Royce," she said in greeting.

"Chief," he acknowledged her with a nod of his head, and went to his desk.

In her office, Kerry started in on the officer reports and found out that they'd finally arrested Abby Franklin for solicitation. She read the name of the john: Walter Jackson, forty-eight. She didn't recognize his name and hoped he was from out of town. The arresting officer, Jake Rivers, had made a notation that Abby had been transported to the county jail. Kerry hoped Abby would at least get drug rehabilitation out of her stay in jail. She'd known hookers who'd been on the street to support their drug habit, and when they got clean went on to lead productive lives.

There was a knock at her door.

"Come in," she called.

Paul Robertson strode in. He smiled at her. "You asked about the crying scenes," he reminded her.

"Yeah. Sit down, Paul."

"Miss Bess came by to see Tad Armstrong, Saturday afternoon. I couldn't hear what was being said, but they got into a heated argument and she left crying."

Kerry didn't condone listening in on the prisoners' conversations with visitors but, in this case, she wished Paul had caught that conversation. First Ike came to her house pleading Tad's case; then Miss Bess went to see him in jail and left an emotional mess. It made her wonder whether or not they were telling her everything.

She pursed her lips. "Interesting. You sure you didn't hear anything?"

"Just him repeating the word, 'no,' " Paul answered.

"And the other crying scene?"

"Abby Franklin's john," Paul supplied. "It was worse

than watching Jimmy Swaggert confess he'd committed adultery. The guy carried on in good fashion. Swore he'd never propositioned a hooker before, to which Abby cried, 'Liar! You're a regular!' She definitely didn't intend to go down alone."

"So, she showed no remorse, huh?"

"Remorse?" Paul asked, incredulous. "She seemed proud. Like it was a badge of honor or something. Didn't even flinch when Jake told her how much time she'd probably pull since drugs were found on her, on top of the solicitation charge."

Kerry hadn't gotten to that in the report before Paul had interrupted her.

"Thanks, Paul," Kerry said with a smile.

"Anytime, Chief," Paul replied as he rose to leave. "Glad to have you back."

Kerry ordered a roast beef sandwich for lunch and consumed it at her desk while she went over paperwork that had piled up in her absence. It was amazing how many E-mails she had, too. Messages from fellow peace officers, notices from police organizations she belonged to, reminding her of meeting dates.

At a quarter past one, her phone rang. It was Dr. Lisa Soto.

"Hey, I heard you were back. How're you feeling?"

"I'm doing great, thanks. How about you and yours?"

"Oh, I'm fine, and so is the family," Lisa said, her tone cheerful. "Remember I told you that there was something about Haywood's blood that didn't sit well with me?"

"Mmm-huh."

"Well, I found out what it was. He had a stimulant in his bloodstream. But not your average stimulant like caffeine, for example. This was a plant. Pure foxglove. Do you know what foxglove does to the body?"

"Foxglove?" Kerry said. She knew she'd read something about it, but it had been a long time ago. Then it occurred to her: The leaves of the foxglove plant were the source of the heart drug digitalis. "It's a heart stimulant, right?" she asked Lisa.

Lisa laughed shortly. "You're one smart cookie. Yes, indeed. Someone pumped him with enough digitalis to make an elephant's heart burst."

"Are you telling me the gunshot didn't kill him?"

"Oh, yeah, the gunshot would have killed him if he hadn't already been dead."

"This is getting a little too strange for me," Kerry said.

"Yes, dear. This is a strange case, all right. Sounds like whoever killed Haywood gave him the foxglove, probably cooked in some kind of food, then made love to him until his heart exploded."

"When you say pure foxglove," Kerry began, "do you mean the culprit couldn't have gotten it from a physician in the form of digitalis?"

"I'm saying it was still in its plant form," Lisa said with a triumphant tone to her voice. "I have tiny, undigested bits of purple leaves here in a specimen jar for you if you need it for evidence. It's disgusting, but sometimes you have to go into the stomach of the deceased to find out if his last meal killed him. In this case, it did."

"Thank you, Lisa! You're a genius," Kerry said excitedly. "I've got to run."

"Glad to be of service," Lisa said. "Take care, girlfriend."

"You, too," Kerry said, and hung up.

Kerry forgot about the paperwork and left her office in a rush. She swept right past Mayor Reginald Washington. He ran after her. "Chief, I need to speak with you about a very important issue."

"Tell it to one of the other officers and I'll get back to you," Kerry said, not stopping.

Reginald stood in the middle of the office, fit to be

tied. "Who does that woman think she is!" he yelled to no one in particular.

"She's the chief of police," Dera said, then promptly answered a 911 call. "Dispatch. What is the nature of your emergency?"

Reginald turned and stormed out.

Kerry didn't even need her car for her next destination. It was within walking distance: Damascus Public Library. She pulled the glass door of the modern building open, and her senses were immediately engaged. The smell of books always relaxed her. She loved books. Her library card was up-to-date. And, come to think of it, she probably had a couple of overdue books out. The librarians knew her by sight.

"Afternoon, Chief," Mrs. Donaldson, a young-looking septuagenarian with a pair of reading glasses hanging on a chain around her neck, called as Kerry passed her desk.

"Hello, Mrs. Donaldson," Kerry paused a moment. "I need to see what the foxglove plant looks like."

That's all she needed to say. Surprisingly agile, Mrs. Donaldson was on her feet and leading Kerry down aisle after aisle until they arrived in the horticultural section. The library had a huge collection of horticultural books because many Damascans took pride in their gardens and were always looking for ways to make their plants thrive.

Mrs. Donaldson picked up a thick book and flipped through the pages.

"Here we are," she said, handing Kerry the book.

"Thank you," Kerry said, smiling at Mrs. Donaldson.

"My pleasure, Chief," Mrs. Donaldson assured her, and made herself scarce.

Kerry learned foxglove could grow up to four feet tall. The flowers could be white, yellow, lilac, or purple. It was the purple foxglove, genus *Digitalis,* species *purpurea,* that was the source of the heart stimulant digitalis. The plant itself was quite pretty with flowers shaped like fingers or, in Kerry's opinion, upside-down bells. The book went on to say the plant was not an easy one to grow and required diligent care in order to keep it alive.

Kerry closed the book and put it back on the shelf. Armed with the information she'd come to the library to get, she left.

A few minutes later she was driving outside of town in the direction of Mason's Auto Parts. She kept her ears and her eyes open in this town. If anyone had foxglove in her garden, this time of year, it was the local root woman.

Even in this day and age, there were people who put their faith in herbs for curing their ailments. Herbs to induce the object of your affection to fall for you. Herbs to make you more exciting in bed. Herbs to thwart an enemy. Herbs to identify an enemy and put a boomerang curse on him: Whatever evil he wished upon you would come back and bite him in the can.

Kerry was within a mile of Viola Kelly's house when she remembered the promise she'd made to Mac: She wouldn't make any calls without backup. Therefore, she pulled the Explorer onto the shoulder of Highway 441, whipped out her cell phone, and dialed his cell phone number.

Mac answered after two rings. "Agent Kent," he said.

"Mac, do you remember where Mason's Auto Parts is?"

"It's a few miles outside of town. Yeah, I can find it again."

"Well, I'm on my way to see Viola Kelly . . ." She told him about Lisa Soto's findings and her own suspicions about Viola Kelly.

"I'll be right there," Mac said.

After hanging up, Kerry sat behind the wheel of the Explorer, trying to pull up a faint memory of a snippet of information her mother had given her about Viola

Kelly. Something about her eyes. She didn't see well? Wore thick glasses? Something.

Mac was there inside of ten minutes. He parked the rental car behind the Explorer, got out and approached the Explorer on the passenger side. When he was in the cab of the truck, he leaned over and kissed Kerry full on the lips. "I haven't seen you since seven this morning."

After that, Kerry needed a moment to compose herself and slip back into serve-and-protect mode. "How did the assistant director take your explanation for staying on longer?"

Mac grinned. "No problem. He agrees with us. Besides, The Sharpshooter struck again, this time in Arlington, Virginia. We lucked out, though, because the victim survived. The Sharpshooter's aim wasn't good enough. The bullet ricocheted off the victim's skull. The victim then jumped the Sharpshooter before he could get off another round, and while they were struggling in a downtown park, a troop of overzealous Boy Scouts marched in. The Sharpshooter had to flee, but not before being positively identified by twenty Boy Scouts, two troop leaders, and the victim. Agents picked him up last night, and they have enough evidence to convict him on twelve counts of first-degree murder. Turns out he's an ex-cop from Arlington."

"Whew!" Kerry said, giving Mac a high five. "Another dirtbag goes down for the count." She straightened up in her seat and started the car. "Okay, let's go shake down a possible accomplice to murder."

"If she suspects that Nicole Haywood used the foxglove in the commission of the crime, you aren't going to get anything out of her. She'll be afraid to implicate herself."

"I thought of that," Kerry told him, a smile playing at the corners of her mouth. "That's why I'm going to con dear old Mrs. Kelly."

Viola Kelly was sitting on the couch in her living room, her feet up on the sofa as well, enjoying a rerun of *The Jeffersons* and smoking a joint. She'd read the National Institutes of Health report about the use of marijuana for glaucoma in which it stated that there was no evidence that marijuana could be used to lower intraocular pressure any better than the drugs on the market for that purpose. They had their studies, and she had hers. And in hers, the use of pot had been a resounding success. She swore by it.

The knock on her door, in the middle of the afternoon, startled her so much, she dropped the toke in her lap, burning a hole in the leg of her black slacks. "Damn!"

She picked up the half-smoked joint, ran and flushed it down the toilet. Returning to the living room with a can of Glade air freshener in her right hand, she generously sprayed the air in the living room.

When she finally made it to the door, a bead of sweat had broken out on her forehead.

Kerry stood on the porch, back straight, wearing mirrored sunglasses, a grave expression on her face. "Good afternoon, Mrs. Kelly. We're here to ask you a few questions about the murder of Johnny Haywood."

"We?" Viola asked. She ran a shaky hand through her salt-and-pepper 'fro.

Kerry stepped aside for Mac. He was so tall, Viola couldn't even see his face without stooping a little and looking under the top of the screen door. "Hello, Mrs. Kelly," Mac said, his voice as deep as Michael Clark-Duncan's of the film, *The Green Mile*. Viola's heart was off and racing. "Question me?" she cried. "Why me? I don't know anything about that poor boy's death."

She still hadn't unlatched the screen door. Kerry removed her glasses and looked Viola directly in the eyes. "We've arrested Nicole Haywood, Mrs. Kelly. The coroner has determined that Johnny Haywood died of digitalis poisoning."

Viola clutched her heart. "Oh, no! I thought she shot him!"

Kerry's hand was on the door handle. She hadn't come here to give the woman a heart attack, she'd just wanted to get at the truth. Then she smelled something burning. Peering around Viola, she saw smoke coming from the hallway.

"Mrs. Kelly, do you have something on the stove?"

"No," Viola said, defensive now. "Why do you ask?"

"Because there's smoke coming from your hallway."

Turning to look behind her, Viola's face went ashen. She must have missed when she tossed the bud into the toilet and dropped it in the wastebasket next to the commode instead. She ran to the bathroom. Sure enough, the trash in the wastebasket was smoldering, more smoke than anything else. She picked up the basket and held it under the bathtub tap. Running water over the whole mess, she sighed with relief when she saw that the only damage would be to the wastebasket.

Going back to the door, she said, "I didn't put out my cigarette well enough before putting the butt in the trash."

"Better watch that," Kerry admonished. "Now, why did you say, 'I thought she shot him' after I told you Johnny Haywood had died of poisoning?"

"That's what the *Herald* said, that he died of a gunshot wound to the head," Viola said, nervously. Her palms were sweating, and the buzz from the marijuana, though it had partially worn off when she saw cops at her door, made her feel lightheaded.

"Mrs. Kelly, FBI Special Agent Kent and I would either like you to step outside, or allow us to come inside. We can't talk through your screen door."

"I ain't got nothin' to say," Viola insisted. "I'm an upstanding citizen. I've never been in trouble with the law. I lead a quiet life. I mind my own business. Keep my nose out of other people's business."

"I don't think you understand me, Mrs. Kelly. Nicole Haywood claims that you gave her the leaves from a foxglove plant. She says you instructed her on how to use them. Told her how much to give her husband in order to cause a heart attack. She said she paid you handsomely for your advice."

"She's lying!" Viola vociferously contended.

"Then you don't mind if I check your garden for foxglove plants?" Kerry said. She produced a folded piece of paper from her front pocket. "This is a search warrant." She held Viola's gaze. "Now, if I have to search your house and grounds, and I come up with the plant, it will be much harder on you than if you went ahead and told me everything you know and cooperated fully. There is no law against selling herbs from your home. If you say you sold it to her, but you had no idea what she planned to use it for, then you're off the hook. But if I have to waste precious investigative hours searching the premises . . ." Kerry trailed off, as if she were weary of it all, and rapidly losing patience.

Viola unlatched the screen door and stepped back from it. "Come in," she said.

Kerry and Mac followed her into the living room, where Viola directed them to two barrel chairs facing the couch. She sat on the couch and folded her hands in her lap and lowered her eyes. "I ain't never give nothin' to nobody that would harm them. And I wouldn't have this time, either. But she threatened me."

"Threatened you?" Kerry asked. "How?"

Viola's eyes looked huge behind her spectacles. "I was in my garden one afternoon a few days before Johnny was found dead. She must have come to the door, and since I didn't answer, she took it upon herself to walk around back to see if I was in the yard. Well, when she came upon me, I was harvesting some marijuana fronds. She knew what they were, of course. After that, her attitude changed because she knew she had me. She wanted to know if I had a plant that would knock out a full-grown man. I told her I didn't have anything like that. My plants and herbs were for medicinal purposes, not for making anyone lose consciousness. All the while, she's closely examining all of the plants in the garden. Touching them, even yanking off some leaves. I asked her not to do that because some of the plants were very fragile. Then she came to the purple foxglove. She looked at that plant; then she looked back at me, and I knew she knew exactly what it was for." Viola stopped, removed her glasses and covered her face with both hands. Tears came to her eyes. She wiped them away and replaced her glasses. Looking at Kerry, she continued. "Foxglove has always been used in my family as a heart stimulant for the old ones. You know, they're feeling poorly, short of breath, and you'd make them a cup of foxglove tea and they'd pep up. But a little bit went a long way. I explained to her that if she gave whomever she was planning to knock out a cup of foxglove tea, that it wouldn't relax them; instead it would revive them. But she just started plucking the leaves off the plant and putting them on a paper towel she got from her purse. She plucked nearly every leaf off the plant. Then she boldly walked through my house, muddy feet and all, without being invited. When she got to the front door, she looked back at me and said, 'If you tell anyone I was here, I'll tell the police about your happy weed, old woman.' Then, she left."

"I take it you have glaucoma," Mac said gently.

Viola gave him a grateful perusal. "Yes, I'm afraid of going under the knife. What if they make a mistake and I wind up blind?"

"Does the marijuana help?" Kerry asked.

"For hours afterward, I do see things clearer," Viola replied. She sighed tiredly. "I never sell it. It's for personal use only. And I only have a couple of plants. I'm not growing it in bulk out back."

"Listen," Kerry asked, "is that everything? Your whole conversation with Nicole Haywood?"

"That's all of it," Viola confirmed. She sat wringing her hands for a full two minutes before Kerry said another word.

Rising, Kerry told her, "Because you've been so good about cooperating with us, I'm going to see what I can do about keeping you out of this, Mrs. Kelly. I'm referring to the marijuana. If what you've said is true, you didn't give her the foxglove, she took it. In that case, you can't be liable for what she did with it. At any rate, please be available to testify against her in a court of law when that time comes."

"Oh, I will," Viola promised, standing on somewhat shaky legs. "Thank you, Chief. I'll never forget this."

Viola closed and locked the door behind Kerry and Mac, then went to roll herself another joint. She had to have *something* to relax her.

TEN

Mac wondered at the perplexed frown on Kerry's face as she drove back to where his car was parked beside Highway 441. Hadn't they solved another piece of the puzzle?

"What's the problem?" he asked. They sped by a forest of pine trees. At four in the afternoon, the sky was nearly clear, the air thick with humidity. But it hadn't rained in more than twenty-four hours and the earth was drying out. Since Sunday representatives from the American Red Cross, Habitat for Humanity, and HUD had all been in town working to find homes for the displaced Santa Fe River families. Mac knew that couldn't be weighing as heavily on Kerry's mind as it had been the past two days.

"The problem is," Kerry began, "in order to keep Mrs. Kelly out of this for as long as possible I'm going to have to suppress evidence. And since you were present when I promised Mrs. Kelly I'd try to keep her out of it, I'm hoping you'll turn a blind eye, at least for a while anyway."

"Then you're not going to arrest Nicole?" Mac surmised.

"Not until I clear up some loose ends," Kerry said. They arrived at the spot where they'd left the rental. She pulled behind it and switched off the engine. Turning to Mac, she said, "If I go to Nicole Haywood with what I have, what would she do? Deny it? She's too smart for that. No, she'd say she gave Johnny the foxglove all right, but it didn't have the desired results, he went berserk like you see users of angel dust behave, beat her up and left the house. Maybe the foxglove killed him later, but not in her presence. Besides, we've already got the gun with Tad's prints on it. She might have tried to poison Johnny, but Tad finished him off. I, for one, believed Mrs. Kelly."

Mac nodded. "I believed her, too."

Kerry's hand went to her thigh. The wound on her arm rarely bothered her, but the one on her thigh throbbed off and on throughout the day. She couldn't take the pain pills her doctor had prescribed while on the job because she needed to be alert.

"The Tylenol doesn't help?"

Kerry smiled at him. "It dulls it a little. I'll take some when I get back to the office."

Mac leaned over and kissed her mouth. "All right, be macho if you want to be. But I plan to spoil you tonight. A soak in the tub, a rubdown afterward, a pedicure. I owe you one, remember?"

"That's right, you do," Kerry confirmed, remembering their bet on the bank of the Ichetucknee the night Paul Robertson had gone down and found Johnny Haywood's Mercedes.

She kissed his chin. "Thank you for backing me up today, Mac."

"Anytime, Chief," Mac said as he opened the car door and climbed down.

Kerry waited until she saw him get into his car and drive away before following him back to town. Mac left her with a warm feeling inside, almost making her forget the pain in her thigh.

As she drove down Main Street, she saw that merchants were taking advantage of a sunny day by putting up the colorful banners announcing the upcoming street fair.

With the murder investigation taking up most of her time, plus her recent injury, the event had slipped her mind. Then, she remembered the mayor coming into the station just before she'd excitedly run off to check out a lead. Maybe what he'd wanted to see her about concerned the street fair.

She glanced to the right and saw Dale Preston Sr. walking on the sidewalk in the direction of his downtown office. She didn't know how he did it, but he managed to look comfortably cool in a suit and tie even in this sweltering heat. It must have been ninety degrees in the shade today. Only the second week of August, it would be warm until mid-September when the nights would begin to become cooler. Then in October the weather would change to cool days and cold nights. That was her kind of weather. The fall of the year, when leaves turned orange and red, and the sky was a robin's-egg blue. Crisp breezes. Sweater weather. Cold nights during which she could actually start a fire in her fireplace and cozy up with . . . Mac, hopefully.

Mac. Now there was a subject to ponder.

She stopped the car at the red light, and for some reason, her attention was drawn to the parking lot of the Winn-Dixie. The white Jeep Cherokee. When the light changed, she made a right turn and pulled into the Winn-Dixie parking lot and parked in front of the white Jeep Cherokee. Getting out of her car, she walked around and read the car's tag. It was a vanity plate, like Johnny Haywood's had been. RCHBCH. It didn't take the brain power of an Einstein to figure out what that meant.

Nor was she surprised when Jenna Preston walked up with two plastic bags filled with groceries. Jenna smiled at her, her full red lips parting to reveal pearly-white teeth.

"I keep running into you everywhere," she said.

Kerry smiled, too. She glanced down at Jenna's bags. One bag had disposable diapers in it, the other had milk, orange juice, and baby wipes. Meeting Jenna's eyes, she said, "Yeah, imagine that. I hardly ever see you, and now we've run into one another twice in the past two weeks."

Jenna's eyes went to Kerry's bandaged arm, then she quickly looked away. "I was sorry to hear you'd been attacked by that pit bull. It must have been awful for you. I'm glad to see you're up and about."

"Well, thank you, Jenna. I appreciate that. How is Dale, and your father?"

"They're both fine. Daddy is real busy getting ready to defend Tad Armstrong in court. Wasn't that something? Tad being arrested for Johnny Haywood's murder?"

"Yeah, that was something," was all Kerry would say on the subject. She placed her right hand on the butt of her gun. "I'm sure I'm holding you up, Jenna. I was just going to run in and pick up a carton of milk. See you."

Jenna couldn't wait to leave. "Okay, you take care, Kerry."

Eyes narrowed, Kerry turned and walked across the parking lot to the supermarket. When she stepped through the electric doors and turned back to look at the spot where she'd left Jenna, she saw the white Jeep Cherokee speeding out of the parking lot and turning left on Highway 441, in the opposite direction of Nicole Haywood's side of town. She laughed shortly. There was no way those disposable diapers and wipes belonged to Jenna. Since Kerry was in the supermarket anyway, she went to check out what kind of fresh fruits they'd gotten in today.

When Mac left Kerry, he drove out to State Road 231, parked the car far off the road and got out and walked near the turnoff to Edgewood Estates, the new subdivision where the Haywood home had recently been built. Still a mostly wooded area, he had no trouble staying concealed while he approached the Haywood home, camera in hand. This was his third day of having the house under surveillance.

There were four cars parked in the driveway now: A black late-model Lexus, a gold-tone late model Toyota Camry, a huge tan late-model Lincoln Navigator, and a white late-model Cadillac Seville. Nicole's relatives? Probably. Yesterday he'd gotten photos of several well-dressed African-American males. The only female he'd seen going in the house was a middle-aged woman with short, beautifully styled silver-streaked hair. She'd hugged Nicole at the door, and Mac had noticed a resemblance between the two women. He assumed that was her mother. The older woman had been carrying Nicole's son, Jack, in her arms when she rang the doorbell. Two burly black men stood behind her, waiting to follow her inside.

Mac's attention was drawn to another arriving vehicle: A white Jeep Cherokee.

He took photos of the occupant as she stepped out of the car and hurried to the door of the house. Nicole Haywood briefly hugged her at the door and let her in.

He noticed Nicole was still wearing widow's black.

When it started getting dark, Mac walked back to his car and drove to Kmart. He intended to wait while the photo technician developed the pictures; then he would go clean up at the inn then meet Kerry at her house.

Kerry parked outside of Tad Armstrong's modest two-bedroom home. Painted white, trimmed in yellow, it was well kept and the yard had the best-looking lawn on his street. Flowering trees dotted the corner lot, the fence around the house had climbing roses on it on the south side, and in the back, wild jasmine.

There was a car parked in the driveway. The garage door was down. Kerry knew Tad owned a late-model Pontiac, but he rarely drove anywhere except to transport his mother to church and back home again. He preferred riding his bicycle around town for the exercise. Kerry didn't know if she'd get much out of Annie Armstrong concerning who could have stolen Tad's .22-caliber pistol and framed him with it. But she had to try. She waited until Paul pulled his squad car behind her Explorer and joined her on the porch.

She knocked.

The door was immediately opened by a petite brunette with sparkling brown eyes. She appeared to be in her early twenties. Kerry was surprised to see her deputy actually blush when the woman said hello and invited them inside.

Closing the door behind her, she unnecessarily identified herself as the visiting nurse who was there to give Mrs. Armstrong physical therapy. Her white pantsuit and white oxfords, plus the name tag on her chest, all identified her as a nurse. "Mrs. Armstrong is in her bedroom. If you will have a seat, I'll go get her," Holly Gordon said. She smiled at Paul before leaving the room.

"Thank you," Paul said, his voice cracking.

Kerry fought the impulse to tease Paul about his reddened cheeks after Holly had left the room. She didn't know why Paul was acting embarrassed. He was within his rights to find a woman attractive. He was a bachelor at twenty-nine, and as far as she knew, he'd broken up with his last girlfriend more than six months ago.

"She's nice," Kerry said as they sat down in the comfortably furnished living room. Early American couches and chairs in a flowery pattern that wasn't too hard on the eyes. Clean and neat. The mantel was covered with family photos. Kerry rose to go look at them. Stuck in the corner of one framed photo was a snapshot of Jack Haywood, a toothless grin on his cherubic face. He was really a handsome little boy. But then both of his parents were attractive people. She was suddenly sad, wondering what would become of him with his father dead and his mother in prison. Plus, one side of the family, his mother's, involved in the drug trade. What became of children like that? Were they raised by the grandparents if they were in good health, or were they put in foster homes? She knew it could go either way. Some children wound up in good homes but others wound up bounced around the system until they came of age and went out on their own.

Kerry heard the squeak of the wheels on a wheelchair and turned to see Mrs. Armstrong being pushed into the living room by the friendly Miss Gordon.

"Hello, Kerry," Mrs. Annie Armstrong said.

Kerry was struck at once by the dignity Annie Armstrong possessed. She sat up straight in her chair. Her iron-gray hair was pressed, the old-fashioned way, with a hot comb, no doubt. It had been twisted at the back of her head and was pinned there.

The style reminded Kerry of the hairdo she'd always seen Mrs. Rosa Parks wear. In fact, Annie Armstrong was nearly the same complexion and was as petite as the venerable Mrs. Parks.

Kerry went and clasped Annie's hand in hers. "I'm so sorry about your present troubles, Miss Annie. But I'm trying my best to clear up the situation."

"Yes, Thaddeus told me that you would be coming here to ask me a few questions, and I'm glad to answer them. So, you go right ahead and ask."

Miss Gordon cleared her throat. "If you all will excuse me, I'll be in the kitchen filling out my report."

She left, but not before smiling at Paul.

Paul looked at Kerry, then looked in the direction Miss Gordon had gone.

"If you'd like to ask Miss Gordon about the other

visiting nurses while I'm questioning Miss Annie, Deputy Robertson, that would be a big help to me."

"Sure, Chief," Paul said quickly and rose.

"Lovely children, both of them," Miss Annie said in Holly and Paul's absence. "Holly is as loving as she is pretty. She's been coming here since I came home from the hospital nearly seven months ago. She makes sure I get my exercise. I'm lazy about that. But she tells me if I don't use it I'll lose it, and I definitely want to be able to do for myself as long as I can."

"That is important," Kerry said, thinking of her own mother's mother, Grandma Sally, who was eighty-four and still living alone and driving a car. The last time Kerry had broached the subject of her Grandma Sally hanging up her driver's license her grandmother had thrown her out of her house and told her not to come back until she learned to respect her elders. Kerry had driven back to Hawthorne the next day and apologized, but made Sally promise to call her if she was going on any long trips. Sometimes Sally would get it in her mind to visit an old friend in Tampa, which was around seventy miles from her hometown, and get on I-75 and go! Kerry was a nervous wreck worrying about her octogenarian grandmother on the interstate with all those tractor trailers and senior citizens in motor homes, all flying down the road at eighty miles per hour.

Sitting back down and turning toward Miss Annie, Kerry said, "I'm going to be blunt with you, Miss Annie, because I know you want your son back home with you, and that's what I want as well. I need you to work backwards and tell me who has brought your midday meals to you for the last two months. Mr. Tad told me he remembers his gun was in the gun case two months ago when he cleaned it. But since he doesn't use it often, he has no idea when the .22-caliber pistol went missing."

Miss Annie's brows drew together in a frown. "It's usually Bess who brings me lunch every day. She stays and chats for about an hour. I'm very close to Bess. She's been a friend of this family for many years."

"Yes, I know, and having Mr. Tad accused of her son's murder is very hard on her."

"She doesn't believe he did it, either," Annie said, defiantly lifting her chin.

"Her son, Ike Jr., came to see me and told me as much," Kerry said. She pursed her lips. "Okay, Miss Bess usually brings you lunch. But have there been any times she couldn't make it and someone filled in for her?"

"No, never," Annie replied.

"Not one time?"

"You can set your watch by that woman," Annie said proudly.

Kerry looked into Annie's light brown eyes, how her very countenance seemed to shine with an inner light when she talked about Bess Haywood.

"You really care for her, don't you?"

"I couldn't love her more if I'd given birth to her myself," Annie said.

"That's high praise," Kerry returned. She rose and went to get the photo of Jack Haywood. Returning with it, she said, "I suppose it was Miss Bess who gave you this photograph of her grandson, Jack."

Annie nodded, and with a determined aspect in her eyes said, "Bess's grandson, and *my* great-grandson."

It took a moment for the meaning behind what Annie had just said to dawn on Kerry. She had to sit down. Annie reached for Kerry's hand and squeezed it, giving her some of her strength. "That's right, Kerry, my boy is accused of killing his own son."

"So, when I came here that night to arrest Mr. Tad, you all were in mourning," Kerry said, her voice low and respectful. She met Annie's eyes. "Why didn't Mr. Tad tell me this?"

"He and Bess have been keeping it a secret for so

long that he felt he had to consult with her before telling anyone." She sniffed. "But I didn't make that promise, and if my telling you this will save my son's life, then the cat's out of the bag. I don't care who knows. Thaddeus didn't kill Johnny. He loved that boy. It was his fondest wish that Johnny would turn his life around. Now, that'll never happen." Tears rolled down her cheeks. Kerry stood and put her arms around the old woman's thin shoulders. "Don't you worry, Miss Annie. I'm going to catch Johnny's killer. I promise you."

Annie sniffed and gave Kerry a watery smile. "Then let's get down to business, Chief Kerry."

Kerry sat back down, ready to listen to whatever Miss Annie had to say.

"You want to know who could have stolen Thaddeus's gun and framed him with it. Well, like I said, Bess always brought me my meals. There are two visiting nurses: Holly and a black nurse by the name of Kiana Everett-Merrick, and I know you trust her. Kiana has been wonderful all summer. She comes once a week. Holly comes three times a week."

"Is there any time when the house is empty? Does someone come to take you grocery shopping during the week when Mr. Tad's at work, for example?"

"Oh, I see what you're getting at. The only times this house is completely empty is on our weekly shopping day, which is Saturday. And Sunday, when Thaddeus drives me to St. John A.M.E. So, I suppose someone could have broken in here without our noticing. But that's the only way Thaddeus's gun could have left this house."

"Okay, I can work with that," Kerry told her. "And, actually, it makes more sense, because with a memory like yours, there's no way the culprit could have come in here when you were home and not be remembered."

Miss Annie smiled graciously. "Well, thank you, dear."

Kerry rose. "We'll be going and let you get back to

your therapy. Thank you for your time. Our conversation was very enlightening."

"I'm glad to have been of help, Kerry. Please tell your parents I said hello."

"I'll be sure to do that," Kerry said, and went into the kitchen to awaken Paul from the spell of the siren in the nurse's uniform.

Tad Armstrong's hearing was that afternoon, and Judge Frances Putnam allowed him bail since he had no previous record, and was not considered a flight risk because his mother was an invalid. Besides, Judge Putnam had known Tad for nearly thirty years. If Tad had killed Johnny Haywood then the whole world had turned on its ear overnight.

Kerry wanted a private word with him before he was released, however.

She had Royce Clemons bring him to her office. She'd chosen Royce because she'd decided to start giving him more responsibility. It was difficult not to show favoritism to Paul Robertson because he was so efficient at his job. But she thought if she started asking more of Royce, he might step up to the plate and deliver. Perhaps it would also go a long way toward dispelling some of the resentment he seemed to have for her or, rather, the fact that she held the position he wanted.

Royce was respectful toward Tad as he led him into the office. He paused to nod at Kerry, then left. She thanked him with a smile, and directed her attention to Tad. "Please sit down, Mr. Tad. There's something you should know before you go home."

"There's nothing wrong with Momma is there?" he asked worriedly.

"No," Kerry immediately replied. "Miss Annie's fine. She and I had a nice chat this afternoon. She was very animated and seemed to be feeling great."

"Oh, good," Tad said. He closed his eyes a moment. "So many bad things have been happening, I just assumed . . ."

Kerry thought she should just tell him what was on her mind. The man was already stressed to the max and she was only adding to his stress by procrastinating.

"Miss Annie told me that Johnny was your son," she said quickly.

Tad slammed the palm of his hand down hard on Kerry's desk. "She had no right!" he angrily exclaimed. Trembling with rage, he paced the floor.

"She had every right," Kerry disagreed, getting to her feet. "Your life is on the line here. Convicted murderers still go to the electric chair in Florida, or had that bit of info slipped your mind? I know you want to protect Miss Bess's honor and all that, but unless you start telling me the truth, and the whole truth, I'm not going to be able to help you."

"It wasn't Bess's honor we were worried about."

"We? Meaning you and Miss Bess?"

"Yes."

"Then what *are* you worried about?"

"How the boys are going to take the news when they learn I'm their father, and Ike Haywood wasn't."

Kerry squinted at him. "Are you saying all of Bess Haywood's sons belong to you?"

"All four," Tad replied, looking Kerry in the eyes. "Ike was apparently unable to give Bess children."

"And you and Miss Bess had a years-long affair?"

"Bess and I have been in love since we were teenagers. I would have married her, but we argued soon after she graduated from high school and she eloped with Ike Haywood to spite me. I joined the Army, went to 'Nam. When I returned Ike had done his first stretch in prison. Bess and I ran into each other, realized we still felt the same way, and that's when the affair started. She got pregnant with Ike Jr. Ike assumed it was his. He went back to prison . . ."

"And you and Miss Bess resumed your affair."

Tad nodded. "For a while there, every time Ike went to prison Bess would turn up pregnant. I started doing things with the family. Doing the things a father would in Ike's absence. But the boys thought Ike was their father and, for some reason, they idolized him."

"To impressionable boys, being a con and a criminal seems glamorous," Kerry said.

"Yeah," Tad concurred with a sad sigh. "And a Vietnam vet who was rumored to have returned less of a man than he'd been before, was a source of ridicule."

"It must not have been easy for you and Miss Bess to maintain the ruse," Kerry sympathized. "It's all going to come out now, though. Either way: Whether you're the one on trial or the real culprit's on trial. It will have to come to light. You know that, don't you? Please don't blame your mother for telling me. She loves you. She did the right thing."

"They'll wind up losing respect for their mother, and hating me," Tad feared.

"They're grown men. They deserve to know the truth. And you deserve to be recognized as their father. From what Ike Jr. told me, they loved you when they were children. It will probably take them a while to get used to the notion, but time heals wounds."

"We'll tell them soon," Tad said, turning to leave.

When he opened the door, Kerry saw Bess Haywood waiting in the outer office. She followed Tad out and greeted the petite woman who was dressed smartly in a short-sleeved navy-blue pantsuit and navy-blue flats. Kerry didn't know how Bess was holding up under everything, but she supposed that was the mark of a strong woman: to bend under pressure, not to break.

"How are you, Miss Bess?" Kerry asked respectfully.

"I'm holding up, dear," Bess said. "I've just returned

from the funeral home. Since the ground is drying out, they say we can go ahead with the funeral this Saturday. It'll be held at two P.M. at St. John."

Kerry walked outside with Bess and Tad. She saw that Ike Jr. and Harold were waiting in their mother's car, Harold behind the wheel. She acknowledged them with a nod of her head. Both of them returned her nod.

"How is Nicole holding up?" Kerry asked Bess as they walked to the car.

"Don't get me started with that girl. She wanted to cremate my boy when the Browns told her because of the flooding they wouldn't be able to bury Johnny for a few days. She told them to put him in the crematorium. As if she had better things to do and couldn't take the time to put her husband away properly." Bess humphed. "Doesn't matter anyway because it's the insurance policy I had on Johnny that's paying the bill. I went down to Brown's Funeral Home as soon as the body was released and wrote them a check."

Kerry couldn't help it, she had to know: "How did Nicole take your stepping into her shoes and arranging her husband's funeral?"

"She was livid," Bess answered with a surprisingly smug smile on her face. She looked Kerry in the eyes. "Miss Annie told me you and she had a talk this afternoon. Well, you should also know that my daughter-in-law and I don't get along. I've rarely been to her house for anything, and the times I did go out there and found her at home, the place was a sty, and that child was being neglected. I told her about herself on more than one occasion, so there's no love lost between us. But, if she thinks she's going to pack up and move away and keep me away from Jack, she's a bigger fool than I thought because I will go to court and take that child from her before that happens."

Kerry knew, then, how Bess was holding up under the

pressure. Her grief had been replaced by anger. Bess Haywood was taking no prisoners.

A little past seven that night, Kerry left the police station for home. Her body was weary, but her spirit was strong. She'd made progress today, and all roads led to Nicole Haywood. The only thing left to do now was to give her enough rope to hang herself. Mac, Paul, and, now, Royce were taking turns watching the house. If Nicole tried to blow town in the middle of the night, she'd be stopped before she reached the city limits.

The thought of chasing her down made Kerry smile as she placed her key in the driver's side door of the Explorer.

"Kerry!"

Spinning around, she saw Dale running across the street toward her.

He was casually attired in Dockers, a short-sleeved cotton shirt, and Rockports. Grinning down at her, he said, "I'm glad I caught you. I wanted to see for myself how you're doing." He pulled her into his arms and his cologne wafted over her. It had been twelve hours since she'd had a shower, and she didn't have faith that her deodorant was still doing its job, so she didn't want him to get too close.

Gently, but firmly, extricating herself from his arms she took a step backward and returned his smile. "I'm fine, thanks. A little sore, but that's to be expected."

Dale gazed up at the purple-gray sky for a moment. "It's wonderful the rain stopped, isn't it?"

"It sure raised my spirits," Kerry readily agreed. She leaned against the Explorer and crossed one leg over the other. "How've you been doing, Dale? I haven't seen you since that morning you and Mac got on my nerves."

"I've been keeping busy," he said. "And I haven't

called because I figured that's how you wanted it. We did break up, after all."

"Technically, we were never a couple," Kerry reminded him, keeping her voice low.

Dale's dark blue eyes narrowed. He pressed his lips together as if he were trying to decide whether or not to say what was on his mind. "It finally dawned on me where I've seen your drill instructor before. I was having dinner with my client in D.C. one night when Kent walked in with a beautiful woman on his arm. The senator told me that Kent was one of the initial agents who investigated the murder of the woman he was accused of killing. The woman was an aide in the senator's office. The senator had had an affair with her but, as it turned out, it was her present boyfriend who killed her when she told him she was leaving him."

Kerry didn't want to hear all of that. She wanted him to rewind to where he'd mentioned a beautiful woman on Mac's arm. However, she wouldn't admit that to Dale. "And you're telling me this because?"

"I think you should know whom you're dealing with."

"Tell me something, Dale."

"Fire away."

"When you were in D.C. did you hear about a serial killer who shot his victims in the head and carved 'Better Off Dead' on their chests?"

"Yes, I did. It was a big news story for a while."

Kerry didn't say anything else because it occurred to her that her department had never leaked exactly what words had been carved into Johnny Haywood's chest. That didn't mean Collie Mason hadn't told anyone, or the Carr boy. She sensed that Dale didn't know anything about it though. She was willing to bet, however, that he'd mentioned the gory details to his kid sister over the phone one day when they were chatting long distance. And Jenna *would* run straight to Nicole Haywood with it.

"I've got to go, Dale. I'm tired and I want to get off this leg."

Dale reached out and grabbed her good arm. "When he leaves, I'll be here."

"Please don't wait on me, Dale. Go out and meet someone and get married and have kids with her. I'm moving on, you should, too."

"You love him that much?"

"I'm not going to discuss Mac."

"Just think, Kerry. A lot of years have passed since you were in the corps. He's not the same person. Do you know how he lives? Whom he sees? Why it took him so long to come back? Is he back to stay, or is this a nice summer distraction? Don't be a fool for the memory of love, Kerry. Nostalgia is nice, but it's all smoke and mirrors. That time is past. How can you even be sure you loved him back then?"

Kerry wrenched her arm free, opened the door of the Explorer and climbed inside. "I'm a big girl, Dale. Don't worry about me."

Dale stepped aside as she threw the car in reverse.

"You're not too big to get your heart broken," Dale called after her.

Kerry sped out of the parking lot.

Ten minutes later, she was pulling in her driveway. Getting out of the car, she hurried across the lawn to the house. She wanted to bathe and dress before Mac arrived at around eight, and Dale had already put her behind schedule. Dale. He was such a lawyer! Whittling away at her confidence where Mac was concerned. Planting doubt where there had been none. Okay, so maybe she was afraid what she was feeling for Mac was not real, but that she was so enamored of the memory of their love, she'd do anything to get it back. Wasn't that a fear any couple who met again after years had to contend with? After all, did you recall every moment of your time together in the past? No, absolutely not. What you remembered was how the other person made you feel. How good it had been to be together. And the sex. You remembered whether the sex sucked rocks or not. Because if it had been horrible you'd never entertain the idea of getting back together in the first place.

Unlocking the door and clicking on the foyer light, Kerry settled on that one question: Was she confusing love with lust? An age-old query. Damn Dale for putting the question in her mind: How did she know she had loved Mac back then? Just the other day she'd admitted to Mac that she had been too young and inexperienced to know her own mind.

Kerry began unbuttoning her uniform shirt as she made her way to the bedroom. In the bedroom, she removed her gun and locked it away; then she hung her utility belt in the closet on a hook. Going to sit on the bed she bent and untied her shoes and slipped out of them and put them in the closet.

The shirt and slacks went on hangers. Her underwear in the dirty clothes hamper.

She got the bath table and set it next to the tub. On it she placed her cell phone, a caffeine-free Diet Coke, a thick bath towel, and a washcloth.

After running water in the tub and adding bath salts, she stepped in and carefully sat down. She'd been advised not to get the wounds wet, to keep them covered and swabbed with the liquid antiseptic she'd been given. So she had to keep her right thigh and her right arm out of the water. The rest of her was rejoicing as she settled into the hot water. Her muscles practically sighed with contentment.

She picked up the cell phone and dialed her parents' number. When her father answered, she said, "Hi, Daddy. How you doin'?"

"Hey, baby. I'm just fine. How're you feeling?"

"I'm sitting in the tub, trying to get the soreness out of my muscles."

"You've been through an ordeal. You'll be back to normal soon."

"I'm looking forward to it. Is Momma there?"

"She's in the kitchen. Hold on, I'll tell her to pick up the extension in there."

"Hi, sweetie, what's up?"

"Can you talk?" Kerry asked.

"Sure. What's on your mind?"

"Hold on, I'm gonna get Kiki . . ."

The phone rang three times at the Merrick house.

"Hello?"

"Kiki, you busy?"

"Not too busy to chat. What's up?"

"Hold on, this is a three-way."

"Momma?"

"I'm here."

"Hey, Momma."

"Hello, Kiana. What are you up to, Kerry?"

"I want to ask you two a question, and I want blunt, honest answers. Don't candycoat it. Just shoot from the hip, all right?"

Kiana laughed. "Do I ever give it to you any other way?"

"How do you know when you're in love and not just enjoying a man's loving?"

"Well, sugar, they go hand-in-hand," Evelyn jumped right in. "I'd heard all that rot about you can love a man even if he's bad in bed all my life. Your grandmother told me that I didn't have to enjoy myself in the bedroom. Just lie there and take it. As if it were some nasty medicine." She laughed heartily. "No, baby, sex is healthy. Enjoy it while you can. Physical attraction, physical love are important to a union. However the longer you're together you come to realize that the physical act, or the frequency or duration of it, isn't as important as the emotions behind it. That's where you start differentiating between love and lust."

"The retired schoolteacher has put in an appearance," Kiana joked, referring to their mother's tendency to use long words when she really got going.

"Still," Evelyn continued, ignoring her older daughter, "lust is a powerful emotion. God had to populate the world, after all."

"That's why He made sex feel so good when it's done right? To make sure we'd want to do it on a regular basis?" Kiana asked with a note of laughter.

"I don't want to get into a discussion about religion. We'll be here all night," Evelyn said. "Your baby sister sounds confused. Why don't you tell her at what point you knew you were in love with that fine man of yours?"

"Mmm," Kiana mused aloud. "I think it was when he visited at Christmastime and I met him at the airport in Gainesville. I saw him from across the room and, I swear, I could have ripped his clothes off right there and had my way with him."

"Sounds like love to me," Evelyn said, laughing softly. "I suppose you took him home and had your way with him."

"Nope. We waited until I went to visit him in Connecticut."

"So, *that's* when you got busy," Evelyn said. "You had willpower."

"Well, I don't have any," Kerry interjected. "That's the problem. I don't know if I'm in love, or I just want to be in love because Mac makes me feel so good."

That's when her mother and sister started tossing questions at her.

"When you were in the hospital and Mac's was one of the first faces you saw when you woke up, were you happy to see him, or just happy to be alive?" Kiana asked.

"Oh, God, I was happy to see him," was Kerry's reply.

"Did he look like he was upset by your condition?" Evelyn asked.

"He had tears in his eyes," Kerry answered.

"Okay, we're going to get down to the nitty-gritty," Kiana warned lightly. "If you and Mac were living together and he started leaving his socks lying around, stepping out of his drawers and leaving them on the bathroom floor, what would you do?"

"I'd make him pick them up," Kerry said honestly.

"You're in love," Evelyn and Kiana said in unison.

Evelyn explained. "Because if it was just lust, you'd pick them up and think his behavior was cute. But since you love him and you want to live with him for as long as you're both alive, then you know that behavior has to go. Therefore, you try to alleviate the problem."

"That, my dear, is the difference between love and lust," Kiana said. "You think Gabriel leaves his drawers on the bathroom floor? Not if he doesn't want to hear from me!"

Kerry laughed. She'd known that even if her mother and sister couldn't provide her with a definitive solution to her problem they would, at least, make her smile.

ELEVEN

Mac pulled up in front of the florist's shop, the only one in town, and uttered an expletive. Closed. He had to keep in mind that he was no longer in the city and able to find fresh flowers at all times of the day or night. Even in his U Street / Shaw neighborhood in D.C. there was a twenty-four-hour market that carried them.

The only store that stayed open twenty-four hours around here was the 7-Eleven on Archer Road. He knew because he'd gone there at three A.M. for a beer one night when he couldn't sleep, too quiet. One beer usually relaxed him enough to sleep.

He spotted someone moving around in the store. A middle-aged woman in a white apron. He climbed out of the car and dashed to the door, knocking frantically. The woman went to the door, a frown marring her attractive features.

"Are you crazy?" she asked in a charming Irish-accented voice. "It's after eight. We close at seven-thirty." She pointed at the sign on the door. "Next time, get here earlier."

"Please, my girlfriend loves roses," he pleaded. He withdrew his driver's license and held it against the glass door for her to see. "I just need a dozen roses. I'll pay cash."

She looked at the driver's license, then at him several times. "Maceo Kent." To Mac's surprise, she unlocked the door and told him to come in. She smiled up at him as he walked past her into the store. She closed and locked the door. "You're dating our police chief, Kerry Everett, right?"

Mac grinned at her, amazed. "I've never seen it in action before, but it must be true: Everybody knows everybody else's business in a small town."

The woman, a blonde with gray eyes, her hair going gray now, began walking toward the back of the store. "You bet it's true. My daughter's Doreen Wilkins. She knows the Everett girls pretty well. I've never met them, but if Doreen likes them, that's good enough for me. Come on back. I've already refrigerated the roses for the night, you can tell me what you want and I'll make up a bouquet."

"Doreen? Scott's wife?"

"You know Scott, but you don't know Doreen?"

Mac went on to tell her how he'd met Scott on work detail at the Health Center during the Hurricane Sonia crisis. While he talked and pointed at which colors of the long-stemmed roses he wanted, Mona Carpenter created a multicolored bouquet of roses, baby's breath, and fern fronds.

A few minutes later Mac paid her for the flowers, thanked her profusely, and left.

He was smiling thoughtfully as he pulled away from the curb. He could get used to this town and its people. No wonder Kerry loved it here. He'd been doing some serious thinking ever since they'd made love again. What Kerry had said about his wanting to guide her career after she left the corps was true. His father was a military man as well. More than thirty years in the Marine Corps. His two brothers, Nestor and Oscar (their mother was from the Dominican Republic and had given her children Spanish names), were marines before him. Mac had grown up watching his mother follow his father from marine base to marine base, all over the world. Uncom-

plaining. Happy, it seemed to him, to support her husband in his endeavors. Mac knew now that he'd expected
the same of his woman. He had thought he was being
magnanimous by suggesting she become an FBI agent,
like him. If law enforcement was in her blood, she should
be allowed to work in it. But he should, somehow, be
nearby to protect her should something go wrong. How
he'd planned to arrange their being assigned to the same
field office, he didn't know. He obviously wasn't thinking clearly. When you're in love, you just want to keep
the one you love with you.

Which was why he was going to tell Kerry, tonight,
that he was willing to support her in whatever she chose
to do. Live here in Damascus forever, or move to D.C.
with him. Or live somewhere in between. Location didn't
matter as long as they were together.

He'd had to face a hard truth: He wasn't married today
because he'd never gotten over Kerry. Sometimes you
never get over your first love. And even though he'd been
twenty-nine when he and Kerry split up, she had been
the only woman to fully claim his heart. Now that she
was back in his life, he wasn't going to do something
stupid and screw it up. This time forever.

He had one last stop to make before heading to Magnolia Street, and Kerry's arms.

Kerry had Dido's CD on the player. The singer's haunt-
ingly beautiful voice sang, *"I want to thank you for making this the best day of my life."* Kerry was sitting on the
bed applying lotion to her feet. She wanted them to be
nice and soft in case Mac was serious about giving her
that pedicure. After her bath she'd dressed in a willowy
summer dress in a feminine, flower print. It was strapless
and the hem fell a couple of inches below her knees.
She'd smoothed apricot-scented lotion all over her body.
And her wavy hair was loose and rather wild about her

head. A bit of rose-colored lip gloss kept her lips moist and kissable. She was dying for one of Mac's kisses right about now.

As if on cue, the doorbell rang. She walked, barefoot, through the house to the front door. After a quick peek through the peephole, she flung the door open. Mac stood on the porch with the most beautiful bouquet of roses she'd ever seen grasped in one big hand, and balancing a hot pizza in the other.

He handed her the roses, which she gratefully accepted, drawing them into her arms.

"Mac, they're gorgeous, thank you," she breathed, and kissed his cheek.

With the delicate fragrance of the roses and the heady aroma of the pizza fighting for dominance in her olfactory senses, Kerry drifted, with Mac, to the kitchen. "How was your day after we parted?" she asked while tiptoeing to reach a vase on the top shelf.

Mac was busy getting plates for the pizza. "I've got some photos I think you're going to be very happy with."

Kerry grabbed hold of the vase and turned to face Mac. "No! You actually caught them together?" Meaning Nicole and Jenna.

Mac smiled and wriggled his brows at her à la Groucho Marx. "Not only did I catch them together, but I caught them in a very familiar embrace. Kissing at the door."

"On the lips?"

Mac laughed. "No, on the cheek." He paused. "You think it's that kind of a relationship? At any rate, Nicole's relatives were about. Their cars were in the driveway."

"It was just something that popped into my head when you described it as a familiar embrace, as if the kiss were more than a buss on the cheek," Kerry said, running water in the vase. On the counter she removed the cellophane from the roses and placed them, without separating them, into the large vase. She loved the arrangement and didn't want to spoil the effect.

She then went and placed the vase on her foyer table so that they would be the first thing anyone would see upon entering the house. Mac watched her, a plate with a slice of pizza on it in his hand. When she turned back around, he handed her the plate. "I'm assuming you haven't eaten, you look so damn good." He sniffed her hair. "And you smell even better than you look. You've been primping." He licked his lips. "For me?" As if she were a delectable treat he was about to devour.

"Perhaps," Kerry said, her whiskey-colored eyes teasing him. Holding the plate out to the side, she sidled up to him and let him wrap his arms around her waist. Her luscious breasts were about to spill out of that dress. He squeezed her tighter, hoping they would. Mac was wearing Kerry's favorite jeans on him: Button-fly. Sort of low on his washboard stomach. The pale yellow shirt was short sleeved and buttoned down the front. Cotton and very soft to the touch. Kerry momentarily buried her nose in his chest. He'd been doing some pampering himself. He smelled good enough to eat. All male with a dash of sandalwood. She planted a kiss on his chin. "Let's eat, Mac, I'm famished."

Mac had grown tumescent and was not ready to let her go, but he was a big boy and would practice patience. He released her and followed her back into the kitchen.

Kerry recapped her day for him over a dinner of salad and pizza, washed down with Diet Cokes for both of them. Mac passed on the beer since he had no intention of getting drowsy any time soon.

"All of the Haywood boys?" he asked, his tone disbelieving when she told him about Bess Haywood and Tad Armstrong's ongoing affair. "I can see why they were in no rush to tell that secret. It's going to upset a lot of people's lives."

"As my Grandma Sally would say, 'They're grown-ass

men.' " Kerry quoted. "They'll get over it. The important thing is, this bit of information will work for Tad if it ever goes to trial. Which, if I have anything to do with it, it won't."

She then told him about Nicole's attempt to have Johnny's body cremated.

"You think she's still under the impression she's gotten away scot-free?" Mac asked.

"I'm counting on it," Kerry said. "You see, she's got to hang around for the funeral for appearance's sake. I'm sure she's climbing the walls right about now. Wondering when she's going to be able to get out of town without it looking too suspicious."

"So," Mac said, "what sort of goodies do you think she has stashed as a nest egg?"

"I can't imagine," Kerry said truthfully. "But we once busted a drug dealer in Miami and a search of his house produced over a million dollars in tens, twenties, and hundreds. Plus lots of other neat stuff such as stocks and bonds. He was a financial wizard. I doubt if we'll uncover that much in tiny Damascus. But, you never know."

"This town becomes more fascinating the longer I stay here," Mac said with a smile.

Kerry laughed shortly. "Ah, Mac, stay a while longer and I'll show you things that'll curl your hair." She eyed his closely shorn head. "Of course, that might prove a bit difficult with your particular style. But I think I can pull it off."

Mac ran a hand over his well-shaped head. "You don't like the cut?"

Kerry rose and walked around to his side of the table and placed her hands on his temples, gently massaging as she moved upward, her fingers slowly, lanquidly, sensuously manipulating his scalp. Then she kissed him on the top of his head. "Mac, I adore every inch of your body."

She went to remove her hands from his head, but Mac

clasped her wrist and pulled her to him. Kerry stood, Mac's face buried in her bosom. The touch of Mac's mouth on her warm skin sent shivers through her body. Mac only wanted to hold her a moment. Her words had left him weak with longing. *I adore every inch of your body,* she'd said. Did she know how much that meant to him? To be loved by someone as wonderful as she was? To be given a second chance to get it right this time?

He kissed the tops of her breasts. His right hand was on her hips. Then it was pulling up her dress. Kerry's heartbeat, in the meantime, was easily detectable in the throbbing pulse between her legs. Blood pumped, pooled there readying every synapse in that area for physical stimulation. Her breasts, too, seemed to swell in expectation, the nipples hardening.

Mac's hand was underneath the dress now, pulling down her panties.

Kerry shivered slightly and spread her legs to facilitate the removal of said panties.

"I want to feel you," Mac said. Using both hands, now, he gently rolled the silken panties down past her hips and past her thighs, being careful not to come in contact with her bandage, until finally they pooled at her feet and Kerry stepped out of them.

Mac thought of taking her right there on the kitchen table, but it wasn't high enough for his purposes. Instead he lifted her onto the large, empty space on the breakfast nook.

Here Kerry was eye-to-eye with him. Kerry didn't know where Mac was going with this but was willing to go along for the ride. He'd always been inventive when it came to loving her, and she'd never regretted one moment. She watched him now her eyes gone dreamy, she was in such a state of arousal.

Mac kissed her mouth until her lips looked as swollen as her female center felt at that point. His hands were on her dress zipper. Down it went, and since Kerry was not wearing a bra, when the dress collapsed into her lap her heavy breasts spilled into Mac's eager hands.

Every now and then, between kissing, suckling, and nibbling her breasts, he'd check the expression in her brown depths to see where she was. Fully alert? Mildly transported, or wholly in the throes of passion? He would not take her to the bedroom until he saw evidence of her impending "little death," as they referred to orgasm.

If death was anything like sex was between the two of them, he didn't know why so many people were afraid of it.

He lifted the skirt of her dress and gently coaxed her legs apart. Her sex looked moist, glistening, swollen. He wanted to bend and taste her, but resisted. It was time to move this to the bedroom. He reached for her, and Kerry went into his arms, wrapping her long legs around his waist. Mac walked with her to the bedroom, enjoying the enticing weight of her body against his all the way.

In the bedroom, he lay her on the bed and began coming out of his clothes. Kerry went to rise to help him, but he shook his head no. He wanted to look at her looking at him as he undressed. Needed to see the desire mirrored in her eyes. It sustained him. Fed him in more ways than one. Kerry lay on the bed, her dress half off, her breasts heaving, her eyes on every movement of Mac's body.

Mac finally stood before her unclothed, his manhood erect and heavy. *I'm a big girl, I can accommodate that,* Kerry thought wickedly. It's what she thought every time she saw Mac fully aroused.

Somewhere inside there was also the panicked Miss who primly thought, *What am I getting myself into?* Until he was inside of her, and then she was that wicked woman again savoring every thrust.

Mac went to the nightstand drawer and got a condom. He handed it to Kerry who quickly sheathed him. He moved in her hands. Kerry ran her hand along the length of him. Then she took him by the backs of the arms, his muscles hard as rocks there, and pulled him onto her.

"The dress," Mac said. Kerry lifted her hips and he deftly pulled the dress from under her and deposited it on a nearby chair. He kissed her between her breasts, working his way down to her belly. All his senses were heightened. He loved the pebbly skin of her aroused nipples. They were a sensate treat for his tongue. The earthy smell of her skin, her womanhood, mingled with the apricot odor of the lotion or bath oil she'd used. All of these things made his senses reel.

"I love you, Mac," Kerry said breathlessly.

Mac hadn't expected this. Not this soon. But as he plunged into her softness, he said with an equally breathless sigh, "I love you, too. I never stopped."

Tuesday morning, Kerry awakened at her usual time: five-thirty, and had the urge to go running. The doctor had advised her against any strenuous exercise until her thigh wound healed, however, so she opted to walk instead.

There was no change in her route. There *was* a gun strapped to her good leg, hidden underneath the dark blue drawstring athletic pants she had on, though. She wasn't looking for trouble, but, be it beast or man, this time she was going to be ready for it.

To her amazement, Harold Haywood blew the horn of his mother's car and waved at her as he headed out of town with the rest of the commuters. She'd never seen Harold going anywhere this early in the morning. Could he have a job? If so, Miss Bess must be relieved. Maybe Johnny's death had had a profound effect on his younger brother.

She paused after she passed the kudzu jungle, intrigued by the stitch in her side. Her injury must have taken more out of her than she'd imagined. Drinking from her water bottle she gazed up at the clear, blue sky. Mid-August was definitely shaping up to be dryer than the beginning of the month.

The pain in Kerry's side eased up a bit and she continued walking. She blamed the humidity for her increasing feeling of breathlessness as she approached Deeks's place. But when she passed the seven-foot fence, her stomach muscles tensed and she felt nauseous.

Suddenly, barking came from the other side of the fence. Or, more accurately, yelping. A six-week-old golden retriever happily came loping up to the fence, followed by a harried Lewis Deeks. "I'm sorry, Chief Everett, she got away from me," Deeks said as he came and picked up the puppy.

Kerry was initially confused. What was he doing, trying to psyche her out? The puppy got away from him? She squinted at him through the fence. "Do you think this is some kind of a game?" she asked, her tone deadly serious. "Your dog attacked me and tried to kill me and then you get another one and let it run out here just like the other one used to? You think you can intimidate me?"

"I swear before God, that's exactly what happened, Chief," Lewis insisted. He rested his chin on the top of the puppy's furry head. Looking at Kerry through red-rimmed eyes, he continued. "I got Atta Girl from someone who abused her. I was trying to train her to be more gentle. But once a dog has been beaten down the way she'd been beaten down, it's hard to reverse the damage. The man who owned her trained her for illegal dogfights. I got her when he died, and his wife was so afraid of the dog she threatened to shoot it in the head to be rid of it, if I didn't take it off her hands." He stopped and put the puppy back on the ground. "I know how strange I must seem to a lot of people. I keep to myself."

"You raise a Confederate flag every morning," Kerry couldn't help interjecting.

"That's out of respect for my ancestors who died in

the Civil War. It's not because I hate black people, Chief
Everett. I'm a Southerner, and I'm proud to be a Southerner. Everyone who respects the Confederate flag
doesn't necessarily have to be a racist. Just as every black
person who raises the tricolor African flag doesn't want
to go back to Africa to live. We're all Americans. We
have the right to fly any flag we wish to on our own
property."

Kerry had hold of the fence as she was talking to
Deeks. Before she knew it, the puppy had stood up on
its hind legs, its paws on the fence, and licked her fingers.

Seeing the overture, Deeks continued his case: "Isn't
communication the key in getting to know someone from
a different background, Chief?" He held her gaze. "I
can't apologize enough for what happened to you. And
I hope y'all catch whoever cut the lock on the gate and
let Atta Girl out. But, I am not a mean and hateful man,
and I'm tired of people assuming I am."

Kerry stooped and scratched the puppy under the chin
through the fence. She really was an affectionate pooch.
Rising, she said to Deeks, "All right, you've had your
say. You're right, we base a lot of our opinions of others
on assumptions, and that isn't good. I've had to fight
against being stereotyped every day of my life, especially
in this job." She peered down at the puppy. "What's her
name?"

"Janie, after the main character in my favorite Zora
Neale Hurston book."

"Their Eyes Were Watching God?" Kerry asked, as-
tounded.

"From the opening sentence, that book held me en-
thralled," Deeks said softly, reverently. "She was a beautifully lyrical writer. A talent before her time. You know
she died poor? Can you imagine that? The gifts she gave
the world and she had to be buried in a pauper's grave?
It's ludicrous."

Kerry stood there a long while arguing the merits of literature with Lewis Deeks and playing with Janie. She was ever grateful for life's little surprises.

"Chief Everett, I've just heard some disturbing news," Mayor Reginald Washington said, blocking Kerry's path as she walked into the police station. Kerry sidestepped him and kept walking. His short legs were no match for her long ones. He had to practically jog to stay with her.

"What news was that, Mayor Washington?"

"Tad Armstrong could be innocent." Reginald was breathing hard by the time they reached Kerry's office and she closed the door behind them. She gestured to the chair in front of her desk. She went around, sat down, and turned on her computer. "I'm listening," she assured him, eyes meeting his, then back to the computer.

"I already said it, 'Tad Armstrong may be innocent,' " he repeated irritably.

Kerry looked at him. "And that's a problem for you? I don't understand." The man was certifiable. He had nothing better to do all day except bother her?

"The street fair starts Friday," he explained as if he were laying it out for a child, or an adult with less than normal intelligence. "And you may not have the real killer in custody. To me, that's a problem, Chief!"

As nervous as he was, Kerry figured he must grind his teeth in his sleep, poor guy.

"Mayor, you have my report for security at the fair on your desk. Have you taken the time to read it? Main Street will be blocked off. We'll have officers strolling through the crowd the entire time the fair is going on. Plus, there will be one central location, as indicated on the fair's map, should a citizen need to report any misconduct during the event. If that isn't enough, we'll put an officer in a tower with a rifle."

"I don't think you're funny, Chief," Reginald said, his

light colored eyes bugging out. He breathed deeply and exhaled. Somewhat calmer now, he said, "You seem to be taking all of this as a joke. But if one resident gets hurt at the fair, the city's liable. And if I'm given hell, I'm going to make certain you get your fair portion."

"I'm sure you will, Mayor," Kerry said, rising. "But until then, I've got work to do. Don't let the doorknob hit you where the good Lord split you."

With that, she sat back down and pulled up last night's officers reports.

Mayor Washington saw himself out.

Kerry was pleased to see that the past night in Damascus was a quiet one. No arrests. Two tickets for traffic violations. One call on an altercation between a husband and wife, which had ended amiably.

Scanning the duty roster, she saw that Paul was presently watching the Haywood home, and Royce was on patrol. It was time she started putting a little pressure on Nicole Haywood. She'd start by filling her in on the recent findings concerning her husband's death. Nicole would, undoubtedly, be grateful for the information.

When she was within a mile of the Haywood home, Kerry phoned Paul and asked him to meet her at the house. Paul's cruiser was at the curb by the time she turned onto Nicole's street in the Edgewood Estates subdivision. Nicole's retinue was still in place. Besides her black Lexus, three other cars were in the driveway.

A short, fat African-American woman in her late fifties answered the door. She wore an apron over a pair of slacks and a blouse that were clean but well worn. On her feet were leather brogans. That was the only way Kerry could describe the work shoes she'd seen on so many women in the service industry.

"Yes?" the woman asked in a tired voice. Her springy gray hair was combed back from her face in no particular style. Dark brown eyes regarded Kerry curiously and perked up when they settled on Paul. She was obviously not too old or too tired to know a good-looking man when she saw one.

"I'm Chief Everett, and this is Deputy Robertson. We're here to speak with Mrs. Haywood."

"Wait here, I'll see if she's able to have visitors."

Kerry and Paul waited on the stoop in ninety-degree heat. Kerry turned to Paul. "So, did you call Nurse Gordon yet?"

"We have a date Friday night after I get off fair duty," Paul said. "So, please, please, don't make me work overtime."

"I'll see what I can do, but the mayor was just riding me about security this morning. He seems to believe that if we don't catch Haywood's killer before the fair commences, the killer will go on a killing spree at the fair; then he'll go down in history as the mayor of a town where there was a bloodbath."

"You ought to deputize him, and put him on patrol. On foot, of course. He could stand to shed a few pounds."

The woman returned and ushered them inside. "Mrs. Haywood will see you in the living room, and she asked me to offer you iced tea or lemonade."

Kerry spoke for them both. "No, thank you."

"All right," the woman said, pointing to the left. "It's right through there."

Kerry led the way, Paul staying alert.

The house was still immaculate, due, Kerry was sure, to the presence of the woman in the brogans. Nicole rose when she and Paul entered the room. She was wearing a sleeveless black pantsuit that sported a double-breasted tunic. Three-inch black leather sandals completed the chic look. The extra inches brought her nearly eye level with Kerry. Her hair had been professionally styled since Kerry saw her last and now lay in layers around her attractive face.

There were four other people in the room. A middle-aged woman with silver hair and impeccable style. She was also dressed in a tailored pantsuit, hers in gray, and heels, also gray. Kerry couldn't miss the resemblance. Nicole had the same slanting, brown eyes, pert nose and full-lipped mouth. Plus, they were around the same height.

Three African-American males in various sizes sat around the room. The TV was tuned to ESPN, the bane of a woman's existence since sports programming was on twenty-four hours a day. They didn't even look up from the set until Kerry spoke.

Then, three sets of eyes were riveted on her.

"Is there someplace we can speak in private?" Kerry asked Nicole. "I'd like to fill you in on the progress of our investigation."

"This is my family," Nicole said, spreading her arms to encompass them all in a gesture of togetherness. "It's all right to speak in front of them. I'd tell them everything after you left anyway."

She smiled warmly and indicated that Kerry and Paul should take a seat. The only place left to sit down was the sofa whose back was to the room's entrance.

"We'll stand, this shouldn't take long," Kerry said. "But, perhaps, you'd like to sit down."

"No, if you're standing, so will I," Nicole said pleasantly.

She walked closer to Kerry. Paul remained near the door.

"The coroner has determined that Johnny didn't die of the gunshot wound after all," Kerry began, keeping her voice low but clear. "He died of digitalis poisoning. The coroner says whoever did it deliberately gave him too much of it and then made love to him until his heart stopped."

Nicole's eyes stretched in horror. Her hand went nervously to her throat. "Was it painful?" Her eyes were already tearing up, she was so upset by the way her husband had met his end. "It sounds like it could have been painful."

"Oh, yes, the pain must have been excruciating. He had to have been clutching at his chest, saying he couldn't breathe, gasping for air." Kerry stopped. "I'm sorry. This must be hard for you to hear."

She placed a hand on Nicole's shoulder. "There's more."

"M . . . more?" Nicole stuttered.

"It turns out there was a reason why Tad Armstrong was always after Johnny to straighten up and live right: Tad is actually Johnny's biological father. He's the father of all of Bess Haywood's sons. It's a long story, but now that this has been discovered we've reopened the case and are actively looking for someone else. It's highly unlikely that Tad killed his own son whom he, and everyone who knows him, swears he loved very much. Therefore, we're now looking for someone clever enough to not only kill Johnny, but frame his own father for the murder." Kerry paused for effect. "Unless, of course, the murderer simply slipped up and it was never his intention to frame Johnny's father for the murder. He just didn't know Tad was Johnny's father. Which is the most logical explanation since Johnny didn't know, himself."

"He certainly never mentioned it to me," Nicole said in a small voice. Her beautiful brown eyes had taken on a caged-animal aspect. Kerry bent her head to peer into them. "Nicole, are you all right?"

Nicole swayed on her feet. Her eyes rolled back in her head and she would have fallen to the floor if Kerry hadn't moved swiftly and caught her. The silver-haired woman sprang to her feet and helped Kerry gently lower Nicole to the floor where the woman sat down, allowing her lap to be used as a pillow for Nicole's head. Nicole's eyes fluttered open.

"Momma?"

"Yes, baby, I'm here. Do you need us to call nine-one-one?"

"No, just get *her* out of here, I can't take any more of her gory details."

Kerry knew when she wasn't wanted. She and Paul left. She smiled all the way back to the police station. After which she phoned Mac and told him all about her encounter with the black widow.

"The only thing I regret is that Jenna wasn't there to hear it," Kerry told him. "But I'd wager that Nicole was on the phone with her not five minutes after I left."

"She might not wait until after the funeral to flee now," Mac suggested.

"If she tries to run, there will be an APB out on her before she gets past the city limits," was Kerry's reply. "Her best bet is to play it as cool as possible. She must know that if I had her dead to rights, I would've gone there to arrest her, not to bait her. Like you said, Mac, we've only got circumstantial evidence. Otherwise we wouldn't be playing this cat-and-mouse game with her. No, she'll play it cool."

"Now that you've told her about the digitalis, maybe you ought to assign a car to Mrs. Kelly's place. You never know, Nicole might get desperate and try to off the only person who can connect her with the drug."

"Great minds," Kerry joked. "I've already assigned a deputy to watch her place. He's supposed to go out there, let Mrs. Kelly know what's going on and get back to me."

"Good," Mac said. "Now, we wait, huh?"

"Now, we wait," Kerry concurred.

They didn't have to wait long, however.

When Deputy Royce Clemons knocked on Viola Kelly's door, there was no answer and no indication that there was anyone about the place. He made a circuit of the property, going from the front porch to the garden in the backyard. Nothing.

Royce got on the phone and called Kerry with his report. "There's no one out here, Chief." He was standing on the front porch as he said that. The weathered boards gave a bit under his one hundred seventy-five pounds.

At the office, Kerry was frantically turning pages in the local phone book. She found Viola Kelly's number and told Royce. "Listen, stay on the line. I'm going to use my cell phone and call Mrs. Kelly's number and see what happens."

The phone rang three times; then the answering machine kicked in. "Hello, this is Viola. I can't come to the phone right now. My sister's sick in Denver, or that could be Detroit or Daytona or even Dayton, Ohio. My mind ain't what it used to be. At any rate, I'm getting my black ass out of town for a while. If this is Chief Everett calling: Sorry, honey, but if she'll kill her own husband, she'll kill me. And though I know you'd try to protect me, you can't be everywhere at once, now can you? I'll be back when I think it's safe. Or I might not be. Who knows? Denver or Detroit, Daytona or Dayton's pretty this time of year. Bye."

TWELVE

"Mac, I want to show you something. How quickly can you pack an overnight bag?"

It was Wednesday afternoon and Kerry was going to leave the office early. She rarely did that, but today was special. Or as special as she was prepared to make it. With Viola Kelly safely out of town she felt comfortable enough to leave the Haywood case in the capable hands of her staff for a few hours. Besides, she would be less than an hour's drive away, and they were instructed to phone her if Nicole Haywood so much as bundled up Jack and put him in the car.

After going home and packing a bag for herself, she swung by the inn and picked up Mac. At half past three, the day was brightly lit and hot. Less humidity in the air. In fact lately there had been a touch of fall in the air in the evenings. A visitor to the area might not be able to detect it, but any native Floridian, who prayed continually for respite from the heat, felt the difference right away. Some started turning the air conditioner off at night and sleeping with the windows open. Kerry was one of those people. She opened her windows at the drop of a hat, welcoming even the slightest cool breeze.

"Where're we going?" Mac asked, looking at her profile as she drove out of town.

"It's a surprise. Don't you like surprises?"

"If it involves you naked on a bed, I do."

"It involves me naked in water."

"I can get with that," Mac said, his voice husky.

Kerry laughed shortly. "Yeah." She gave him a sensual perusal before turning her attention back to her driving. "So can I."

She turned right on Highway 441. "This place is special. It's in the middle of the woods, and there's a spring on the property. A clear spring. It's beautiful, Mac. So pristine, even in this day and age. Being there makes you want to take care of the Earth. Makes you wonder why everybody doesn't care enough not to use our waterways as garbage receptacles. Did you know that the Santa Fe River, alone, has three dozen springs? At O'Leno State Park, which is near here, it goes underground and follows subterranean passageways for three miles. The spring on the property where we're going goes underground too. I don't do any cave diving. Too dangerous. Especially if you're not experienced. I've known of experienced divers who've drowned in underwater caves around here."

"The place belongs to a friend?"

"It belongs to someone close to me, yes."

Mac turned toward her. "Kerry, if you're taking me someplace to let me down easy, I'd rather you tell me now."

"Let you down easy?"

"Tell me you didn't mean it when you said you loved me. It was just the excitement of the moment, and what we've rediscovered couldn't possibly be real after a ten-year separation."

"You've given that some thought, huh?" She smiled at him, and kept driving.

She would not deny or confirm his accusations. Instead she told him what their destination meant to her. "I chanced upon it about two years ago. I was hiking in the Ocala National Forest. Some girlfriends and I. My best friend, Bess—another Bess—I guess we southerners like that name. Anyway Bess Calhoun and I have been best friends since second grade. She recently relocated to California. Her husband's an electrical engineer and was offered the position of a lifetime. Bess is a writer and can work anywhere. Not that that would have stopped her from going with Adam, because it wouldn't have. Bess believes in going with her gut reactions. That's why she married Adam after knowing him about three months. They've been together seven years now."

She paused, knowing she was rambling, but unable to stop herself. Mac watched her with a half-smile. Enjoying her company even if she was being mysterious. "We have so much to catch up on, Mac. I just wanted you to see a different side of me. See me out of my normal environment, if only for a few hours. We'll spend the night out here and tomorrow we'll go back to being law enforcement types. But for tonight, we're just Kerry and Mac, okay?"

"You were saying you chanced upon the place two years ago," Mac reminded her of where she'd ended before she'd gone off on a tangent. "Was Bess with you when you found the . . . place?" He didn't know whether they were going to a lodge in the woods, a cabin, or would have to pitch a tent. He didn't care. It was nice putting himself in her hands, though the control freak in him was freaking out. Which was why he kept asking questions.

"Yes, Bess was with me. And two other women friends I went to UF with."

"Does this place have running water and indoor plumbing?"

Kerry laughed delightedly. "Mac, you're such a city boy. But, yes, it does. It's very comfortable. It even has air-conditioning."

"Okay. Just so I don't have to fight a bear for dinner. Florida does have bears, right?"

"Black bears, yes. Though their populations are dwindling. You're always hearing about a bear that wanders onto a highway and gets killed. Encroaching civilization is causing their extinction."

After driving south for nearly an hour, Kerry turned west and for the next five miles all they saw on either side of the road were trees. Pine trees everywhere. Shortly after that turn, she made another, winding up on an unpaved road that was surprisingly smooth due to the packed ground. Mac could see the cabin now, in a clearing up ahead. Kerry was on the half-mile stretch of road that led to the cabin. She pulled in front of the house and switched off the engine. "We're here."

Mac opened his door and got out. Stretching, he breathed in the pine-scented air.

"The place smells like Pine-Sol," he joked.

The cabin was made of pine logs. The wood had been treated so that it retained its vibrant light-brown color. There was a detached garage several yards from the cabin. And a storage shed sat about fifty yards behind it.

"That's not the outhouse, is it?" Mac asked, totally serious.

"I told you it has indoor plumbing, Mac," Kerry said, smiling at him. "For God's sake, you're an ex-marine. You're supposed to be able to survive in the wilderness with just a pocketknife."

"I'm not gonna have to do that, am I? Because I didn't bring my pocketknife."

Kerry laughed and went around the car to get the bag of groceries she'd brought with her. It was heavy. She put it in Mac's arms. "Here, I'll get our bags."

The yard had been meticulously landscaped. On either side of the walk leading to the cabin the lawn was a plush, green carpet. The backyard was deep and edged by a six-foot-tall wooden fence.

"The Ashtons, the couple who owned this cabin, had lived here for thirty years off and on. They were from

Maine, and spent winters down here. But more than two years ago Mr. Ashton developed Alzheimer's and they couldn't live way out here with no close neighbors, so they had to find a buyer for their dream home. It wasn't easy for them to give it up. And it wasn't easy for me to buy it, knowing how they felt about it," Kerry told Mac as she led him onto the porch.

"Yours?" Mac asked.

"Mine," Kerry said proudly. She put the key in the lock and turned the doorknob.

They stepped onto a highly polished pinewood floor. Kerry set the overnight bags on the foyer table, leaving the front door open, but securing the screen door. Walking over to the unit on the wall, she switched on the air conditioner. "I like to open all of the windows for a few minutes to let the stale air out while the air conditioner's running."

Their footfalls resounded throughout the structure. "You bought a cabin in the middle of nowhere." Mac placed the bag of groceries beside the overnight bags on the foyer table. "Why?"

"I'll explain it all later, Mac," Kerry promised. Her eyes were lit from within with pleasure. She was enjoying this little intrigue. She walked close to him and pressed her jeans-clad thigh to his. Peering up at him she placed her hand on his chest, feeling his heartbeat. Mac lowered his head and kissed her forehead. "Okay, I'll be patient. Lead on."

After a quick repast of chicken sandwiches, they put on their hiking boots and took to the woods. It was nearly five o'clock. Figuring they might be returning after dark, Kerry took along a flashlight. Mac was glad to see the path they were taking was well-beaten. It was unlikely they'd get lost.

"Remember I told you I chanced upon this place two years ago?" Kerry asked. "Well, Bess, Cleo, Jackie, and I were hiking and came upon a natural spring. I looked on the other side and saw what was obviously a hewn-out path in the wilderness, you know? So, we decided to go around the spring and investigate. We came out on the other side at the cabin. The Ashtons were stunned to see four black women walking up to their cabin. But they were very gracious and invited us up onto the porch to share their iced tea. We got to talking and after they learned I was the chief of police in Damascus, they confessed that they were in Damascus practically every weekend. They enjoyed browsing antique shops. Downtown Damascus is full of antique shops. The next time they were in Damascus they looked me up and we became friends."

Mac truly was in awe with the natural beauty of the woods. After all the recent rains, the forest was more lush than usual. The ground was still moist, but didn't give much when you walked upon it. Birds flew above their heads. Every now and then, he'd see squirrels leaping from branch to branch, wary of the humans invading their space.

"I've seen three types of birds and squirrels. What other sorts of animals are we likely to encounter?" he asked.

"We've mentioned the bears," Kerry began with a smile. "This area is also home to the wild turkey, bobcat—you don't want to meet one of those, they're fierce. Otter, deer, possums, raccoons, my Grandpa Frank used to hunt coon. He'd skin them, gut them and cook them over a pit in the yard. We kids used to think he was Davy Crockett or somebody like him. I'm referring to my mom's father, Grandma Sally's husband. Now, those two were something else together. They'd been married sixty-five years before Big Daddy passed a year ago. He died not long after Dionne and Kevin were killed. The family was devastated a second time."

Finally, they arrived at a clearing and in the center of the clearing was a glistening pool of water. Kerry immediately sat down on the bank and began removing her boots.

When they were off, she stood and began removing her jeans.

"What are you doing?" Mac asked, brows knit in surprise.

"I'm getting undressed," Kerry said, looking at him with a mischievous glimmer in her eyes. "Won't you join me?"

Mac didn't have to be asked twice. He *had* worked up a sweat during the walk out here. "Okay, but don't be surprised if some hiking enthusiast walks up on us."

"Are you kidding?" Kerry shot down the notion. "It's Wednesday evening. Most hikers in this area do it on the weekend."

"All right," Mac consented, but didn't sound convinced.

"Knowing what cold water does to a man, don't expect much," he jokingly warned.

Kerry had stripped down to her birthday suit while Mac was talking. She went to him and pulled his T-shirt over his head. "I'm not trying to seduce you, Mac, I just want to go for a swim with my man."

As soon as Mac's hands were free, they were on her breasts. "You might not be thinking of seduction, but your body's built for it."

Kerry licked her lips. "We didn't bring condoms on this expedition, so behave."

Mac reluctantly let go of her breasts to go into his jeans pocket. "I was a Boy Scout before I was a marine. I'm always prepared."

Kerry gazed down at the condom in his hand, then up into his eyes. She hastily began unbuttoning his jeans. No use wasting a perfectly good condom.

Sometime later, they were lying on the bank of the spring, atop the bed their clothing made, Kerry's head on Mac's chest. "All our lives our mother drummed into us the importance of saving. She encouraged us to keep piggy banks as children, and every few months we were taken to our local bank and the money we'd saved was put into savings accounts with our names on them. By the time we got to high school, we all had part-time jobs and we were required to save part of our salaries. Well, because I skipped college for a while, opting for the Marine Corps instead, my savings continued to grow untouched. And then when I left the corps, I left with a nice lump sum, which I invested. I went to UF on a basketball scholarship. It isn't often done but I was a walk-on, which means—"

"You weren't recruited out of high school like most college athletes are." Mac supplied the answer.

Kerry smile up at him. "Right. Anyway, I had three years on the other freshmen. Three years in which to hone my skills."

"You were a damned good basketball player," Mac admitted. "You used to rack up on the weekends, betting the guys they couldn't beat you."

Kerry laughed. "You knew about my extracurricular activities?"

"I knew. You were a novelty to the guys, you know. I think half of them bet you in order to see you move. You had moves, girl."

"I still love the game, but I don't get the chance to play much. I'm thinking of starting a league in town. For school girls. Anyway, back to how I bought the cabin. You see, I figured I'd use my savings to pay for my education. By that time it was in the tens of thousands. But since I went to school on a scholarship, it was once again unnecessary to touch my savings. Then, I went to a broker and he turned me on to stocks and bonds. I'm not wild about stocks, but bonds I can get with. Anyway, to make a long story short, I'd managed to save a lot of money over the years. And when the Ashtons told me they were selling their property, I made them an offer and paid cash for it. I have a mortgage on the house in Damascus, because actually having a mortgage has tax benefits. Sometimes it's the only deduction I have at the end of the year."

"You're a regular financial whiz," Mac complimented her. "You make a man proud."

"That was how I bought it. Here's the reason why: For years I was waiting to meet that special someone. But it's difficult when you're in my line of work. Some men have admitted to feeling emasculated by me, Mac. I despaired of ever finding the right guy. So, when I turned twenty-nine, with the big three-oh right around the corner, I decided I'd have to be my own prince charming. Give myself the moon. Make outlandish promises to myself, and make them come true. I wanted the cabin, and there was no reason to wait on my mystery man to come riding in to buy it for me when I could afford it myself."

"Sisters are definitely doing it for themselves," Mac said. "And it can make a weaker man feel less than a man."

Kerry pushed up on her elbow, concerned now that she'd revealed something about her personality that might send Mac running for the hills. But she was who she was and there was no denying it, or hiding it. "What about you, Mac. Does the fact that I'm independently wealthy—"

"Oh, you're independently wealthy, now, not just the owner of a nice nest egg?" Mac joked. He turned onto his side, facing her. "Kerry, you could be as rich as Oprah, and I'd be your Steadman. I'm not put off by the fact that you have money. To begin with, I'm not exactly a beggar myself. I've invested over the years, too. Money is a cushion to fall back on. I live modestly, like you do. I own a condo in D.C. I helped put my younger brothers and sisters through college. I give to several charities such as the United Negro College Fund. With all the information at our disposal today, there's no reason why a black man can't be as successful as he wants to be."

"Amen," Kerry said, climbing on top of him, rising and pulling him up with her. "Time for that swim." She turned, ran and dived into the sparkling water.

Mac hung back. "How's the water?"

"It's *glorious,*" Kerry said, dazzling him with a sexy grin.

Mac dived in. "Damn, woman, this water is freezing!"

Kerry's laughter rang throughout the forest.

On Saturday the weather was as close to perfect as it had been in a long time. Kerry had two deputies work funeral detail, but she and Mac were going as civilians. When they arrived at St. John A.M.E., the parking lot was already full, cars spilling out onto the street and, in some cases, in nearby residents' yards. Kerry supposed Johnny Haywood's notoriety had drawn the crowd. Of course there were sincere mourners who were there to support Bess Haywood and, now, Tad Armstrong. Because the news that Tad had been Johnny's father had spread like wildfire through the town. This was better than watching one's favorite soap. It had drama, mystery, and intrigue, what with the real killer still being on the loose.

Kerry and Mac had to stand at the back of the church during the service. Kerry saw Nicole Haywood sitting in the front row, her mother and a brother flanking her. She had Jack on her lap. The boy was abnormally quiet. Perhaps he sensed the solemnity of the moment. Looking around the church, Kerry also spotted her own family sitting a few rows behind Bess Haywood and Tad Armstrong and their sons, Harold and Ike Jr., Evelyn, Buddy, Kiana, Gabriel, and Courtney had all attended.

It was a closed-casket ceremony. An oversize portrait of Johnny, obviously his high school graduation picture, was sitting on a stand near the casket. Kerry didn't know why people couldn't find more recent photos of the deceased. But she'd seen it so many times. Even if the deceased was eighty years old, the photo on the program was usually from a much earlier year.

Reverend Darton gave an impassioned plea for all who were not right with God to get right today. A funeral, he said, was not for the dead but for the living. Because the dead know nothing. But the living know that they are dying. If he didn't make a few converts, Kerry would have been surprised.

After Reverend Darton took his seat Mrs. Tracy Newbold, the lead soprano, rose to stand in front of the choir and when she opened her mouth to sing you couldn't hear a pin drop in the church. "This world is not my home. I'm just a passin' through. My treasures are laid up somewhere beyond the blue," she sang. Men, women and children were moved to tears.

Mac took Kerry's hand in his and gently squeezed it. She was fighting back tears too. "Are you a chief or a mouse?" he whispered in her ear.

"Right now, I'm a mouse. This is too sad," Kerry whispered back.

After Mrs. Newbold melted back into the choir, the entire choir sang "Amazing Grace." Following a rousing rendition of that American classic, funeral director Jeri Brown rose and asked for testimonies from family and friends. Any remembrance they had of Johnny that they wished to share. It almost looked as if she'd have to make another plea when Harold rose and said, with tears glistening in his eyes, "I know a lot of y'all are here because of the way my brother was killed. Butchered like an animal. Or maybe you came because you heard rumors that he was a drug dealer, and you wanted to see how a drug dealer is put away. But he was my brother, and I loved him. I'm gonna miss him. And I want whoever killed him to roast in hell!"

"Harold," Bess said quietly, pulling him back down beside her. She put her arms around him. "Shhh, baby, it's okay."

Emboldened by his brother's words, Ike Jr. rose to say something, too. His muscles strained against the dark suit he had on. Kerry could see some of the women craning their necks to get a glimpse of him. "Just like everybody else, my brother was a lot of things. He liked to laugh. He loved his family, even though he chose to go the wrong way in life. I did, too, and served my time for it. I'm not ashamed to stand up here and tell you that. But who in here hasn't sinned?"

"Amen!" an elderly woman shouted from the back of the church.

"We hear you, brother," a man with a deep bass voice called out.

"All I'm saying is," Ike Jr. continued, "everybody, no matter what he's done, has somebody who loves him. And me and my family loved Johnny. He meant something to us, even though he didn't mean anything to his murderer. To his murderer he was nothing. That's all I've got to say."

He returned to his seat.

Jeri Brown looked over the church, hoping to see someone else stand up. Then she saw a petite woman all in black, her features obscured by a veil attached to a wide-brim hat, slowly rise from her pew.

"I have something to say," the woman announced, her voice strong and bold.

In the back of the church, Kerry's ears perked up. She nudged Mac.

"I'm here to confess to my part in that boy's death."

General cries of shock and surprise rose up among the assemblage.

Kerry, having recognized the voice of the veiled woman, went to the podium and whispered something in Jeri Brown's ear. Jeri left the stage.

"Please, everybody, settle down. The woman came here to speak, and we should let her speak."

Nicole's mother stood and pointed a finger at Kerry. "You staged this." She turned to those gathered. "This woman has been harassing my daughter. Nicole is a nervous wreck after what she told her about the manner in which her husband died. It took every ounce of her strength to come here and show respect, respect for the man she loved. Whatever that woman has to say was told to her by your chief of police."

"That's a lie," Viola Kelly shouted. She pulled off her hat.

Nearly everyone in the room knew her by sight.

She looked all around her. "I see a lot of faces I know in here. You come to me in secret looking for solutions to your problems and I try to help you as best I can. Have I ever charged any of you for anything I ever did?"

"No!" cried a church mother who went to Viola for blackberry root. It pepped her tea up, gave her vigor.

"Have I ever given anyone anything that would harm you?"

"That tea you gave me gave me the runs," one woman spoke up.

"Ain't that the reason you came to me, because you were stopped up?" Viola countered. "That got you going."

"And going," the woman said.

Laughter relieved some of the stress in the room.

Kerry was watching Nicole Haywood who had given Jack to her brother beside her, and looked as if she were prepared to bolt at the first opportunity.

In the center of the church, Viola Kelly cleared her throat. "Nicole Haywood took the leaves from my foxglove plant and fed them to her husband. That's what killed him, according to the coroner. I stand here before you, and before God, and that's the reason I'm doing this, and tell you I didn't give it to her. But maybe I'm liable, too, because I didn't call the law after it happened. I was too afraid . . ."

While everyone else had given Viola their rapt attention, Nicole Haywood had risen and was trying to sneak out the side door. However, when she passed Bess Haywood, who was also sitting in the front row, Bess stuck out her foot and Nicole tripped, landing on top of Johnny's casket. The legs of the support that held the casket collapsed, the casket tipped to the side, and, since the lid was not secured, it fell open. Johnny's body fell on top of his wife.

Nicole's piercing screams reverberated off the walls. "Get him off me, get him off me. I did it, I killed him. Just get him off me."

Kerry allowed the funeral director and her assistant to remove Nicole's husband from on top of her; then she pulled Nicole to her feet and led her out of the church.

Mac met her at the exit and handed her a pair of cuffs, which she quickly slapped onto Nicole's wrists.

Two hours later they had a full confession. Jenna Preston was arrested for her role in the murder. She'd helped to dispose of the body, and had supplied the information about the Sharpshooter's modus operandi. Which had been inadvertently given to her by her clueless brother. She'd also been the one to cut the lock on Lewis Deeks's gate, allowing Atta Girl to attack Kerry.

Nicole had been the one to break into Tad's house and steal the gun. She said she had watched the house a few days before her chance had come. The reason she'd chosen Tad was because many people in town had witnessed his altercations with Johnny on the street. That, and the rumors that Tad hadn't been wrapped too tight since his return from Vietnam.

Armed with a search warrant, Kerry, Mac, and several deputies discovered Nicole's motive for the murder carefully packed in an oversize briefcase and stowed in the trunk of Nicole's Lexus: Five hundred fifty thousand dollars in twenties, fifties, and hundreds.

In the end, it was always about the green.

If confession is good for the soul, then these girls' souls must be singing, Kerry thought later that evening as she sat in her office listening to their statements. Dale and Dale Sr. were there, as well. Dale acting as Nicole's attorney, and Dale Sr. as his daughter's. Mac stood in the back, observing the proceedings.

"It wasn't exactly premeditated," Nicole said tiredly. Her mascara was running from a recent crying jag, otherwise she looked composed. Jenna, sitting next to her, was silent, eyes downcast. She couldn't even look her father in the eyes.

"I mean, sure," Nicole continued, "I'd stolen the gun two weeks earlier, with the intention of shooting Johnny with it but, after I'd stolen it, I couldn't go through with it."

"Why did you have to drag my daughter into this?" Dale Sr. suddenly erupted, shooting out of his chair and glaring down at Nicole.

"She didn't force me to do anything, Daddy!" Jenna cried, going to stand between her father and Nicole. "If you want to blame somebody for all of this, you can blame me. I was the one who put the idea into Nicky's head."

Dale Sr.'s face went ashen. He peered into Jenna's beautiful dark blue eyes, eyes so like his own, trying to find some regret in their depths, a smidgen of remorse. He found none.

He turned away from her and stumbled back to his chair. Dale, concerned, stood and helped his father to his seat. A look of utter helplessness passed between the two men. Neither of them knew what they could do to save Jenna this time.

Jenna had the floor. She paced as she spoke: "Nicky never would have poisoned him if she'd had the nerve to shoot him. But, she didn't."

"So, I poisoned him," Nicole said from her chair. She and Jenna looked into each other's eyes. Jenna gave a nod, and Nicole went on: "When Johnny came in that night, he was in an amorous mood. I wasn't having it. I told him I wanted to talk. He needed to quit the business, or I was leaving." She glanced at Kerry. "That part was true, Chief. I really did want to get out of the business. I didn't want Jack growing up around it. I'd had to, and I'd hated it. If I'd known Johnny was in the business before I married him, I never would have married him, and that's the truth. But, he promised me he wasn't in it any longer when we started dating, and I believed him. Recently, though, I found his money-hiding place. I foolishly wanted to confront him then and there—'

"But I cautioned her against it," Jenna put in. She was so wound up she couldn't stop pacing the floor. "You see, Nicky and I met at a meeting for abused women. We were both getting beaten on a regular basis by the men in our lives. I left mine, but getting rid of hers wasn't that easy."

"Whenever I told Johnny I was going to leave him, he'd laugh in my face," Nicole said, her face screwed up in a frown, remembering. "That night, though, something in me snapped. Once Johnny realized I was actually serious about leaving this time, he slugged me and raped me. Then, afterward, he demanded to be fed."

"And, boy, did she serve him one hell of a last meal," Jenna said with a cruel smile on her lips. "He never got up from the table."

"I phoned Jenna in a panic." Nicole picked up the story.

"When I got there, Johnny was slumped forward on the table wearing only a pair of jeans and a stunned expression. That's when I went into action. I told Nicky I had a plan. I took the .22 and we propped Johnny up, and I shot him right between the eyes. I'm only sorry he was already dead when I shot him and he couldn't feel it going in."

"I don't understand," Kerry said. "Why would you go with two different scenarios? Set it up to look like the serial killer the FBI was after had done it, *and* use Tad Armstrong's gun, thereby implicating him? It doesn't make sense."

"I didn't know where Nicky had gotten the gun until *after* I'd put the bullet in him," Jenna answered.

"Things were happening so fast, we weren't thinking, just reacting," Nicole explained. Her hand trembled when she smoothed her hair back. "I'd never killed anyone before. I didn't realize how sick it makes you feel. How weak and panicked."

Weak and panicked, that's how Kerry felt the next morning when she had to tell Mac good-bye. They stood on her porch in a tight embrace, neither of them wanting to let go. Mac buried his nose in her wild hair. Inhaled the sweetness of her warm skin, still fresh from the shower she'd taken this morning.

He kissed the side of her neck and murmured, "I'll be back as soon as I can wrap things up in D.C. I have some vacation time coming."

Kerry met his gaze. Her own eyes were teary. "Mac, what am I going to do without you? Even for one day?"

"You're going to do what you do best, take care of everybody in this little town that I've come to love," he told her with a gentle smile.

"You mean you don't want to live someplace else?" Kerry was confused because they hadn't made any decisions yet.

"And take you away from the one place where you feel totally at peace?" Mac asked. "No, baby, after watching you operate the last few days, I'd be a fool to even suggest it." He kissed her forehead, and smoothed a few strands of hair out of her face. "Kiss me now, so I can go. The sooner I leave, the sooner I'll be back."

Kerry happily obliged.

Things returned to normal in Damascus, or as normal as they could be with the most infamous trial ever to take place in the small town going on. Dale Sr. excused himself as Jenna's attorney, and Dale asked a colleague from D.C., a young African-American woman by the name of Billie Roman, to take the case as a favor to him. Billie was a fireball in the courtroom and succeeded in getting Jenna a reduced sentence from the one the jury had recommended: life in prison. Jenna got ten years with the potential of parole in five with good behavior.

Nicole didn't get off as easily. She got twenty years with the possibility of parole in ten with good behavior.

Because Nicole's family was involved in the drug trade, Bess Armstrong (she'd dropped the "Haywood" when she married Tad) was granted custody of little Jack. Bess agreed to take Jack for visits with his mother at the women's facility in Ocala on a monthly basis.

Some of the best news came in late August of that year when it was announced in the *Damascus Herald* that Doreen Wilkins had undergone a kidney transplant and was recovering nicely.

Then, in early September, Kerry learned that Dale was dating Billie Roman and she'd moved to Florida to be with him. That news did her heart good. Dale deserved some happiness.

Speaking of happiness . . .

EPILOGUE

The marriage of Kerry Anne Everett to Maceo Luis Kent took place on Saturday, September eighth. It seemed rushed to some people, but not to those who knew them and loved them.

The guests totaled in the hundreds, and the walls of St. John A.M.E. Church seemed to swell with them. Kerry and Mac recited their own vows, which were indicative of their life together.

Kerry remained chief of police for several years, then quit to run for sheriff of Alachua County. She won and became the first woman, and the first African-American, to become sheriff.

Mac was assigned to the local FBI field office. He continued to rise in the ranks and eventually was offered the position of assistant director in Washington, D.C., which he declined. He enjoyed his life in Florida with his wife, two daughters, and three sons.

Dear Readers,

Thank you for picking up one of my books. I hope you enjoyed Kerry and Mac's story. I know I got a kick out of writing it. Drop me a line or two with your comments.

My next full-length book will be Solange and Rupert's story. You met them in A SECOND CHANCE AT LOVE. Look for their story in the summer of 2002.

Until then, dear reader, keep turning those pages . . .

Many blessings,
Janice Sims

P.O. Box 811
Mascotte, FL 34753-0811
E-mail: Jani569432@aol.com
Web site: http://romantictales.com/janicesims.html